SHOOTING FOR STARS

For Ezra.

Shoot for the stars, little buddy.

Published by Peachtree Teen
An imprint of PEACHTREE PUBLISHING COMPANY INC.
1700 Chattahoochee Avenue
Atlanta, Georgia 30318-2112
PeachtreeBooks.com

Text © 2024 by Christine Webb

Jacket art by Maggie Edkins Willis
Design by Lily Steele
Composition by Lily Steele and Lucy Ricketts
Edited by Jonah Heller

Printed in March 2024 at Sheridan, Chelsea, MI, USA.
10 9 8 7 6 5 4 3 2 1
First Edition
ISBN: 978-1-68263-601-5

Library of Congress Cataloging-in-Publication Data

Names: Webb, Christine, author.
Title: Shooting for stars / Christine Webb.
Description: First edition. | Atlanta, Georgia : Peachtree Publishing Company Inc., 2024. | Summary: Teenage science-minded Skyler teams up with film club member Cooper to defy her father and video an application to study in space.
Identifiers: LCCN 2023050609 | ISBN 9781682636015 (hardcover) | ISBN 9781682636848 (ebook)
Subjects: CYAC: Fathers and daughters—Fiction. | Interpersonal relations—Fiction. | Scientists—Fiction. | LCGFT: Romance fiction. | Novels.
Classification: LCC PZ7.1.W41785 Sh 2024 | DDC [Fic]—dc23
LC record available at *https://lccn.loc.gov/2023050609*

SHOOTING FOR STARS

CHRISTINE WEBB

PEACHTREE
Teen

My first trip to the principal's office is for something ridiculous, and I'm only a month into my senior year. I would've guessed I'd be in here for something more exciting, like accidentally blowing up one of our science labs or hacking the teachers' gradebooks for a friend. Or getting caught on the school's roof targeting the Orion Nebula with my telescope or genetically modifying some cafeteria food to taste less like cat puke. But no, I'm here because of the fuzzy rat who is sitting in my hoodie pocket. She's a blue rat, which is kind of a misnomer because her fur's actually a bluish gray. Anyway, she wasn't bothering anyone, so this principal's office visit feels a bit over the top.

As I sit in the overstuffed chair in front of the secretary's desk, a few things flash through my mind:

1. These chairs are more comfortable than the ones in calculus, so this situation could be seen as an upgrade from where I was ten minutes ago.

2. Is my dad going to be mad or think this is funny? Getting a call from the school saying your daughter is in the principal's office is not usually a good thing, so I'm guessing mad. My stomach twists.

3. It's a bummer that Five's food is in my locker. She's wiggling around in my hoodie, and she's probably hungry. She hasn't eaten since breakfast.

I pat my hoodie pocket gently, hoping it comforts Five. Then again, since she doesn't know she's in the principal's office, maybe she doesn't need comforting. A banner on the wall displays our school's logo next to our motto: EXPECT EXCELLENCE.

The secretary, Mrs. Ling, taps away on her keyboard, ignoring me—just another kid who missed excellence. Her eyes look like years of staring at screens have dulled them, and ten dollars says the apple on her vest isn't the only pin in her collection. If she were an element, she would be radon: a product in the decay chain of uranium and thorium.

I started classifying people according to what periodic table element they would be in elementary school, when Jon Blatnik called me a poophead. I researched the grossest thing in the world in order to find a good comeback. Turns out livermorium is known as the smelliest element, so that's what I called him. He started crying because he thought I put a Harry Potter curse on him.

Pretty soon, I'd matched everyone in my class with a square from the periodic table. It made me feel like I finally understood people. For example, livermorium? Extremely radioactive. So of course Jon Blatnik would lash out at me sometimes—it's in his nature. This elemental conclusion allowed me to tolerate him, and I've been classifying people ever since.

The door to the office behind the desk opens, and Mr. Grant flicks a piece of lint from his red-and-black striped tie. "Skyler Davidson?" He looks around like a doctor surveying a waiting room, but in a row of empty chairs, there is only me.

"That's me." I raise my hand. Five wiggles in my hoodie, so I put my other hand in there and give her a scratch behind her ears.

The principal's office is a bit of a letdown. There's a poster of a tropical island and a framed picture of Mr. Grant's degree from some college that must be small because I've never heard of it. His metal desk fills about half of the office, and there's a clear glass bowl of chocolates in the left corner. I help myself to a Crunch Mini. What's so scary about the principal's office?

Mr. Grant frowns at my Crunch bar. Maybe those weren't supposed to be for students. Well, half of it's gone, so I'm not putting the other half back now.

"Skyler Davidson . . ." He says this like he's trying to buy time while looking at the papers in my very thin file. He probably has no idea who I am. In a high school of five thousand students, principals usually don't bother with ones like me. He reaches for his reading glasses.

I recite my stats like an athlete, hoping we can speed up this process. "Senior. 4.0 GPA. No previous infractions unless you count the time in seventh grade when my science fair project started that tiny fire in the corner of the gym, but I don't know if that ever made it into my cumulative file."

Mr. Grant looks at me over the top of his reading glasses, then shuffles through another couple of pages. "It appears that it did not."

"Oh, good." That means it won't show up on college applications. I finish off the Crunch bar except for a tiny corner that I slip into my gray hoodie pocket. I eye Mr. Grant's candy dish again and spot a Butterfinger, but there's no reason to press my luck.

Apparently finding nothing remarkable in my file, Mr. Grant folds his hands on his desk and looks at me. "Would you care to explain what happened in calculus, Ms. Davidson?"

I hold up one finger to show that he needs to wait until I'm finished chewing. After all, it's rude to talk with my mouth full. "No one cared about Five until Chelsea freaked out."

"Your teacher reported that you . . ." He looks at the discipline slip one more time to make sure he's reading this right. "You brought a rat to class?"

"Technically, yes." I pull Five out of my hoodie pocket and put her on my shoulder. She's holding the small piece of chocolate between her paws and chewing. She pauses for a minute, her bite bulging in the side of her mouth. She looks around, finds the principal's office as unimpressive as I did, and then goes back to chewing.

Mr. Grant squints a moment and then shakes his head. "Right. I see. And you brought the rat to class because . . ."

"Because she needs electrolytes four times a day. Which I explained to Chelsea *and* to Mrs. Batts, but I don't think they got it." As if on cue, Five sneezes. She uses a paw to wipe her whiskers and pink nose. "See? If this turns into an upper respiratory infection, she'll be in trouble. Her predecessor, Three, died of a URI, and I'm telling you—it looked unpleasant."

"I see."

It doesn't look like he does.

"Chelsea saw me putting a dropper of Gatorade into my hoodie pocket, and she asked what that was all about. So I showed her Five. She screamed and acted like I've been digging around in sewers or something, but rats are the cleanest rodents out there. If you ever find yourself in a sewer, Mr. Grant, you should go where the rats are. It will be the cleanest part of the sewer."

"Is that so?"

"Yes, it is. There has been lots of research done about this. Plus, rats are extremely smart. They're great pets. Watch this. Five, sit."

Five keeps chewing on her piece of chocolate and doesn't move.

"We're still working on it. But they're smart, seriously."

Mr. Grant takes a deep breath. "Is Five . . . part of a project you're working on?"

"My science fair project: the effects of creatine monohydrate on muscle growth in rats. She runs on a treadmill for ten minutes a day, and I'm attempting to prove that the creatine monohydrate will expedite her gains in muscle mass. We've been training for weeks. It took me forever to even teach her to run on a treadmill, but now she can do up to level 2.1. That's roughly five miles per hour. Pretty impressive if you ask me. It's worth the extra attention she needs right now, especially seeing as there wouldn't be enough time before the science fair to train a successor rat." I hold up the Gatorade bottle like I'm Alexander Fleming with some freshly discovered penicillin.

Mr. Grant stands up as my dad comes through the door.

"Sky, what's going on?" Dad is still wearing his white lab coat. His silver-rimmed glasses frame his alarmed blue eyes. "I got your text that I needed to come in."

"I brought Five to school because she needs her electrolytes. Apparently that's not okay, and I was hoping you could bring her home."

My dad puts his fingertips to his forehead. "Sky, you know you can't bring a rat to school."

"You said you didn't have time to give her Gatorade. Was I supposed to let her waste away?"

My dad runs his fingers through his overgrown blond hair. We don't look much alike. I have my mom's dark hair and dark eyes. I'm also short like she was. My dad is tall and lean. He claims he was ripped back when he played golf in high school, but I doubt it. Hours of fine-tuning microscope slides for the past twenty years have taken away from all the time he spent doing any exercise. He recently started going to a local gym a couple of times a week and said he's "turning over a new

6

fitness leaf," but we'll see how long that lasts. It's not usually very long.

"I'm sorry, Mr. Grant," my dad says. "I'll take Five home."

He plucks her from my shoulder and puts her on his. Then he shakes Mr. Grant's hand, and Mr. Grant eyes the massive bottle of hand sanitizer on his desk.

"Are you going to give her the Gatorade?" I ask. The bottle is about half empty, and a dropper is secured around it with a blue rubber band. "Five milliliters at a time? Please?"

My dad closes his eyes and puts his hands together with his fingertips at his mouth, like he's praying to the God he doesn't believe in and asking how on earth he ended up with such a weird kid. It's his fault, really. All of my rats have been from his micro-biology lab.

He sighs and turns to me. "I'll give Five the Gatorade. Today only. My bacteria cultures are probably wrecked for the day anyway since I had to come here." He rolls his eyes, annoyed but not mad. Life is always interrupting his cultures. Those bacteria are fragile little buggers.

"Thanks, Dad." I smile. For a guy who routinely gives rats diseases as part of his job, he has a soft spot for them every once in a while. Or maybe it's just a soft spot for me. Whatever it is, I'll take it. I turn to Mr. Grant. "So, am I good to go back to class, or . . . ?"

Mr. Grant's eyes are squinted, and his mouth is slightly open.

My dad takes advantage of the pause and says, "Is this candy up for grabs?" He takes the Butterfinger I was eyeing, holds it up before opening it, and says, "Thanks. I forgot to eat this morning."

The wrapper crinkles as he unwraps it, and Five's nose wiggles in anticipation.

Mr. Grant regains his composure. "Thank you for coming in, Mr. Davidson. I'm glad you can agree that Skyler's retention of a rodent in class is highly inappropriate."

"Definitely," he says while still chewing the Butterfinger. He turns to me and attempts a stern look. "You're grounded for a week."

We both try to hide smiles. Grounding me is pointless since I'm always home anyway. My dad's phone pings, and he pulls it out of his pocket to read the text.

Mr. Grant adjusts his glasses and searches my paperwork as if the answer to the appropriate disciplinary action is in there. Finally, he looks up. "It looks like you have it handled, Mr. Davidson. Skyler, don't let me catch you with animals at school again, got it? If you bring another rat to my office, I'll have to suspend you."

"Yes, sir." I attempt to look properly chastened.

He puts my papers back in my file. "You can head back to class."

Before we can leave, my dad's phone pings again, and his demeanor changes as he answers a text. He picks up Five and puts her back on my shoulder. "Um . . . That patient I was telling you about with the bizarre fungal infection? The doctors are going through some more testing. I have to get to the hospital."

"What about Five?" I ask.

"Sky." My dad's voice has gone into business mode. "This is a *human* patient. I think we can agree that's a bit more important than Five's Gatorade?"

"But I don't think I can bring her back to class." I glance at Mr. Grant.

He shakes his head. My dad is preoccupied, his phone absorbing all of his mental focus.

"Can I go home?" I ask. "It's already fifth period."

"That's fine," my dad says. He's already reaching for the door. He hits a number and puts it to his ear. "Hello, Charlie? Yes, it's me." He walks out, leaving me alone with Mr. Grant.

I guess my dad wasn't as mad as I thought he would be. In fact, it seems like he barely cares that his kid landed in the principal's office. I should feel relieved about this, but the relief feels a little tainted with . . . something else. I don't know. Could it be disappointment? Sure, I don't want to be in trouble, but at least he could *care*. Defend me, or defend the school, or somehow invest in the situation a little bit. But he's already gone.

I look toward the closed door and then back at Mr. Grant. Five starts licking my ear, which tickles, but I don't laugh. "So . . . can I go?"

Mr. Grant sits heavily into his plushy desk chair. "You are dismissed."

I'm never home by 2:15. It feels weird to be skipping class. Outside my bedroom window, my street looks like it always does: cookie-cutter stucco houses with red-tile roofing and pebbled yards harboring scraggly trees and an occasional cactus. Standard, boring suburb in Las Vegas Valley.

Still, the architects can't make the insides of our houses look alike. For example, Julie next door has an entire wall of shelving to display her vintage troll dolls. My house has a make-shift microbiology lab in the basement for when my dad either has to bring work home or does his own hobby research here. Sometimes I mention our basement lab when the neighbors are out and about, and I'm pretty sure it's why we don't get invited over much. It's fine with me. The one time we ate at Julie's, shortly after we moved in ten years ago, she talked about the history of trolls for a half hour. I kept wanting to interrupt with "There is no history of trolls because TROLLS ARE NOT REAL," but that would have been rude. Instead, I complimented a blue-haired troll's sparkly tutu in an effort to be nice. Julie ordered me a replica and dropped it off the next week. It sits in my room in a cracked beaker.

I flop onto my bed and start scrolling through Instagram: MIT, CalTech, and Harvard; NASA astronauts; SpaceX; the Hubble Space Telescope and the Webb Space Telescope. I followed a couple of girls from my QuizBowl team once, but they posted too many things about what they were having for dinner and "#blessed" selfies. #Unfollow.

A NASA post stops me. I sit up in my bed and read it again. "Five, does this say what I think it says?" Five runs to the side of her cage and looks outs expectantly like she always does when I call her (seriously, rats are the smartest).

This post can't be real.

I boot up my laptop, as if seeing this information on two screens will make it more valid. I check NASA's website to confirm that the post isn't some hacker pulling a prank. It takes me a second to find the right information page, but then there it is, on a blue background with white stars:

> NASA seeks teenager for Teen in Space intern-
> ship. One teenager to be chosen to assist in
> research on the International Space Station
> (ISS) next summer. See application instructions
> for full details.

The application details are straightforward. The intern needs to be a healthy teenager (check), available for training and a two-month research flight next summer (check), and committed to astronomy research (CHECK!). Applicants need to include a three-minute video on why they should be chosen for this project. I don't know how to make a video, but it can't be that hard.

NASA says they're doing this internship because they want to "invest in young minds" and "encourage the scientists of our future," but I know the real reason why. I follow the Russian Federation's space agency, Roscosmos, on Instragram, too, and a few months ago they posted about putting up the youngest cosmonaut to ever work at the International Space Station: Viktor Ilyokavich, age twenty. While we didn't see much of it on the news, I bet our super-competitive president was all over that. This is probably NASA's direct response to Roscosmos. You send a twenty-year-old? We'll throw a teenager up there. #AmericaFirst.

This is like being five years old, playing Candy Land with my mom, and I just got the Queen Frostine card. That's the one that basically lets you skip the whole board and go straight to the end. Since middle school, I've had my whole life planned out: get into the Massachusetts Institute of Technology like my mom did, graduate with honors like my mom did, get into their astrophysics doctoral program like my mom did, and then be accepted to NASA's space program to complete the research that my mom *didn't*.

A car accident when I was in third grade brought an abrupt end to her promising career in astrophysics. Some people shoot to change the world, but she was going to change the universe.

I crash onto my bed, grabbing a familiar doctoral dissertation I've read too often. It's hardbound in black with gold lettering on the side: FORMATION OF STRONGLY MAGNETIZED NEUTRON STARS AND IMPLICATIONS FOR DIRECTIONAL ASSISTANCE IN INTER-PLANETARY TRAVEL. Below it is the Massachusetts Institute of Technology logo and then my mom's name: Renae Davidson. The gold ink has started to smudge on her name because I've run my fingers over it so often, but I do it again now.

"I'm going to get there," I whisper to the name. "I'm going to finish this for you."

Just last week, my MIT dreams were in jeopardy. My SAT scores came back significantly lower than I expected, and I was wrecked for that whole night. One of my QuizBowl teammates said that doing poorly on one test is no reason to binge-watch seven hours of *My Fast-Food Life*, but she got nearly a perfect score. Also, her mom isn't counting on her like mine is.

I've been too ashamed to tell my dad, especially since he paid for all those prep classes, but now it's like I have another chance.

What kind admissions board would turn down a NASA intern? I can pretend like those SATs never happened.

It's nine o'clock by the time my dad gets home.

"Good news," he says. "They think the treatments have worked. We'll keep doing follow-ups, but looks like we zapped it. I wish I could magnify bacteria a million times so I could punch it in the face." He smiles at his joke, but the dark circles under his eyes betray how many late nights he's spent at the hospital trying to solve this one.

"I made you dinner," I say. "Chicken piccata. It's in the oven on warm."

"Oh yeah." He slaps his forehead. "Food. Thanks. What would I do without you?"

If I didn't cook, my dad would either die of starvation or live off the Chinese take-out place that's a mile from our house. He's a loyal follower of General Tso.

I sit on the barstool next to my dad while he eats. "You're not going to believe what NASA announced today." It's hard to sit still. Before he asks what it is, I slam the printed copy of the announcement on the counter. "I might be going to space next summer."

He takes a drink of water and another bite of chicken while he reads the article. His eyes should be widening by now. He should be hugging me or cheering. Instead, his eyebrows furrow.

He picks the papers up to read them again. Then he puts them down, swallows his bite, and says, "Interesting."

Interesting? This is probably the most exciting opportunity I've ever had, and all he says is "Interesting"?

"Dad, are you serious? This is NASA. The big leagues. The dream. The fact that you collect antique petri dishes is 'interesting.' This is . . . I don't know. This is monumental."

"SkyBear." I hate when he calls me SkyBear. The nickname doesn't even make any sense. "I don't know if this is a great idea."

It feels like someone pulled the barstool out from under me. "Not a great idea? How is this not a great idea? We've been talking about this for years. I could finish Mom's research."

"And I support you in that." He holds up his hands. "When you're old enough. When you have the background and the necessary knowledge."

"Dad, I know more about neutron stars than most grad students. I've read every single piece of literature that I've been able to find. There are notebooks in my room full of notes and flow charts of what needs to be done to get the data mom needed."

"I know." He sets his fork on our granite countertop. "But NASA isn't for teenagers."

I wave the papers. "It is now!"

"It's not." He wipes his mouth. "Space travel is dangerous. To be honest, I've always figured you'd change your mind. Or maybe there would be technology that would allow you to finish Mom's research from here. I already lost your mother, Sky. I can't lose you, too."

"I'm not dying, Dad. I'm going to space."

"No, you're not." His mouth is set in a hard line.

"Wait, are you saying I can't even apply for this?" That was the last thing I expected. As a matter of fact, I hadn't even considered it.

"Apply to college, not NASA. That's what normal teenagers do."

My guilt morphs into anger. "So I'm a normal teenager now?"

When my mom died, I went straight from child to adult. There was no teenager. The summer after third grade, our electricity got shut off. That's when I learned what a bill was. Now I'm in charge of paying all of them. That fall, I built a Barbie dream house out of pizza boxes and Chinese take-out containers. A toilet paper tube served as Barbie's telescope. My dad wasn't as impressed as I'd hoped, and cookbooks started coming from Amazon soon after. He had a few "cooking dates" with me, but as his nights at the lab stretched longer, the cooking became more of a solo affair. While waiting for my dad to come home each night, I would study my mom's dissertation. It was my bible—it had all the direction I needed in life, and I worshipped the author. My dad would come home, apologize for being late, then tell me what a great kid I was and promise to be home sooner next time. We would talk about neutron stars and bacteria while he ate the plate of food I left in the fridge for him, and life wasn't all that bad. Not bad, but not normal.

"Sky, that's not what I meant."

"Then what did you mean?"

"Just please don't. Leave this one alone. You know it's a publicity stunt because of Viktor What's-his-name."

"Viktor Ilyokavich. So what? It's my break."

My dad takes a deep breath. "Mom's not here to appreciate you even if you do finish the research, SkyBear. You have to move on."

Hot tears sting my eyes. "Like you have?"

My mom's Chanel perfume still sits on his dresser. Her necklace with a Saturn pendant is next to it. Her reading glasses are still in the drawer of her nightstand, right next to the book she was reading before she died. The bookmark will never move to the next page.

After my mom died, it was a slow evolution to friendlessness for my dad. "Let me bring you dinner" turned into "Tell me if you need anything," which eventually became "We haven't seen you in forever, man." And then one day, no one checked in anymore.

"We all have our own ways of coping. I'm not hurting anyone by dedicating time to my work." It looks as if he's talking to his plate.

"I'm not hurting anyone by trying to finish mom's research."

"It's too risky. You can't do it." He takes a drink of water as if this is settled. Like he's washing back the bitterness of the words coming out of his mouth.

"I can't do it? Now suddenly you're parenting me? You haven't told me what to do since I was ten years old."

"That's because you always do what you're supposed to. You're an easy kid."

"Maybe it's time I became difficult." I take a drink of his water and set the glass down a little too hard. "This is my dream, Dad."

He doesn't forbid me to do things. He's working so often that he probably wouldn't even notice if I started making what my teachers call "negative life choices." The last "crazy party" I had was for my birthday, and it included Five and me helping my dad with his research. My cake (which I made) was in the shape of an Erlenmeyer flask. I even put a little indentation at the top for a baking soda and vinegar reaction to make it foam over. It was really cool, but it made the cake taste kind of gross.

Wait a minute. I'm eighteen now.

As a legal adult, he can't stop me from applying even if he wants to. The thought is triumphant and terrifying. "I'm an adult, you know," I say. "You can't technically stop me."

My dad's shoulders sag even farther down. He puts his elbows on the counter and his head in his hands. When he looks up, his eyes are glassy. I'd prefer he was angry. I wasn't ready for glassy. My dad is classic tungsten—the element with the highest melting point. It takes a lot to break him down.

"Please don't do this, Sky. You can't put yourself in this kind of danger. If you didn't come home, it would kill me."

My love for my mom and my love for my dad battle inside me. To abandon this chance might mean abandoning the only opportunity to finish my mom's research. There have been so many whispered promises to her: to her photos, to her gravestone, to her dissertation, to the night sky itself—I have promised all over the place that the research would be finished. Then again, my dad's right. She won't know whether or not her research is ever completed. And although I'm willing to risk my life in pursuit of this research, I saw what losing a family member did to my dad. We stayed at the gravesite so long that first night that the sky was a dull predawn gray when he nudged me awake, picked me up, and trudged back to our car. Then he cried at the steering wheel until the gray turned to a pale rose. I remember patting his shoulder and saying, "It's okay, Daddy. Don't cry." Not because it was okay, but because seeing my stoic dad falling apart made it feel like I was losing both parents. In a way, I did. But my love for my dad means that I would do anything to keep him from going through that again. He wouldn't have anyone left.

"Fine." I cross my arms and study the chicken piccata. "I won't apply. I'll focus on college." My eyes are still burning as I crumple up the printed pages and throw them in the trash on the way up to my room.

It's the first time I've ever lied to my dad.

The next day after school, I'm in Walgreens staring at a wall of cosmetics with no idea what to buy. I researched until past midnight about how to shoot the video for my NASA application, and a common tip was that makeup is important since camera lights can "wash out your skin tone." Looking sickly could be a fatal error, seeing as one of the main requirements is that the intern must pass a series of physical tests.

There should be a one-stop makeup pack called Youthful Vibrancy. Sadly, this doesn't exist. I checked.

My notebook is open to my shopping list of necessities. I thought the lip-gloss part would be easy. Turns out there are seventy-two choices of lip gloss, and that's just in the Revlon section. Also, what's the difference between lip gloss and lip shimmer? Do I want glossy or shimmery? Does it matter that normal lips are neither of these things?

I half-heartedly pick up a lip gloss and examine it, a specimen of bottled beauty. It looks like a tiny test tube. I turn it over and see the name: Champagne Bubbles. Champagne bubbles? Who wants their lips to look like an alcoholic beverage? Not me. I put it back and try another one: Poppy Pout. So I can be a disgruntled flower. Great. Who names these?

Also, is lip gloss seriously $8.99? For a minuscule tube of hydroxylated lanolin and polybutene? You've got to be kidding.

I'll figure out lip stuff later. Foundations should be easier since it's a matching game to see which ones go with my skin. My notes tell me that I need a "highlighter" and "shadow" in order to "contour." It's like I'm doing a chemistry lab on my face.

A girl who looks about thirteen walks up behind me. She expertly navigates the cosmetic maze and grabs a black eyeshadow, a gray, and a light neutral. This sounds familiar. A quick check to my research notebook confirms. "Ah, a smoky eye?" I say. "A sultry blend of color with soft shading to exude flirty appeal?"

"Um, yes," she says, eyeing me like I'd been speaking in a foreign language.

To be fair, it feels like I had been. She grabs some eyeliner and mascara. How does she know exactly which types to get?

Most girls learned about makeup when their moms or friends did makeovers with them at middle school sleepovers. It never felt like I missed out on much by not doing that, but suddenly I miss it. Can you miss a memory that you don't have?

Five foundations are all I can hold at once, so I pick five that are near my skin color and then balance them while looking through my fingers to see which one is closest.

A woman about my dad's age walks over and takes a bottle from the wall. She dabs a bit of the makeup on her wrist. Is that how I'm supposed to figure out what color I am? Makeup can be sampled like cheese cubes at Costco? Does every woman on earth know how to do this besides me?

Perhaps this is how Chelsea (a helium if I ever met one) feels in science classes. It's a new feeling, and it sucks. I look around, hoping for a familiar face to decode this situation for me. Even Chelsea would be great, but there's only me—my ignorance on display under the harsh fluorescent lights. Like Chelsea looking at a blank physics test, I'm in trouble.

Later that night, it's a good thing that my dad is at the hospital again instead of home. I'm on my third try of doing makeup contouring, and it is *not* as easy as they make it look online. A peek in the mirror startles me. It looks like I tried to do tiger makeup for a Halloween costume, but the tiger wasn't the prettiest one in the ambush. Also, my eyeliner is in jagged lines around my eyes, and I've poked at them so many times that they're turning red. I look like a strung-out raccoon. And also a tiger. Whatever I am, it's not cute.

Time for yet another tutorial. Four hours and $87.56 have been lost on this cosmetic endeavor, but it will all be worth it when I'm in space. The channel I've stumbled on is called *Kisses from Charli*. Barf. I've heard the girls at school talk about this one. Apparently Charli lives in Las Vegas. Chelsea ran into her once at the mall. We all had to hear about it for like three days.

"Hi, girlies!" Charli says to her viewers. She talks with a southern twang. "Are y'all ready to get gorgeous?"

Her dark brown hair is braided to keep it out of her face, and her bright eyes are framed by huge lashes (they're probably extensions—I learned about those in the last video). She's wearing a lacy white tank top, which seems like a terrible idea when dealing with all of these pigmented substances; my jeans are already smeared with foundation, and there's eyeshadow on my T-shirt. She starts her tutorial, but it's impossible to keep up. It's like those cooking shows where everything's premeasured.

Charli says, "Y'all go over these lines with your beauty blender . . . and snap!" Then she snaps her fingers and everything is perfectly blended into something that resembles skin, only better.

I growl in frustration and try to wash off the makeup again. It should come off with water, but it doesn't. I've gotten three different kinds of soap in my eyes, and there's probably a layer of skin missing at this point. There has got to be a better way.

Great question for Google: How do I take off makeup?

Answer: makeup remover wipes.

Dang. Should have thought of that. There's the possibility of going out to get some, but one look in the mirror assures me that's a bad idea.

Maybe I've overreacted on the need for makeup. I'm a super-healthy teenager, so maybe I'll naturally look like one—as soon as I'm able to cut through all this goop. In order to feel like something's been accomplished tonight, I turn my attention to lighting. That's got to be easier.

My iPhone is set up on a stand to film my video. Two floor lamps from the basement make my room brighter than ever, and both nightstand lamps have their shades tilted toward my desk. My desk chair is spotlighted like a molecule under a bright microscope. My plan is to do a monologue about neutron stars and why this research needs to be completed. Sitting at my desk will make me look sophisticated and smart. There's a galaxies poster behind my desk, so that sets an intellectual-looking scene. Once I get my monologue and voiceover completed, I'll throw in a dash of edits and—snap!—perfect application video.

Once the phone's recording, I rush to my desk chair and then feel ridiculous for rushing. After all, that part will be cropped out.

"Hi. My name is Skyler Davidson. You should pick me for NASA's Teen in Space internship because I'm passionate about neutron stars, and I have some research that would be useful to the team at the International Space Station." I smile like I'm incredibly friendly and would get along with everyone at NASA. There. Stop recording. Let's see how this turned out.

I'm appalled. My Hollywood lighting is all wrong. The right side of my face is brighter than my left. Some backlighting from my desk lamp has made my usually smooth hair look frizzy. The focus of the video goes in and out twice in my few-sentence monologue, and my ghoulish makeup doesn't help the overall effect.

I unscrew both lampshades from the nightstand lamps and move the desk lamp. My dad has a nightstand lamp, so I throw that one in the mix. There's another desk lamp in the office, so it joins the party. Pretty soon I have eight lamps in the room, and I even put a flashlight on top of Five's cage. Beaker Troll gets one, too. When I sit at my desk, it's like I'm at an eerily silent press conference.

One of those black-and-white snapper things they use to mark the start of a scene would be useful right now: "NASA application demo video . . . take two. Marker!" Record. Mosey over to my desk in no rush at all because that part will be edited later.

"Five? Your question?" I squint at her cage, picturing her with a tiny press badge and a clipboard. She's probably in her hut with her paws over her eyes. "Why yes, good question, Five. Why should I be the one to represent the United States? For starters, I love hot dogs. Also apple pie. Can't say I'm a fan of baseball, but that's negotiable. Neutron stars are my specialty, and I can confidently say I know more about them than any other eighteen-year-old on the planet. Beaker Troll? Question?"

Trolls really are creepy. Even though I can't see its eyes with all this light, I can feel them.

"Yes, Beaker Troll, I know it's a risk, but it's a risk I'm willing to take. It's for my mom, you see. She's very supportive of this mission. And you should not show up to a press conference wearing only a tutu. Have some decency."

Okay. Stop recording. Deep breath. This one is sure to be better.

Whoa. Now it's so bright that I'm completely washed out, and the dark makeup lines on my contoured face look like scars. No wonder Beaker Troll looks horrified.

The feeling of lost isolation hasn't gone away since the makeup aisle. "This will be funny one day—right, Five?" My voice breaks as I say it.

I reach into Five's cage and pet her in between her ears, which she likes. Not that I should care what she likes. She's a *scientific specimen*. I shouldn't even call it "petting her between her ears," since that makes her sound like a pet. I was . . . poking at her cranial muscles to check for tissue growth. That's better.

Her round eyes look so content that I check her cranial muscles again.

"You ready for the treadmill, Five?" I pick her up and plunk her on my shoulder. "Let's do science."

I survey the mess of makeup and haphazard lamps. After all my video research, I'm good for nothing. Not makeup, not lighting, not even recording in focus. I can invest in better equipment and better makeup (please, no), or I can admit the inevitable: if I want this internship, I'm going to need help.

3

"Is this the film club meeting?" I ask. A student I don't recognize is holding a clipboard at the entrance to the band room. He has curly shoulder-length hair and chains on his black jeans. Does the film club have bouncers?

His eyes don't leave checklist he's marking. "Yeah. Are you one of the actors for the shoot today?"

I try not to laugh. "Definitely not."

Clipboard Dude looks up and waits for me to explain why I'm there. Oops. I should have said yes. No, wait. Then I might have had to be in whatever they're filming. Honesty is my best bet.

"I need to talk to your cameraperson."

"Which one?"

Dang. There are choices? I'm about to say I don't care which one, but maybe he won't let me in if it's clear I don't know any of them. Seems like tight security with a clipboard and all.

"I forgot the name. It, um, starts with an *R*? Or an *M*?"

Clipboard Dude looks up, like he's trying to remember. "Big Mike graduated last year . . . don't think we've got any *R*s. Just Stevie, Bryce, and Cooper on cameras today."

"Cooper! That's it. Because of the *r* at the end. That's what I was thinking." I try to look as helium as possible. "Cooperrrrr. The *r* stuck with me." I do two eyelash bats for effect. This is humiliating. Come on, Clipboard Dude. Let me in.

He raises one eyebrow. "I'll see if Cooperrrrr is available. Hold on."

The band room has been transformed. Well, I assume it has. Not positive I've ever been in the band room.

A lot of music stands are pushed together in a mangled mess in one corner. The back wall is built with barred lockers that hold instruments. About halfway down that wall, the makeover begins. The floor is littered with pastel-colored balloons. Fabric drapes elegantly in the background to cover up the caged music equipment. A trellis is set up, and giggling girls in prom dresses are posing under it. There's a lot of glitter, sequins, and cleavage.

My jeans, tennis shoes, and QUIZBOWL STATE FINALS T-shirt seem grossly out of place. Usually this wouldn't bother me, but combined with the fact that I'm on a film set seeking help from a perfect stranger, I feel quite small. I take a step back and lean against solid brick behind me.

People are rushing around the actors and cameras in a blur. Who knew there were so many people involved in shooting those weird school commercials we see in morning announcements? Maybe it was a bit presumptuous to think I could make my NASA video all by myself.

The producer holds up a megaphone and makes an announcement over the hubbub. "Actors, take five. Crew, reset the scene for the slow dance." Clipboard Dude taps a cameraman on the shoulder and points in my direction before heading back to his post. I eye the door, about to make a run for it, but then the cameraman, apparently Cooper, smiles at me and does that weird "what up" chin jerk that guys do. Have we met before? I don't remember him, but he's looking at me as if we're friends. He puts his hat on a stool and walks over, his gait confident. Running now would be even more embarrassing than staying and talking to him (probably).

"I hope Doug didn't give you any trouble," Cooper says. "We've had issues with people walking in during filming, which can mess up a whole scene."

"Got it. Makes perfect sense. I totally get that." What am I saying? I had no idea.

Cooper doesn't call my bluff. After an awkward silence, he says, "This is super embarrassing, but I don't remember who you are. I was trying to pretend, but in my experience, pretending to know something ends up with me looking like an idiot. Last year, I tried to talk art with that French foreign exchange student, Belle. Don't know if you knew her. I thought Manet and Monet were the same person. Rolled with it for like half an hour until she corrected me, and then I tried to pretend that she hadn't under-stood me because of our difference in accents. *Of course* I knew they weren't the same. The whole thing was kind of a mess. So . . . I'm gonna be honest. I don't remember you, but you don't seem like the type of girl a person would forget. Perhaps I was abducted and had my brain wiped—it's the only explanation. Humblest apologies." He does a fake bow.

Oh boy. Definitely should have gone with Bryce or Stevie. The *R* could have been Brrrrryce, after all. Too late now.

"You don't know me." That comes out sounding way creepier than I intended. "I mean, hi, I'm Skyler Davidson." I hold out my hand to shake his, because this is a business transaction after all.

He shakes my hand. "Cooper Evans. But you already knew the Cooper part?" He cocks his head, waiting for me to explain.

Cooper's quite a bit taller than me (then again, most people are). His brown hair is styled, but not in a way that took apparent effort. It looks like he woke up ten minutes before walking out the door and thought, "Crap, I have to do something with my hair." It sticks out at weird angles, but I don't hate it. His eyes are a dark gold that fades to green, like before he was born his chromosomes just couldn't make up their mind.

A tiny diamond stud glints from his earlobe, which means he owns at least one more earring than I do. None of the QuizBowl guys have earrings. Who does he think he is, a pirate?

Come to think of it, he does look like a guy from a pirate movie—one of the hot, young pirates, not one of the weird zombie ones. His build is lanky, and he's wearing a blue shirt advertising some obscure movie. Maybe it's one of those independent films.

I'm not the type of girl to have a crush, but I can say that he is objectively attractive. Simply based on . . . the attractiveness quotient or whatever. *Kisses from Charli* would probably say something about his chiseled jawline.

We'll shake hands again when we decide on the terms of this deal, right? At the very least, there will be a thank-you-for-your-time handshake. How have handshakes been so boring before now?

Crap. It's my turn to talk, and I'm staring at his dumb can't-make-up-their-mind green-gold eyes. Can I get away with saying I'm here to volunteer for the film club? The actual reason seems ridiculous now. But I can't work a camera, I'm hopeless with makeup, and I don't own a sequin, let alone a whole dress covered in them.

"I want to discuss a film project with you," I say. "This video could change space travel as we know it."

Cooper smiles. He either had braces in the past or has fabulous genetics. He also has pronounced dimples.

"Space travel, huh? Does that mean you know the aliens who wiped my brain? Because you still haven't explained how you know who I am. Doug said you asked for me by name."

"Oh, that. It was a lucky guess."

He lifts one eyebrow. "You *guessed* my name was Cooper?"

"You look like a Cooper."

"What if I told you my middle name is Cooper and my first name is Sam?"

"You're not a Sam."

"That's why I go by Cooper."

"Is your first name really Sam?"

"Nope."

For the love—we're not getting anywhere. "Well, Sam-slash-Cooper, I legitimately didn't know who you were until one minute ago. I was afraid Doug wouldn't let me in if I didn't say who I was visiting, so I weaseled him into telling me your name. I'm in dire need of a cameraman."

"Dire need? That sounds dramatic." He crosses his arms.

Can't say I blame the guy for being skeptical—this whole interaction has been derailed from where it was supposed to go. Time to pull out the big guns.

"Yes, dire. Here's what I'm working with at the moment." I pull out my iPhone and click around until I find what I need. There. Play.

Cooper looks over my shoulder. I can smell his cologne. It's fresh and earthy, almost citrusy, and it reminds me of summer. I debate moving the phone so he'll lean in closer.

"Whoa. Is that you? What's on your face?"

"Long story. Don't ask. The point is: I have to get to the International Space Station, and I'm not doing it with this video. I need professional help." I drop the phone to my side and face him. I may or may not be in his personal space. Is there a strict dimension requirement on personal space? Does it get smaller for certain people?

He doesn't step back, which is a good sign. "How is any video, professional or otherwise, going to get you to the International Space Station?"

"There's an internship being sponsored by NASA, and applicants have to—" Wait a minute. The video is still playing.

From somewhere near my knee, I hear myself say, "Why are you wearing only a tutu to a press conference? Have some decency." Ack! PAUSE.

The video pauses with my mouth half open and one of my eyes sort of shut. Can't get it in my jeans pocket fast enough.

"You were filming with someone wearing only a tutu?"

"It was no one. Beaker Troll. Again, long story. Super long."

Cooper laughs. "I have . . . all the questions."

The producer comes over the megaphone again. "Two minutes to filming. Get where you're supposed to be, people."

Time to get down to business. "I need to finish my mom's research on neutron stars." I unzip my backpack and pull out some papers. "Here's a copy of the application guidelines, and I included a few information sheets about the research. So you can get acquainted with the subject matter." This felt way cooler last night when I was making the packet.

He flips through the pages and eyes my T-shirt. "QuizBowl, huh?"

"It looks good on college applications if I have an extracurricular activity."

"Are you good at it?"

I shrug. "I'm the captain, so maybe? We get most of the science ones right."

"Mmmm." He's deep in thought as he reads the application requirements. "Do you think you have a shot at this internship?"

"I wouldn't be applying if I didn't."

He flips to some of the later pages in the packet and reads out loud. "Electrons become degenerate, meaning that electrical and thermal conductivities . . . What does this even mean?"

"It explains how neutron stars work. I thought it might be helpful for you to know about them."

He skims a few of the papers as I talk.

"I don't know how much you charge, or what to even offer for something like this. Is there a going rate? Do you have a brochure?" He should have a stack of pamphlets around or something. This is a poor business model.

Cooper hands the papers back to me. It looks like his decision has been made. "I know exactly what I charge."

"Oh, good." I checked my bank account last night, and hopefully he doesn't need more than that. I checked my dad's, too, just in case I need to borrow some money. It's for a good cause (kind of).

"Hour per hour. Even trade."

Now it's my turn to be confused. "What?"

"You're clearly science-y, and I need someone science-y. My sister, Bridget, is a sophomore, and she's in danger of being ineligible for volleyball. She needs to pass chemistry, and if her grade dips under seventy, she'll be benched. You tutor her one hour for each hour I work on this video. What do you think?"

I've never tutored anyone before, but it would look good on my MIT application if I dedicate some time to the . . . less fortunate. Plus, how hard could it be? I can balance chemistry equations in my sleep.

"Deal." We shake hands to seal it. His hand is a little rough, but not in an unpleasant way. Our eyes meet, and I find myself happy that slightly prolonged eye contact is a common feature of a sealing-a-business-deal handshake. I wonder about what element he is, but it's too soon for me to call it. I hope I'll spend enough time with him to find out for sure. I break eye contact, and he drops my hand.

Seriously, who invented handshakes? They need a thank-you card.

Cooper's smiling face grows serious. "One thing, though." He pauses, like he's thinking hard about how to make this request. "When we film, can I wear more than a tutu?"

My hand flies to my face, but I'm smiling. "Oh my gosh. Yes. Stop making this weird."

He laughs so loud that a couple of the sequined actresses look over, then shakes his head. "Can you start tonight? Bridge has a quiz in two days."

"What's her grade right now?"

"Seventy-two. And they play their rivals next week."

Eeep. I was hoping for a bit more of a percentage buffer. "You're awfully invested in your sister's volleyball career."

"I don't care much about volleyball, but I would do anything for my sister." He tries to smile, but his lips stay closed this time. His jaw clenches, like he wants to say something but can't. He looks at the floor for a second, lost in something, then swallows and looks up. His eyes have lost their jokey smile from earlier, replaced by something that resembles pain. "It's how family works, right?"

I think of my dad and what he would say if he knew I was here right now. I try to nod enthusiastically. "Right."

4

Bridget's room is painted in our school colors (purple and gold—two walls of each). Her bedspread is purple. Her throw pillows are gold. Posters on her wall advertise beach volleyball tournaments from last summer and the one before that. She has a framed picture of her team on her dresser, and the dresser is decorated in colorful paper with quotes such as "Our game is tighter than our Spandex" and "You can hit on us, but you can't score."

"Those are locker signs," Bridget says when she notices me reading them. "We take turns making locker signs before each game and put them on all the team members' lockers. I keep them and hang them on my dresser. I think I might cover the whole thing by the end of the season."

"You . . . really like volleyball." I'm unsure of what else to say. I'm clutching my top three favorite chemistry textbooks and my calculator, and for the second time today, I feel completely out of place.

"It's sort of my life," she says. "That and Andrew." She pulls out her phone and shows me the lock screen: a picture of her kissing a guy with dark hair. He's wearing a gray polo, and his strong arms are wrapped around an enraptured Bridget. You can see her boobs about to pop out of her purple tank top because she's pressed so hard against him. Their eyes are both closed, which I've read is common practice in kissing.

"Isn't he dreamy?" She looks like she wants to kiss her phone screen.

"Why do people close their eyes when kissing?"

Her glowy reverie is broken. "Um . . . I don't know. It's what people do." She looks back at her phone as if the idea had never occurred to her, but yeah, now that I've mentioned it, why are their eyes closed?

The phone is my electronic Petri dish, and I study the picture again. "If you're in love with someone, don't you want to see what they look like up close? Like, 'Stare into my corneas. Perhaps if we're close enough, I could see the rods and cones at the back of your eyes.'" A smile plays at the corners of my lips.

"What?" Her ponytail leans to the side when she tilts her head.

"That was a joke. You can't see rods and cones. There's a crap ton of vitreous humor in the way, and also they're tiny."

She laughs, but she is not skilled at fake laughing. "Here. Look. His eyes are brown." She unlocks her screen, but her phone background is Bridget with a bunch of girls. It's the highest number of faces I have ever seen smashed into one selfie. "Oops, those are my friends from my volleyball team. I forgot I changed my background. Hold on. I'll find a picture of Andrew's eyes."

I've never had a tower of friends like that, but I did have a friend once. Her name was Sasha. Sasha and I ate lunch together almost every day from kindergarten until second grade. She got me a scientist Barbie for my birthday when I turned six. I got her a baby doll because she wanted a little sister. When she moved away before third grade, we promised to write each other letters every day. I wrote her letter after letter with no answer, and she finally responded to say her new best friend's name was Callie and to ask what my new best friend's name was. Also, good news—her mom was going to have a real baby, so now she'd have a real-life sister!

I never heard from Sasha again. I decided she's the element lawrencium. One of the isotopes of lawrencium has a half-life of 2.7 minutes. It wasn't made to last long. There were many times that year when I cried in my mom's lap about not having any friends. She would stroke my hair and say, "It's okay, SkyLight. You'll find more friends. Plus, no matter what happens, you'll always have me to love you."

My mom was dead six months later.

Life's sick like that sometimes.

Bridget finds a picture and shows me her phone again.

"There. Now will you admit he's sexy?"

"Wow. You're so lucky." I try to look stunned by the picture.

"I know." Placated, she puts her phone away. "That's the only kind of chemistry I'm interested in, if you know what I mean."

"Unfortunately, that kind of chemistry won't keep you on the volleyball team."

She wrings her perfectly manicured hands. "That's the problem. I've been playing since sixth grade. I was on varsity as a freshman. I'm hoping for a scholarship to the University of Nevada, Las Vegas, for volleyball, but if I'm ineligible . . ." She wipes her hands on her jeans. "I can't be ineligible."

"Right."

And I can't risk not having my space video.

Bridget's desk only has one chair, a black leather office chair that doesn't look like it's been used often. There's a fluffy purple bucket chair in the corner. "Can I pull this up?"

"Sure, of course." I put my books on her desk while she grabs the chair for me. It's the least ergonomic chair I have ever sat on, but I suffer through it and open the first textbook. "What's going to be on your test?"

Bridget sits down and drapes herself dramatically across her desk. "Acids and bases. The actual worst." She reaches into her backpack and pulls out a piece of green paper. "Here's the review sheet."

I skim the paper and feel confident. I hand her one of the textbooks. "Acids and bases are chapter three in this one. Start there, and we'll see if you have any questions."

She sits up, opens the book to chapter three, and reads about two sentences before saying, "Yeah . . . I don't get this."

"What don't you get?"

"What's a *peh*?"

"A *peh*?"

"*Peh? Pah? Puh? Puh-huh?* How do you say this?" She pushes the book toward me.

"Oh, pH. You just say the letters: *p . . . H.*"

"Oh yeah. I think my teacher mentioned that. What is it again?"

Uh-oh.

An hour later, Cooper knocks on the door. "You about done?" he asks.

Bridget and I have barely scratched the surface of acids and bases, and we've only used one of my chemistry textbooks. About half an hour in, I gave up on Bridget understanding the concepts and resorted to helping her memorize the review sheet. It's going to be her best shot.

"I guess I'm ready?" Bridget says. She seems as unsure as I am. "Thanks for your help."

"Sure," I say. "No problem." I pick up my books, but then I put one back on her desk. "You can use this one tonight if you want. If you think it would help you study."

"Thanks, Skyler." She seems touched, but I have a feeling the book will remain closed until I get it back.

"When are Mom and Dad getting back?" Cooper asks.

"Beats me," Bridget says. "They're meeting a guy about a stroller."

The only type of stroller I know about is a baby stroller. In a family with two teenage children, that doesn't make much sense. Maybe there's another type I'm missing. Curiosity overcomes my fear of sounding stupid. "She's buying a baby stroller?"

"Yeah, my mom flips strollers." Cooper acts like it's normal, not the weirdest hobby ever. "She always brings my dad to Craigslist deals so she doesn't get murdered or whatever."

"She flips them? Like flipping a house?"

"Yeah." Bridget explains this like she's had to explain it many times. "She buys used and then tricks them out—gets fresh parts from the companies, updates the upholstery. She's even done leather interior or lights. Then she sells them for a lot more than she puts into them. People spend an absurd amount of money on baby stuff."

"There's a fleet of strollers-in-progress in our basement," Cooper admits. "But I don't usually show them to a girl the first time I have her over." He's glaring at Bridget.

"Oops, never mind, then." Bridget holds both hands under her chin with her fingers up, framing her face. "We're the ideal family. The picture of Americana."

I want to see this fleet of baby strollers, but Cooper insists we need to get some work done. When we get to the living room, I expect that he'll have cameras arranged and a set ready to go like in the band room today. But there's only a normal old living room, a bag of pretzel rods, and a six-pack of grape soda. I'm not sure what I expected a cute guy's living room to look like, but it seems like it should have been . . . grander. Maybe tall ceilings, walnut trim on some things, I don't know. Not cream walls, mismatched furniture, and an old TV in the corner.

"Grape soda?" I ask.

"It's liquid creativity. Have one." He tosses a can my way, which will agitate the carbonation. Now I can't open it for fear of creating a soda volcano on his parents' white carpeting.

"Where are the cameras?" I ask.

Cooper gives me a look that makes me realize how Bridget must have felt when she asked about *peh*. It's "You've got to be kidding me" mixed with "Oh crap, you're not kidding."

"We're not filming tonight."

"Why not?" I want to get this submitted as soon as possible. It's not due for four weeks, but maybe I'll get bonus points for being early.

Cooper pulls a notebook out of his green backpack. "I have pretzels, grape soda, and a notebook. That's all we need tonight. We're brainstorming." He takes out a pretzel rod and holds it between his index and middle fingers like he's smoking a cigar.

"What is there to brainstorm? I talk, you film."

I think Cooper's trying not to roll his eyes. "A film is art, Sky. You don't make art by dumping a bucket of paint on a canvas. You plan it. You work with it. You make it beautiful. We need to evoke emotion in our viewer—get them on our side. Make them root for us."

"NASA people are scientists, not artists. They don't care about emotions."

"They're humans, aren't they? Humans care about emotions." He stares at his notebook as if reading invisible ideas. "How should we open the scene? Maybe something floral and earthy?" He takes the pretzel rod out of his mouth for a minute, then puts it back in and starts scribbling notes.

"Floral and earthy?"

"Yeah, because we want to end with it in space. So it's a juxtaposition."

I blink at him. "It looks like you're smoking that pretzel."

He looks at it as if he just noticed. "Yeah. This is what I do when I need to be creative. Tons of great cinematographers were smokers, but I'm not keen on lung cancer. So I smoke pretzels. Same creative genius, lower healthcare bills." He bites off the end of it and holds it away from his mouth.

What have I gotten myself into?

Just then, the back door opens. Before I know what's going on, I'm pinned to the ground by over a hundred pounds of furry energy.

"Chewy! No!" The pretzel bag crinkles as Cooper jumps off the couch.

I am getting a saliva facial from the biggest dog I have ever seen. *Seen* is not actually the right word since I can't see him. My eyes are squeezed shut to try to keep his tongue out of them. *This* is a good reason to close your eyes while getting a kiss, but I doubt it ever applies to humans.

Cooper wrestles Chewy off me and pulls him over to the couch. "Sorry about that. Great Danes are huge but friendly. It's Snickers you have to look out for." He nods to the doorway, where another dog, a tri-colored Chihuahua, is giving me the stink eye.

"Nice doggy," I venture.

Snickers growls.

"Do you have pets?" Cooper asks.

I wipe slime off my face with the arm of my hoodie. "Yeah, a rat."

"A rat?" He squints like this is very bizarre, but he's the one with the drool machine and the evil Chihuahua. "Why a rat?"

"My dad's a microbiologist. He uses them in his lab. Sometimes I grab one to keep. This one's number five."

"What's its name?"

"Five."

Cooper snorts. "So original."

Chewy is leaving a puddle of drool on the couch next to Cooper. I see suspicious stains on the love seat and decide maybe I should sit on the floor in the future.

A quick scan of the room tells me there is no hand sanitizer, which is too bad. "Five's a specimen, not a pet. Specimens don't have names."

"Sounds like you just have a pet with a stupid name."

I lean away, looking skeptical. "You clearly don't understand research."

Cooper shrugs. "Didn't claim to." He goes back to writing in his notebook. "Weird pets are sweet. I had a pet bat under my bed once."

My face matches the one he gave me when I said I have a rat. "The . . . flappy kind of bat? Or you pretended a baseball bat was your pet?"

Cooper laughs because one of those is ridiculous, but I'm not sure which one.

"The flappy one, you weirdo. Who would keep a baseball bat as a pet?" He hasn't looked up from writing, but he shakes his head like I'm hilarious. "It was for a science class in sixth grade. My teacher needed a place to keep an injured bat while it rehabbed, so I kept it in a cage under my bed. That was because of the darkness and also so that my parents wouldn't know about it. Eight weeks later, it flew away to live happily ever after with the other flappy bats. My parents still don't know. I'm trying to decide how many years have to go by before they'll think it's funny, but we're not there yet." He finishes writing something in the notebook. "So—earthy and floral? Yes?" He looks up and points next to the loveseat with his pencil. "Watch yourself."

Snickers has sneaked over to the side of the loveseat and is peeking around the corner, sniffing the heels of my socks. I jump in surprise, and Snickers runs full speed out of the room like I shocked him. Then he stands at the doorway and starts yapping furiously.

"Bridge!" Cooper calls up the stairs. "Can you get the pack of paws out of here?"

"Roger that," Bridget answers.

Footsteps sound on the stairs, and then the back door opens again.

"Come on, drool tools!"

Snickers zips out, and Chewy lumbers out behind him.

Bridget pokes her head into the living room. "Sorry, I thought you went downstairs. Good luck on the Salt Lake thing."

"Salt Lake thing?" I look at Cooper. He doesn't look as confused as he should.

Bridget wraps a hair tie around her high ponytail. "Yeah. Thanks so much for helping him with it. We were worried he would never get started. He's got all the creativity in the world, you know? But his drive . . . eh. Sometimes we think it drove away." She laughs at her own joke and heads back upstairs.

The ticking wall clock suddenly feels very loud.

Cooper clears his throat. "I, um . . ."

Now I wish the dogs were back in here so that I could pet them or something while I wait for him to formulate whatever he's about to say. Who's mistaken here? Should I be mad about something?

"I'm applying to the University of Utah film school. It's in Salt Lake City."

"Oh." That doesn't explain anything.

He stares at his shoes and talks like he can't get the words out fast enough. "My application is due in five weeks. I have to have a video for it that showcases someone making a difference in my community. Documentary-style sample, no more than four minutes in length. So when you came along, I thought . . . I mean, if you don't mind, maybe I could . . ."

"You're going to use my NASA video for your film school application?"

He meets my eyes. "Is that okay? Sorry I didn't tell you earlier. I thought that if I was the one doing you a favor, you might tutor Bridget, and she *has* to stay eligible. But I suck at chemistry, and we can't afford a tutor. Let's recall that my mom's full-time gig is *flipping strollers*. My dad runs a tiny camera shop. Anyway, our agreement is a little more even-trade than I let on. Please still tutor Bridget? I'll make the video kick butt with an extra dose of *kick*. Scout's honor." He does the sign of the Catholic cross instead of the Boy Scout sign, but his eyes are earnest.

"Cooper, it's fine."

After meeting Bridget and seeing how much help she needs, I feel it would be a crime against science to leave her in her current state of ignorance. It would be like watching a kitten stuck in a tree, mewing, and me walking by while saying, "Sucks to suck." She strikes me as a rubidium, though it's tough to tell after only one meeting. Rubidium is a beautiful metal, but it's soft and doesn't have many practical uses. It also produces strong reactions. I'll go with rubidium unless new properties in her personality prove otherwise.

"You'll do it?" Cooper looks hopeful. "Seriously?"

"Of course. It's symbiosis."

Cooper's face breaks into a wide smile, and I put an invisible periodic table in front of him. The squares all disappear as I rule them out. Within a few seconds, all the squares are gone. What *is* he?

My silence must be concerning him because his smile flickers. "That's . . . good, right? Symbiosis? Sorry, I hated chemistry."

I smile, mentally erasing the table and deciding I'll figure out his element later. "It means we're helping each other. That's all."

He lets out a huge breath. "Thanks so much, Sky. I majorly owe you." He cracks open another soda. "We could use the dogs," Cooper thinks out loud. "That's earthy."

"I'm not putting your dogs in my NASA video."

"Why not? Everyone likes dogs."

This new development might not work in my favor. Does he have equal control over this video now? "This is a serious video, Cooper. It needs to be scientific. Impressive. Intelligent."

"Okay." Cooper puts down his pencil. "Tell me. What is your vision for this project?"

"I was thinking I'd sit somewhere, science textbooks in my lap, and look very smart."

Cooper is dutifully writing down my notes. When I stop talking, he looks up. "Then what?"

"Then what? It's a three-minute video."

Cooper squints. "It's not . . . great." We're quiet for a minute.

Cooper turns on the TV and flips to the TV Guide channel. "What do you want to watch? Looks like we have *Law & Order: Special Victims Unit* or *Dateline*."

"Um, we're supposed to be working on my application video. Our application video."

"I know. But work can only start when inspiration strikes. We're not inspired right now." He throws me the bag of pretzels. "Dig in. And drink that grape soda you haven't opened. Which show do you want? Wait, I haven't seen this *Dateline*. That okay with you?"

I'm too stunned to say anything besides "Okay."

Some guy is talking about a murder on a dark street in the middle of nowhere, and I tentatively crunch a pretzel. It doesn't taste inspired. Maybe I should just leave.

Forty minutes later, I'm engrossed in the forensic science used to convict the no-good ruthless killer. If they don't have enough evidence, he could run free! He could kill again! I haven't watched anything but space documentaries for a long time (excluding the night after the SAT scores came out). This is cool. I try to take another sip of my grape soda, but the can is empty.

Cooper gets a text. "Ugh. My dad needs me to go to his shop and fix a camera. He always needs me to fix the cameras. Let me see if it can wait ten minutes." He starts typing a text while keeping his eyes on the TV screen.

"He's got to be guilty," I say. "His wallet was at the crime scene!"

Cooper shakes his head. "Circumstantial. It's not going to be enough." He shakes the dregs of the pretzel bag into his mouth.

My phone buzzes. It's my dad.

Where are you? You need to come home immediately.

5

My dad never tells me to come home. He floats between the lab and the hospital except for when I snag him for dinner. Today I'd texted him that his dinner was in the fridge. There was a high probability that it would remain uneaten, but I'd at least put it there. When I called and asked why I needed to come home, he said he had a surprise for me. His voice was weird, like it was an attempt at being cheery but the cheer got strangled.

To my surprise, dinner is on the table when I get there. It's lasagna, salad, and very familiar-looking breadsticks. Olive Garden to-go. I don't see any bag, and the lasagna is awkwardly plunked in a pan. Is he trying to pass this off as home cooking? Why?

"Hi, honey," he says as soon as I walk in. He calls me SkyBear all the time, but never "honey." He looks over his shoulder into the kitchen. "There's someone I want you to meet." He's wringing his hands. A woman rounds the corner.

"Jack, are these the glasses you want?" A tall brunette around thirty years old, maybe younger, is holding our plastic periodic table tumblers. You can hardly call them glasses. Her hair cascades perfectly past her shoulders, but it still has the volume of a just-blown-out look. Her makeup looks like that of a model on the cover of a magazine. She's wearing a multicolored checkered romper—a *romper*—and yellow high heels. I don't remember the last time there were high heels in this house. It might be never. She looks vaguely familiar, but I can't pinpoint why.

I look at my dad like he's lost his mind. Who is the supermodel holding our periodic table tumblers? Am I supposed to eat lasagna with her? Am I supposed to pretend he cooked the lasagna? He couldn't have texted me some sort of heads-up about this?

"Sky, this is Charli," he says.

We all stare at each other in silence. Is this *The Twilight Zone*?

"I spell it with an *i*," she finally says, like this explains everything. She has a slight southern accent. "I was named after my grandfather, which was better than my grandmother. Her name was Maude." She laughs like this is hilarious, and my dad forces a laugh while looking at me.

"Maude, huh? Can't see her as a Maude, can you?" He shakes his head. I swear he's about to slap his knee, happy-grandpa style.

"Right." I nod. "Not Maude." As if her name were the confusing part of this situation. The three of us stare at each other. I still don't know why Charli-with-an-*i* is here. I look between them, waiting for someone to explain.

"Well." Charli breaks the silence by setting the "glasses" down on the table. She seems to have decided that it's her job to explain what's going on. My dad looks paralyzed by the weirdness of all of this. "Jack here has been so kind to me the past couple of weeks, and when I was discharged, I told him that I simply had to spend my first day of freedom celebrating with him. And I've been dying to meet the SkyBear that he talks about all the time."

"She was a very interesting case," my dad adds. "We spent a lot of time together while I tried to study this bacterial infection. I was called in as a specialty consultation two days into her illness, which was lucky for me."

They exchange a look that I can only describe as *gooey*.

I put my hand on my hip. "Seriously, Dad?"

"Sorry." He holds his hands out in apology. "It started with just talking about our lives. I didn't know it would turn into . . ."

"Into what?" I'm not letting him off the hook on this. "Are you guys dating or something?" They would make the weirdest pair ever. Picture a rose dating a dandelion.

"We're taking it slow." Charli smiles at my dad in a way that I don't like at all. "One day at a time, right, Jack? Just like my recovery."

"That's right." He nods and smiles at me. His mouth is smiling, but his eyes are pleading. "She's the patient I had to see the other day when I had to leave your school so quickly. We were afraid some symptoms were returning, but it turns out she's fine. Can we have dinner together? It's just one dinner."

"Yeah, of course." I shake off my backpack and try to shake off the weight building in my chest. Only the backpack comes off.

We settle in around the table, and Charli says, "Shall we say grace?" She holds her hands out for us to each hold one. My eyebrows shoot up. My dad's eyes are pleading again. He's lucky I love him so much.

I hold Charli's hand and notice her ballet-pink fingernails. Not a single chip. She bows her head and closes her eyes. I take the opportunity to mouth, "What the heck?" to my dad.

He tilts his head toward Charli and mouths, "Watch it," back to me.

I know my dad doesn't believe in God. I respect all beliefs, but does that mean that I really have to sit around my own dining room table and say grace?

Yes, apparently.

"Amen!" Charli finishes and drops our hands. She gives me a warm smile and passes the plastic basket of bread. "Breadstick, Sky? Can I call you Sky?"

"Better than SkyBear." I shoot a glare toward my dad. "Thanks."

I take a breadstick. It tastes stale. This might be because the breadstick *is* stale or because food doesn't taste good when I feel like throwing up. My dad takes some lasagna, and I try to look at this situation scientifically. As far as my dad being attracted to Charli, I can see the sexual appeal. I don't like to think of my dad as a sexual being, but it's hard not to see the allure of Charli's perfect body, hair, and nails.

Now I analyze Charli's attraction to my dad. He was apparently her microbiology consult, so maybe it's a savior complex? Like she read too many romance novels about sexy doctors, and now she wants one of her own? But my dad would not be described as *sexy* by any objective measure. Then again, if he's the one who saved her, maybe that overrides the need for aesthetically pleasing physical features? Interesting. I will research this later.

"So, Sky," Charli says, serving herself some lettuce. "Your dad says you like stars?"

I *like* stars? That's like someone saying, "Ice is chilly."

"They're my life."

"Mmm-hmmm." She nods enthusiastically with a mouth full of lettuce. She swallows. "I once had a red dress with black stars on it. I wore it to my freshman-year formal. Still one of my favorite formal looks." She smiles like we're so similar.

What she's doing here is trying to find something in common with me in order to win my approval. It's classic psychology. I see right through you, Charli-with-an-*i*. But I don't think she's being malicious about comparing neutron stars to her formal dress. She's just wildly uninformed.

"Neutron stars aren't star-shaped at all," I say. "They're born from the explosive death of a star that was up to eight times the size of our sun, and then they keep blowing off layers as the star's mass condenses into a smaller and smaller object. Even when it's at its smallest, it's still larger than our sun. It gets extremely compacted." I push my hands together like I'm compacting a neutron star myself. "So compacted, in fact, that the protons press into the electrons, and the positive and negative energies combine to form neutrons. Hence the name *neutron* star. But they're round, not pointy. So, um, your dress wasn't strictly scientifically accurate." Or accurate at all. I'm being generous.

"Right, I see." Charli nods too enthusiastically. "So what I hear you saying is . . . the polka-dot dress that I wore to my cousin Shayla's wedding is the real star dress!"

Oh my gosh.

"This lasagna is great," my dad says, trying to take over the conversation. "Did you make it yourself, Charli?"

"I gotta be honest, y'all." Charli leans over her plate like she's letting us in on a huge secret. "I didn't have time to cook, so I catered it."

Catered is a generous word for Olive Garden, but I'll let her have it.

"Thanks," I say. I'm only saying it because social convention states I should say that here. I'm not feeling thankful.

"We're all busy," my dad says. "Catering works great for us!" He passes me the lasagna dish. "Charli has a very successful online business."

"Really?" I try not to sound as surprised as I feel. "What is it?"

"I'm a vlogger," she says. "I run a makeup and fashion vlog. Maybe you've heard of it? *Kisses from Charli*?"

Wait a minute. I knew she looked familiar, but with so much happening today, the tutorial I'd watched just the night before had already slipped my mind. She's Charli from *Kisses from Charli*? There's a *makeup influencer* having dinner with us? What are the odds of that? About the same as the odds of me happening upon a pile of astatine, the rarest element on earth.

If it was possible, this just got weirder.

My dad laughs. "Sky's not exactly—"

"I've heard of it," I interrupt.

He looks startled.

"Seriously," I say, turning to Charli, "I tried your tutorial on contouring just yesterday."

"You wear makeup?" My dad sounds shocked.

"No." Oops. I can't tell my dad why I was trying makeup. He still thinks I gave up on the NASA idea. "It was an experiment for, um, a science thing." Which is mostly true.

"How did it go?" Charli asks. "You've got phenomenal cheekbones."

"Thanks," I say. There is no such thing as a cheekbone. She's complimenting the prominence that's part of the zygomatic bone of my skull. I suppose if she wants to compliment my skull, I won't stop her. "I did my best with the tutorial, but I would still consider myself a novice."

"Bless your heart. I can help you!" she says. "We can do a makeover sometime!"

Her shoulders relax like she's landed squarely in her comfort zone. Mine tense involuntarily. I do not want any more chemicals on my face. Plus, isn't *Bless your heart* an insult sometimes? Is she being genuine here or trying to be condescending? My eyes narrow.

"I'm not sure that I'm a makeup kind of girl."

"I'm sorry, what did you say?" She pushes a strand of hair back behind her ear like she didn't hear me right.

"I'm not a makeup kind of girl."

"Oh. Right. What do you do for fun when you're not studying stars?"

"I train my rats."

She blanches. "Your . . . rats?"

"I only have one at a time, but rats have an average of a three-year life span. I've had two who died from upper respiratory infections and one that had liver cancer when I got it. My dad gave it the cancer. I tried to cure it as my project for last year's science fair. It didn't work out, but I still won."

Charli stops with her fork halfway to her mouth, wrinkles her nose, and puts it back on the plate. "That's wonderful. Good for you."

Charli leaves after the world's longest dinner and one excruciating game of Scrabble. I played words like *pipette* and *forceps*. She played words like *lip* and *cute*.

"So," my dad says as he washes a "glass." "What do you think? She's nice, right?"

"I guess." I rinse a dish. "She'd look great next to a Ken doll."

"Don't hold it against her that she's beautiful."

"I'm not. I'm holding it against her that she's vapid."

"Come on, Sky. I wouldn't have even let her come over except that you told me to move on. I'm trying to move on."

"I didn't mean with *her*," I say. "Of course I want you to move on. I want you to be happy. I don't mind if you start dating again. But can't you date a scientist? Or an accountant or something?"

"An accountant?"

"Not necessarily an accountant." I wave my hands like he's missing the point. "Just . . . I don't know . . . not a freaking makeup vlogger? Come on, Dad. She's the opposite of us."

"She's not."

"No, Dad, she really is. You collect microbes. She collects mascara."

"Can you try to see her as an artist?"

"No."

He sighs heavily. "I just want to do what's best for us. Charli is smart in a nonscience way, and she's deep when you get to know her."

I almost drop my dish, but I catch it at the last second. "How? How is she deep? *Deep*, as in she's buried under so much makeup that it would take a team of archaeologists to find her actual skin?"

"Hey, that's not fair." Something in his gaze looks broken, and then he puts his head down, studying the fork he's washing.

I hate that he's defending her. I hate that I've hurt him. We wash dishes in thick silence for a few minutes.

"She wasn't wearing any makeup when I met her," he says. "She was so sick. Even her hair looked frail. And she was still so beautiful."

I cringe.

"The doctors couldn't figure out what was wrong, and she wasn't stabilizing. That's when they called me. They thought it might be something bacterial."

"And it was?" As much as I don't like Charli, the science part is fascinating.

"Yes. It was a rare bacterium. We've only seen a few cases in the United States. Once I figured out what it was, it was relatively easy to treat. As you can see, she's fine now." He smiles to himself, like he's proud that he saved her life. He should be proud. My dad is brilliant.

"Where did she pick up this weird bacterium?"

My dad's smile falters, like he knows I won't like the answer. "Our best guess is that it was from a pedicure she got in Dubai."

I slam the dish into the drying rack so hard that I may have chipped it. "Are you telling me that you're dating someone who almost died from a *pedicure*?"

He drops the fork back into the sudsy water and turns off the faucet. The dishes are momentarily forgotten. "Sky. You and I both know that bacteria can enter the body in a myriad of ways. Nail salons can be dangerous. It's not your place to judge whether or not—"

"I'm not judging. You're judging. You're the doctor, right? You judged where that bacterium came from. And then you decided that it was a good idea to bring this woman home for dinner. Do you not remember Mom at all? Can Charli even spell *astrophysicist*?"

"When did you become so rude?" His voice has an edge to it that I haven't heard before. My dad is never angry with me. Is this what it's like to fight with your parents? Goose bumps raise on my arms. I can't fight with my dad. I don't have friends to call and complain to about him. My dad has always been my ally, my friend. If anything, I've been the one taking care of him. What am I going to do after this? Go talk to Five?

I take a deep breath and try to stabilize the situation. "I'm not rude. I'm rational. Men like you don't date women like her. It's unnatural. It doesn't make any sense. The entire world is ordered by logic and reason, right? That's why we're scientists—because we love this. And you're messing everything up."

"You're the one who told me to move on," he reiterates. "You can't suddenly switch and be mad about it."

"Come on, Dad. Anyone else. I'm serious—anyone. She's awful."

"You didn't give her a chance."

"Date my chemistry teacher! She's single!"

"Isn't she the one with the bowl haircut and the long denim skirts?"

"Uh, yeah. But a denim skirt is very ergonomic. It protects against chemical spills. And it looks fabulous under a lab coat."

My dad turns the water on again. "This conversation is over."

It's over? Can he do that? Is this how fights work—someone can just declare it over? I'm not done. He has to see my point of view. How can he possibly disagree with me on this? I open my mouth but then shut it again. As I watch my dad scrub cheese off a fork, it's like I'm looking at a stranger. And I'm scared.

I grab my keys from the counter.

"Where are you going?" he asks. "The dishes aren't done."

"My participation in the dishes is over."

I run up the stairs and throw on a hoodie. I put the hood up, put Five in the pocket, and head out the door without answering my dad when he asks where I'm going.

6

The beauty of living in the desert is that the night sky is often clear. I pull my telescope from the trunk of my car and set it up to watch for meteors. There aren't any meteor showers scheduled for tonight, but you never know.

After about ten minutes, I see one. The shimmering, momentary streak of brightness against the deep black never ceases to amaze me. It's understandable why people make wishes on these. Nothing in the universe is more magical than the night sky.

I'm not superstitious, but I still find myself whispering, "I wish things were normal." I don't fully know what I mean by this wish. Do I wish it was like it was before dinner tonight, before I met Charli? Or before I had to keep secrets from my dad? Maybe before my mom died, and she would be out here with me? I don't know. Any and all of the above. Meteor's choice.

I pull Five out of my pocket and put her on the ground. She looks around, confused, and tentatively sniffs a couple of rocks. She sneezes.

"Stop sneezing," I command. "Come on. You've gotta get better." My eyes feel hot, and I'm so embarrassed. She's just a lab rat. "You're lucky you don't have a family," I tell her. I pull a granola bar out of my bag and give her a corner. "They mess up your life. They just . . . they make you so sad." Some people handle life's problems by getting drunk. Some do drugs. I sit in a desert, cheers-ing granola with a lab specimen.

I look through my telescope again. Nothing. I look at my watch—I should be able to see Mars in about an hour. Five finishes the piece of granola that I gave her, wipes her nose, and looks up at me again. I give her another piece. She sneezes.

I lie on my back and look up at the stars, putting Five on my stomach so she won't crawl away and get lost. Whenever I study the sky, I remember my mom's funeral and how so many people comforted me by saying, "She's in a better place. She's smiling down on you right now." They would look at the sky knowingly, like if I stared hard enough, I would see her face. And I've never stopped studying the sky, even long after my dad explained to me that I wouldn't ever see her up there. Sometimes I feel like I do see her up there. Not her face, but her essence. She dedicated her life to the night sky. In that way, if I dedicate my life to it, too, it's almost like we're together. We're standing side by side and separated by an impenetrable curtain. And out here, when I'm looking at the stars, that curtain feels a little bit thinner.

My phone buzzes in my pocket. When I pick it up, the screen flashes aggressively bright. Shoot. Now I'm going to have to wait to get my night vision back again. It's a text from Cooper.

Everything okay?

I left his house in such a rush when my dad texted me earlier that I never offered a good explanation of why. After all, I didn't have an explanation myself. I text back.

Yeah. I'm fine.

That's exactly what my sister says when she's not fine.

I'm taken aback. "What do I say to that?" I ask Five. She stops chewing granola to look at me, then wipes her nose and goes back to the granola. Before I can formulate a good text response, he adds an *LOL*. He's giving me an out to laugh it off if I want to. Do I want to?

I'm studying stars. It's neither a confirmation nor a denial. Not a great time to chat. I put the phone back in my pocket and take a deep breath.

The phone buzzes again.

Where are you? I'll come get footage.

Footage? It's dark. If he brings any lights, it will wreck the stargazing. He should leave me alone.

Then again, I'm a bit overdosed on alone. My best friend is a rat, I'm not going to get into MIT without a better SAT score, and now my choices are to disappoint my mom by going to a different college and/or make my dad angry by applying to NASA behind his back. Even if I get the internship, his anger about me going will make the achievement ring a little hollow. Not that I won't do it, of course. It's just that my life, which seemed so full of promise a few months ago, now feels . . . alone.

I'm off the 95. About twenty miles out of town toward Sloan Conservation Area.

That's a pretty far drive for this time of night. He'll text back and say that we'll reschedule. It's fine, seriously. I'm not *that* alone, if I really think about it. It's been a rough night, and emotions are so fleeting and untrustworthy. As a matter of fact—

A text pings in.

I'll be right there.

Oh. Okay.

A half hour later, bright lights once again wreck my night vision. Cooper pulls up behind my station wagon and turns off his car. He pops the trunk and pulls some lighting equipment out of the back.

I shove Five back in my hoodie pocket and head over. "Do you need help?"

"Sure," he says. "You take the camera." He hands me a black case with a bunch of side pockets on it. He pulls out one of those white umbrella-looking things.

"Does the film club know you have all of this?"

He stops and smiles at me, proud of himself. "These are mine."

"Whoa." I'm impressed.

"It's one of the perks of my dad owning Norman Camera." He continues taking things out of his trunk.

"Are we shooting a video or building a city?"

"There's a surprising amount of overlap between those two. Planning, construction, finessing the details . . . making sure everything's pretty but still accomplishing purpose. Yeah. We're doing a bit of both." He ducks his head back into the trunk and pulls out a six-pack of grape soda that is now a five-pack. "All that's left is my hat and the pretzels. Can you grab them?"

I pick up the trucker-style cap and read the front. "You showed a film at Sundance?" I don't know anything about filming, and I have no idea where Norman Camera is, but I have heard of the Sundance Film Festival. It would be Cooper's MIT.

"Ha!" Cooper is already sorting out his equipment by my telescope. "That's a negative, Ghost Rider."

"Ghost Rider?"

He looks incredulous, like I couldn't possibly be confused. "*Top Gun?*"

I shake my head.

"You've never seen *Top Gun?*" Now he's shocked. It's like I admitted I'm from Mars.

"I don't watch many movies."

He sighs and walks toward my telescope. "You don't have to have seen many movies to have seen *Top Gun*. It's a classic."

The trunk echoes loudly in the desert wilderness when I close it. "What's it about?"

By the time I get to my telescope, Cooper is already expertly putting his equipment together. It's clear that he's done it so many times that assembling in the darkness doesn't faze him.

"It's about a couple guys in flight school. One of the most classic friendship plots of all time: Maverick and Goose."

"Those are dumb names. Who names their kid Goose?"

"Those aren't their real names. Maverick is this super-independent dude, and Goose is his sidekick. Then there's Iceman . . ."

Pretty soon my telescope looks small under the equipment surrounding it. Cooper turns the lights on, and I squint and shade my eyes. "I won't be able to see any stars with all that light."

"You don't have to see the stars. Filmmaking isn't about reality. It's about appearing like reality. Those are different things, trust me." He puts his hat on his head.

"A hat seems superfluous," I comment. "There's no sun and no wind."

He takes it off and wipes some dust from the patch. "Keeps the dream front and center, you know?"

"Sundance is your dream?"

"Eventually. First I need to get into film school. This stuff is the tip of the iceberg on what I need to know how to operate." He motions to the pile of technology around us. Then he pulls something out of his bag. "Here. Put this on."

It's a tiny microphone with a clip on it. I look down at my hoodie and clip it to one of the strings. I hold up the battery pack. "What do I do with this?"

Cooper finishes adjusting a tripod. He takes the pack out of my hand and unclips the microphone. "The string part is supposed to go under your sweatshirt so that people won't see it. We could clip the pack to the waistband of your jeans and string it through. . . . Would that work?"

"Sure." I clip the battery pack in place and attempt to finagle the microphone. I go up through the front of my hoodie and pull it out of the top. "Where should I clip it?"

"Here." Cooper takes the microphone and clips it in one of the subtle folds of my hood. His fingers brush against my neck. The warm night is suddenly warmer. Maybe I should take the hoodie off. But then we'd be sliding things under my T-shirt, close to my bare skin, and . . .

I'll leave the hoodie on. I guess.

Cooper gets the microphone clipped and hidden. "Here. Clip this back into . . . Whoa. Is your hoodie pocket moving?"

How could I forget? I pull Five out and put her on my shoulder. "Meet Five."

"Awesome." He runs his index finger down her furry back. "Can I try putting her on my shoulder?"

Five looks instantly comfortable on Cooper's shoulder. She sniffs his ear, puts one paw up to his hair, then sits and starts clicking. Rats click their teeth when they're content. I wonder if rats can sense good people and bad people like dogs are supposed to do. Mental note: research this later.

"Here's what we're going to do," Cooper says, walking behind his camera. "You go ahead and do your telescope thing. I'll film. Go about your normal business and pretend I'm not here."

"I'm not going to be able to see anything. There are too many lights."

"Just pretend."

"I'm not good at pretending. Science is cutting through all the pretending and finding out what's real."

He looks up from behind the lens. "You wanna finish that research?"

"More than anything."

"Then pretend." He ducks back behind the camera. "Rolling."

Okay. Pretend. I can do this. The stars are gorgeous through my viewfinder, even though I can't see as many as I could before. Near the horizon, there's still no sign of Mars. It should be here soon.

I adjust the focus on one of the stars. The clarity sharpens.

Cooper calls from behind the camera. "When are you going to do something?"

"This is it. This is all I do."

"Hmmm." Cooper pops the top on a grape soda and takes a long drink. "I've got it." He comes over and plunks Five on my shoulder. "Narrate to her what you're doing."

"I'm not talking to a rat. That's ridiculous."

"Putting a rat on your shoulder makes you unique. Fun. NASA will want unique and fun." He goes behind the camera again without waiting for me to agree with him. "Still rolling. Pretend she's your sidekick."

"But she's a—"

"Specimen. I know." He rolls his eyes. "*Pretend.*"

Five sniffs my shoulder.

"Uh, this is Five," I say to the camera. "She's my rat. Kind of a sidekick. She's the Goose to my Maverick, some might say."

Cooper peeks out from the camera, smiles, and gives a thumbs-up.

I look through the viewfinder again. "Right now we're looking at the Milky Way and waiting for Mars to come up on the horizon."

Ten minutes later, Cooper finally yells, "Cut!"

He switches off his bright lights and closes the weird photography umbrella. (Seriously, what are those? Mental note: research this, too.) The camera goes back in its case.

"That was great," he says. "Definitely shot some usable footage there."

He tosses me a grape soda. Does he not understand carbonation? He's got to stop throwing these.

My phone shows five missed calls from my dad and a bunch of texts that I don't open. With a sigh, I take one last look through my telescope. Looks like Mars will have to wait.

When Cooper finishes putting the last of his equipment in his trunk, he comes back out to where I'm dismantling the telescope. He plucks Five from my shoulder, puts her on his, and then sits with his legs out in front of him, one hand in the dust behind him, and one hand swigging his artificial grape flavoring. He opens the pretzel bag and offers me one before taking one out himself.

"Why are you really out here?"

"I already told you that. I'm looking for stars."

"No you're not." He says it simply, like I just said four plus four is nine. "You left my house in a mad rush after getting a mysterious text, and then a couple hours later I find you in the middle of the desert with a rat you don't need for stargazing. My gut tells me I'm missing something, and I always go with my gut."

"That's a dangerous game."

"Tell me I'm wrong." He raises his eyebrows.

I'm faced with a choice: I could shake him off again and make up something about Five needing electrolytes (though I forgot to bring any with me).

Or . . .

Cooper senses my hesitation. "Come on, Sky. I may not be as smart as you, but I'm not stupid." He sets his can in the dust. "Call it research if you want. I have to learn more about you to capture your personality in a three-minute clip. Now, are you going to open that soda or what?"

I sit cross-legged in front of him and pop the top of the soda, which has settled by now. "You never met my mom." Relief leaves me like the air from the can. "She was the best."

"Yeah?" He sits up.

"Yeah. Her name was Renae. She was an astrophysicist, but she was one of those smart people who didn't care that she was smart, you know? She was so much fun. We baked cookies every Saturday. She would always say, 'Hey, Sky, you up for some kitchen chemistry?' like maybe I wouldn't want to do it that day. But I always did. They were chocolate chip cookies but with three butterscotch chips."

"Three butterscotch chips in each cookie?"

"No, three butterscotch chips in the whole batch. She said that if you got a cookie with a butterscotch chip in it, it meant it was your lucky day. At first, we started with only one butterscotch chip, but then she said we should do three so that there was a chance that my dad, my mom, and I could all have a lucky day that week. Sometimes it worked out that way, and sometimes it didn't. I'm pretty sure she kept track of the butterscotch chip cookies, though. There always seemed to be one in my lunch on a day when I had a test or a presentation or something."

He takes a swig of grape soda. "I would have thought your family wasn't the type to believe in superstitious stuff."

"She was the kind of person who made you want to believe in luck." The fizz inside me comes more from the memories than from the soda. "I'd always use my spoon to scrape bits of dough off the bowl, and she'd say, 'SkyScraper, put that down. You know skyscrapers belong in big cities, not in my kitchen.' But she always smiled when she said it, and then she'd wipe some up with her finger and eat it, too."

"She sounds amazing." He leans forward now, arms wrapped around his knees. Cooper's voice is genuine, not like people who awkwardly say nice things about her because it's sad that I'm that girl whose mom died.

"She died when I was eight. Car accident on her way home from the lab. She had just finished a day extending her neutron star research. The other driver had just finished a six-pack of Bud Light. The cans were in the back of his car. Want to know what was in the back of my mom's car? An Astronomy for Kids kit. It was in this big box. Well, it seemed big to me. I was only in third grade. It had a book and some star maps and even a little telescope to put in my window. It was going to be my birthday present."

"She died on your *birthday*?"

"No, three weeks before. She was the type to plan ahead. I didn't end up celebrating that year."

"Do you still have the kit?"

"I never opened it."

"Why not?"

"It's the last present I'll ever get from my mom. I don't know . . . I guess I didn't want to wreck it? Kids are always destroying their toys. It was sacred somehow. It's in my closet next to my copy of her dissertation."

"Ah, yes." Cooper leans back again. "The research."

"A lot of astronomers think that neutron stars can be used to help in interplanetary travel, especially for long-range space flights. There's a camera on the space station called the NICER—Neutron Star Interior Composition Explorer. If I can access that camera, I can finish the research. It wasn't up there when she was studying."

Cooper drains the soda. "It's a shame the astronomy community lost her. I'm sorry for their loss." He says this with his eyes locked on mine, as if he isn't talking about the astronomy community.

"Anyway, there's this new woman my dad brought home today, Charli, and she's awful."

"How so?" He takes a pretzel rod out of the bag and takes a bite of the end.

"She was wearing a romper. And yellow high heels. And she used the phrase *bless your heart*."

"And those things are . . . bad?"

"No. I mean, yes. Kind of. I don't know."

"She's not your mom?"

"It's not that. I'm not the kid who doesn't want her dad to move on because I'm scared of the evil stepmother or whatever. I want him to be happy, just with someone respectable."

"What makes someone respectable?"

"I don't know. It's not like I've done research on this. I don't have, like, a profile. But if I did make a profile, 'fashion influencer' wouldn't be on it. She's so . . . curium. Definitely a curium. And he's tungsten. They don't match."

He looks at me like I stopped speaking English. "What?"

"It's how I figure people out. They're all elements. Periodic table, you know? She's curium. I thought she was helium at first, but she's not. Curium is formed by smashing helium ions into plutonium. It's glows in the dark all creepy, and it's dangerous. It killed Marie Curie."

Cooper takes the pretzel out of his mouth. "*Everyone's* an element?"

"Yeah."

"What are you?"

"Silicon."

He laughs. "Seriously?" He takes a giant bite of the pretzel.

"What's funny about silicon?"

He's chewing, so he doesn't answer right away. But he's cracking up, and I'm a little on edge. What's so weird about my element?

He swallows his bite, and he points at me with the end of his pretzel. "You're a fake boob."

I laugh in disbelief. "That's *silicone*, you moron."

He narrows his eyes. "I've heard it both ways."

I grab a pretzel out of the bag and use it like a pointer, pointing to an invisible whiteboard as I explain. "Silicon is a naturally occurring element. It's used in many items with fast processors, like computers. There's also silicon in space. The Apollo 11 spacecraft left a silicon disc on the moon with good-will messages from seventy-three countries. It's still there. Some scientists believe that if extraterrestrials are ever discovered, they may exist in a silicon-based life-form since carbon is hard to come by out there. So, on account of my fast processing and that a piece of me will always exist in space, I am silicon." I switch to the other side of me with my pointer, pointing to a new invisible white-board. "Silicone, on the other hand, is a synthetic substance. It doesn't occur in nature at all. It's usually in liquid or plastic, not metal. Its low toxicity and high heat resistance makes it useful in the medical field. It can be found in catheters, contact lenses, bandages, and the like."

"So . . . fake boobs."

"Are you twelve? Yes, it can also be used for breast implants. But it's nothing like silicon."

He takes another bite of his pretzel, processing this. Then he shrugs. "Whatever. Still heard it both ways."

He smiles at me, and his dimples make my stomach do a weird flippy thing.

"What element am I?"

We're interrupted by a pair of headlights coming around the corner. The car pulls up behind Cooper's, and my stomach drops.

It's my dad.

7

"Skyler." The word is heavy with anger and relief. "I've been looking all over." He looks haggard—his hair is sticking up in all directions as if he's run his hands through it way too many times.

Is he going to hug me or yell at me? It might be both.

He notices Cooper for the first time. "Who's this?"

Crap. Cooper. My dad thinks I abandoned the NASA idea. Quick—who is Cooper, and what is he doing out here with me?

"This is my boyfriend."

WHAT. What just came out of my mouth? Words need to be tangible so you can grab them and stuff them back in before they're out there floating around for everyone to hear.

"Your . . . boyfriend?"

Cooper's body tenses. His eyes are huge.

"Yes, my, um, boyfriend. Cooper, this is my dad. Cooper and I were out here so long because we were, um, making out."

"You were *making out*?"

Words, stop. Please stop. I want to dissolve into the desert sand and blow away on the breeze. But at least my words have deflected attention from any possibility that Dad will suspect the NASA video.

I laugh nervously. "It's what teenagers do, Dad. Teens these days, you know? But if you can't beat 'em, join 'em. That's what I always say."

He cocks his head. "You've never said that."

He's right. I haven't. Why can't I stop talking?

"You also didn't know I had a boyfriend. You don't know everything about me, Dad."

His face crumples.

This isn't fair to him (especially since none of it's true), so I try to soften it. "It's no big deal. I mean, we're not serious or anything. He hasn't even gotten to second base."

Cooper hits his hand to his forehead.

My dad's hurt is quickly returning to anger. "Skyler Renae, this is absolutely unlike you. I don't know what's come over you lately, but—"

Cooper cuts in. "Mr. Davidson, I'm sorry. Skyler's out too late. It's my fault. She's been so kind to help me on a project for film school, and I guess we . . . Uh, I don't really know, actually."

He sure doesn't.

Film school. DUH. How did I not think of that? I could have said that I'm helping him with a film school project. For someone of high intelligence, I can be so dumb.

"I think you should head home." My dad's voice is icy as he addresses Cooper, like the subtext is "Head home before I punch you in the face."

"Yes, right." As he heads to his car, Cooper throws me a sympathetic look. It's touching, especially considering how thoroughly I threw him under the bus.

Cooper's car kicks up dust behind it, and I can only imagine what's going through his mind right now. My dad looks a little . . . lost. What does he do with a daughter who stormed out to meet her secret boyfriend? That is one of the most surprising things I could have done (even if I didn't really do it). There's a part of me that wants the truth to come out and wants my dad to hug me and tell me that everything's going to be okay.

But as I learned at age eight, sometimes people say that everything's going to be okay when it won't be. It can't be okay for me to give up NASA, but it also can't be okay to keep hurting my dad like this. Standing in the open expanse of the desert with only blank air between us and the stars, it's not difficult to believe that we're both feeling a bit lost.

When Cooper's car disappears around a corner, my dad turns back to face me. Is he going to yell? What's he going to say? He starts to speak a few times, saying only beginnings of sentences: "I can't . . . I just didn't . . . Hopefully you . . ."

"I messed up," I prompt. "It's okay if you're mad."

Why do I want him to be mad? Perhaps it's because me sneaking out and him being mad about it would be the most normal parent/teenager interaction that we've ever had. Maybe my messed-up life would start to feel normal, even if the normalcy would be the tricky parts. Maybe he'll ground me for real. That would wreak havoc on my schedule, of course, since I have filming to do, but I'm sure we could negotiate something that would work.

Unfortunately, even the normalcy of "dad yells at teenager for secret boyfriend" eludes me. He simply meets my eyes and says, "Let's go home." Then he gets in his car and waits for me to drive away before following me.

"It was too soon for you to meet Charli," he says. We're sitting at the dining room table with mugs of tea. "You should *not* have run off like you did," his eyes flash, "but clearly you weren't ready."

"I don't think I ever would have been ready to meet her." Which is probably true. "You're blinded by chemicals, Dad. It's dopamine and stuff. It's not real."

He closes his eyes and takes a deep breath. "SkyBear, not everything in the world is science."

"Literally everything in the world is science. Science is how the world works."

He turns the tables on me. "So what you and Cooper have— it's just science?" He says *Cooper* like it's a swear word and wrinkles his nose in disgust as he says it. "Nothing more than chemical reactions?"

"Yes."

"Oh. Then you're not in love." He says this with the simplicity of a scientist making an observation in a lab notebook. The thought seems to cheer him. "How long have you been, um, an item?"

"It's recent." Like, within the past hour.

"I see." His eyes narrow through his glasses, and I wonder if he suspects the truth. He's smarter than most people, after all. I study a stray tea leaf.

My dad takes a sip from his steaming mug. "There's something you're not telling me, SkyBear, and when you're ready, I hope you will tell me. You know I love you more than anything on earth, right?"

"I know."

"Or in the universe," he adds with a slight smile.

"I know that, too." I try to smile back.

He takes a deep breath, like this next part is difficult for him to say. "I will stop seeing Charli if it means that much to you. You're my first priority."

Why is he being so nice? How am I supposed to storm up to my room and slam the door and listen to angsty teenage music? How can I fill journals about how my parents don't understand me? With one parent gone and the other trying so hard, it hurts sometimes; I was never destined for a normal adolescence.

Suddenly I feel selfish. My dad has been through so much. If Charli makes him happy, and I'm the only one standing in the way, then that sucks. I want him to dislike her, not sacrifice her on the altar of family unity. Then she's a martyr and I'm the villain. That's not how it's supposed to be.

"No, it's fine. You should keep seeing her."

With any amount of luck, this will only last as long as one of her manicures. They're obviously incompatible; he just doesn't know it yet. Better for him to find out for himself than to blame me for it.

"Really?" He doesn't look hopeful or relieved, but rather suspicious. "That's not what you said a few hours ago."

"Cooper helped me see it differently," I say. That's not totally a lie. "Maybe she's not that bad." Well, that part is totally a lie.

"I think you'd like her if you gave her a chance," my dad says. "She's smarter than you think. She has millions of followers online—did you know that? She's a businesswoman. She has to work with advertisers, endorsements, fans. She works hard."

"Okay." Millions of mindless followers don't impress me.

Except a good number of them can probably do makeup contouring. I now have an appreciation for those people.

My dad sighs again. "What happened to the SkyBear who used to draw me flowcharts of her upcoming day? I used to know all about your life."

"I don't know." I really don't. Somewhere along the line, he got too busy, and I got too focused on school to notice. Our lives became parallel instead of intersecting. "I should have told you about Cooper. I'm sorry."

"Tell me about him now. What element would he be?"

I love that this is my dad's first question. There's at least a dull spark of life to the relationship we used to have. "I don't know yet." But I think I do. Cooper is . . . gold. I don't say it, because it sounds painfully cheesy. Like he's valuable or aesthetically pleasing or something. But, really, he's gold because gold is so malleable. It can be bent or shaped in any direction, and Cooper seems to go with the flow no matter what. It's hard to imagine anything breaking him.

Also, he *is* aesthetically pleasing. Just saying.

"Where did you meet him?"

"School." That's appropriately vague.

"Does he get good grades?"

That's the type of question I would ask.

I answer honestly: "I don't know." For a fleeting moment, this bothers me. What if he's not getting good grades? Am I trusting my internship video to someone whose GPA isn't great? Possibly even *below average*? I remember the dexterous ways that he handled the camera equipment today, and the fear passes. His GPA doesn't matter.

Well, obviously it matters. Because . . . because it always matters.

Except when maybe it doesn't?

My dad asks me a few more questions about Cooper, but with each answer, I'm digging myself a deeper and deeper hole. If I want to be closer to my dad, lying about my life seems a bit counterintuitive. As soon as I'm accepted to NASA, I'll come clean about the whole thing. I'm not lying so much as borrowing the truth. I'm simply giving it to him later. There. That sounds better.

"I'm really tired," I say by way of exiting the conversation. "We should probably get to bed." I grab both of our mugs and bring them to the sink.

"Isn't there something else you'd like to tell me about?"

I freeze, mugs hovering over the sink. "What do you mean?"

"Let's stop having secrets, okay? You know about Charli. I know about Cooper. Let's get it all out on the table while we're here. I was hoping you'd tell me on your own, but if you're not going to bring it up, then I have to."

The mugs clink as they hit the bottom of the sink. He knows.

I turn on the faucet to break the tense silence. "Dad, you have to understand. It's all I've ever wanted. I don't know how to want anything else."

"The dream isn't dead, Sky. You still have a chance."

"I know! And that's exactly why—"

"I already signed you up to retake the test. You'll do better next time. And these new scores will still get to MIT before admissions decisions are made."

Hold up.

"I bought you a present." He goes upstairs for a minute and then clods back down like usual. It always sounds like he's testing each stair to see how much weight it can hold.

He hands me a silver gift. Did he wrap this in aluminum foil?

"It's sort of like wrapping paper," he offers as an explanation. I smile.

The gift is heavy in my hands. I put it on the counter and neatly open it, saving the foil to put on leftovers later. It's an SAT prep book.

"This year's edition," he says excitedly. "It came out last week."

The cover of the book is shiny and perfect. There are no fingerprint smudges. The inside pages aren't dog-eared, Post-it-noted, or highlighted like they will be soon. There's something infinitely exciting about a brand-new textbook.

"Thanks, Dad." I'm touched. This is the kind of thing he'd get me for Christmas or my birthday, not as a just-because gift. "I'm sorry about last time."

"You weren't feeling well. Don't worry about it. Who can focus with food poisoning? You're not a 1440 at heart. That's still in striking range of MIT, though. I bet you'll get it next time."

"How did you know about the score?"

"Online scores were released a while ago. I was waiting for you to tell me."

"I'm really sorry, Dad. For what it's worth, I'm glad you know." I'm so relieved that he wasn't talking about NASA. It's like a fence just came down between us, but I've been building a brick wall behind that fence. Brick walls fall a bit harder.

My dad leans heavily on the table. "You've gotta trust me, okay? I'm here for you. I know you think you're more like your mom, but you're also a lot like me. I will never forget this one time when you were around eleven. We were eating pasta, and you said, 'Isn't it fascinating how hard pasta takes on more and more water until the starch vacuoles burst, making the noodle lose its rigidity?' And I thought, 'That's definitely *my* girl.' You are so much like me, which is good and bad. But know I'll always be proud of you, Sky. 1440 or 1600. MIT or community college."

It's hard for me to fall asleep, and I wonder if my dad's struggling, too. What about Cooper? Social convention says it's too late to text him, so I scroll on my phone instead. I get lost in the vortex of Google news stories about space, and one headline grabs my attention: "NICER slated for return to Earth next year."

Next year? That's too soon! I'm old enough to remember it launching. We threw a huge party on the day they launched it. It was me, my dad, and the two classmates who agreed to come, so it was a pretty major event. That camera is the key to finishing this research—it would be finished by now if NICER had been up there while my mom was working. It can't come down. At the party, I presented my four flowcharts explaining how I was going to get access to it. All four included MIT.

The accompanying news article says that NASA has decided to make room on the ISS in order to load new equipment. They're turning many of their research dollars to explore how to mine minerals from the moon and possibly Mars.

WHO CARES ABOUT MARS MINERALS?

The SAT book was a beautiful gift, but now it feels like someone handed me an oar while someone else was punching a hole in my boat. Even a perfect score won't help me if the equipment won't be there when I graduate. If I don't get this NASA internship . . .

I'll get it. I'm my parents' kid, right? Science is what we do.

My stomach feels twisty in a way that calcium carbonate won't fix.

8

"Any nonzero digit is significant, and zeros are significant some-times. For example, it's significant if it's between two nonzero digits." Explaining significant digits to Bridget is even more diffi-cult than explaining pH. There are two chemistry textbooks and an algebra book open on her desk, and I'm still not sure we're making any progress.

Bridget and I look a strange pair sitting next to each other. Her black pants are so tight that I wonder about her circula-tion, and her neon-purple bra straps peek out from the straps of her pale yellow tank top. Her hair is in a messy bun. Plenty of strands hang loose, but it looks like she did that on purpose. Her fingernails and toenails sport chipping gold paint, and she's wearing a braided anklet in our school colors. I had no idea that anyone besides criminals on probation wore anklets. She's sitting cross-legged on her desk chair.

My hair is pulled back in a tight ponytail, and my faded MIT shirt is so shabby that it can pass as vintage, which is something people pay a lot of money for. That's what Bridget said anyway. My long jeans cover unadorned ankles, and my toenails haven't seen polish in years. There's a basket full of polishes on Bridget's dresser. What color would I wear if I did wear nail polish? Probably blue. Or green. There's a dark blue with some gold flecks in it that looks particularly interesting. It's a night sky in a bottle.

Bridget is working on a problem set. "Seven. Done." She lets her pencil clatter to her desk like a mic drop.

The answers are in the back of the book, but there's no need to look them up. "No, the answer's six. That zero isn't a significant digit." I point with the tip of my pen.

"Why can't all numbers be significant?"

"They just aren't. It's the rules."

"Oh, so because something has been done a certain way forever, we have to do it that way into infinity? What if we had taken that approach to women's rights? You're eighteen. You could be getting ready to marry a neighboring farmer as we speak, and you would never go to space. You'd push out sixteen kids to help you with collecting chicken eggs and milking goats." She says this with the inspirational vigor of someone giving a TED Talk. She puts her hand on my arm like this next part is vitally important. "Because people were forward-thinking enough to stand up for you, now you can study chemistry."

This is probably the part where I'm supposed to stand up and say, "Yeah! Screw significant digits! Do you have a match?

Let's burn these chem books!" Instead I say, "There weren't farms here. We live in a desert."

Bridget sighs, her inspirational speech all for naught. "Then you'd be, what, a gold miner's wife or something? A cactus grower's wife? Is that a thing? You're missing the point. Here's the gist: You wouldn't have any options. But forward thinkers paved the way for you to get here."

My pen still hasn't moved from its placement in the book. "We seem to have moved away from significant digits."

"No, this is completely related. Because who are we to tell numbers that they aren't significant? What kind of message is that sending? We're all significant, Sky. Let's not start labeling things 'insignificant.' That's judgmental." She shakes her head, like I am so unenlightened. It's Bridget teaching me rather than the other way around. She twirls a piece of her hair, bored with my number nonsense.

"It's not being judgmental. It's a way to measure precision. Without significant digits, we wouldn't be able to tell how specific a measurement is. And specificity is important in any chemical experiment."

Bridget goes from twirling the chunk of her hair to pulling it across her upper lip as a mustache. "Not sure I buy it."

"Listen." I sit up straight. "You don't have to like it, but you need to know it."

"No I don't." She opens her desk and pulls out a small note-book. She's self-laminated a picture to the top of it using Scotch tape. "Here's my future. None of that digits crap."

"A gym?"

"It's the Cox Pavilion."

I'm not following. It's definitely a gym. "You're going to . . . own it?"

She rolls her eyes. "It's where I'm going to play for the Runnin' Rebels at UNLV. Starting outside hitter. You watch. That gym will be my life. And when I'm on the bench, which won't be often, I'll sit right . . . there." She points to a small dot of white. "It's close to the net, but not close enough that the coach's yelling will hurt my ears. Prime spot. See? I've planned out the whole thing. Sometimes I lie awake at night, dreaming of the hours I'll spend in this gym."

I bite my lip to keep from pointing out that according to her "life plan," her life ends at college graduation. Does she not have any plans past age twenty-two? Maybe twenty-three or four if she fails some classes? Because let's be honest, that's an option here.

More immediate motivation will work better. "You might not go to college at all if you don't pass chemistry. You definitely won't play in your tournament this weekend."

She reluctantly puts down her notebook and picks up her pencil. "Fine. Teach me how to judge numbers."

Bridget's drive for volleyball feels familiar. Maybe we're not as different as it would seem.

We're four problems into the set when Cooper pops his head in. "Hey, Skyler, my mom wants to meet you. Can you come downstairs a sec?"

My stomach does a flip. Cooper's not my boyfriend, so why should I be nervous to meet his mom? Adults love me. As an only child, I've been conversing with adults my entire life. On my kindergarten readiness test, I tested in with the vocabulary of sixth grader.

Maybe it's because Cooper and I still haven't talked about what happened in the desert last night. We don't have any of the same classes, and I successfully avoided him at school until he texted to ask when I could help Bridget with chem. It was a tricky text, because it relayed the fact that our deal was still on but said nothing about whether or not he was mad at me. If I were him, I'd be mad at me. But I still need his help. Whether he wants to admit it or not, he needs mine, too.

We get to the garage as Cooper's mom takes a stroller out of the back of her black minivan. There are two more in there, folded up. Is that another one in the front seat?

"Mom-to-mom sale," she says by way of explanation. She wipes her hand on her pants and reaches out to shake mine. "You must be Skyler."

"Hi, Mrs. Evans." Mrs. Evans has Bridget's long blonde hair (rather, Bridget has her mom's hair). Her brown off-the-shoulder top matches her eyes, and she's one of those women over forty who still looks good in an off-the-shoulder top. Her jeans cover the tops of . . . Are those cowgirl boots?

"Just wanted to meet the star responsible for helping my kiddos. Cooper says you're helping him with his college video? Neutral stars or something?"

"Neutron. And yeah, we're sort of helping each other."

"Coop tells me you're a super genius. You almost burned down the gym with your project on nuclear fission?"

Cooper remembers what my seventh-grade science fair project was about? Most people who remember it at all remember it as "that thing that exploded." A flush in my face reaches down into my chest. Someone remembered my research. *My* research— that one wasn't even my mom's.

"It's tough to do nuclear fission without uranium, but I tried to model it. It went a bit awry. Good news is that it didn't end up on my permanent record."

"Ah yes, permanent records. Distilling an entire life into only a page or two. I wish schools would get a more well-rounded look at students, don't you? High schoolers are so much more than a GPA."

"Definitely." I nod out of politeness.

"Cooper, can you give me a hand with this?" She ducks back into the van, hauling out a stroller. Cooper is happy to jump into action and away from this conversation. Mrs. Evans unfolds the stroller and inspects it. "I'm planning to park them by the pigeons for now. I've got a couple of paint things to do before they hit the basement with the rest of the fleet." She looks at her watch. "I'm selling a guy a Bugaboo in fifteen minutes. Dad's meeting me there. Skyler, can you grab the one in the front?"

The stroller in the front is Jeep brand. Since when does Jeep make strollers? It's got some rust around the bolts and a ripped top.

Mrs. Evans notices me eyeing the rip. "I've got fabric to fix that. It's way easier to do a top than to do the upholstery. Plus, for the price I got it, it's worth the risk." She says this with the authority of a stockbroker.

Cooper is already headed out of the garage, and I follow him with the risk-worthy Jeep.

"Set them here," Cooper says, putting his stroller next to a small wooden hutch with wire cages coming out either side.

"So your mom said . . . these are pigeons?"

"Yeah. I was filming this piece a while back as extra credit for English. I did a retelling of *Romeo and Juliet* using the dogs. Chewy was Juliet, and Snickers was the tiniest, yappiest Romeo in history. It was great. The part when they fell in love wasn't dramatic enough, probably because they're dogs. I woke up in the middle of the night with this brilliant idea—*doves*. If you release doves, everything looks romantic and magical, right? But no one online was renting doves. There was a guy selling white homing pigeons, which look like doves. You can't tell the difference. I bought four, planning to resell them, but one was a nesting pair. Now I've got a dozen. They fly around, but they always come back to the coop at night." He opens one of the sides, and a couple of pigeons shuffle out before flying up into a nearby tree. "Cool, huh? Turned out to be a terrible idea for the project, since dogs chase birds. Snickers went nuts and tried to chase all of them at once. They're lucky he wasn't tall enough to catch them."

"You randomly bought pigeons? You parents didn't kill you?"

Mrs. Evans's voice floats out from the garage. "Cooper! Can you grab this Graco?"

At the same time, the window to Bridget's second-story bedroom opens. "Sky, does 0.0034 have five significant digits or two?"

"Two," I call.

Cooper motions in the general direction of his house. "My family's never been conventional. Plus, doves are handy for movie sets."

"You said they were pigeons."

"They look like doves. Ask a hundred people what animal this is, and ninety-seven will say it's a dove."

Fascinating. "Did you conduct that experiment yourself?" Who was his sample set for this survey? Because if it was drunk people on the Las Vegas Strip, they were equally likely to say it was an eagle or a parakeet. People in our suburb have limited exposure to doves, so their recognition of them would be based entirely on cinematic representations, which would reinforce his theory. If he polled people online from across the country, I'm surprised more were unable to differentiate between them.

Cooper smiles as he unfolds the Jeep and parks it next to the other stroller. "No, ya nerd. It's a made-up statistic. Don't you know that 87.6 percent of statistics are made up on the spot?"

"That's completely untrue." My life is in a strange place. I'm standing next to two run-down baby strollers parked outside a pigeon coop and debating statistical analysis.

He shrugs. "Seventy-eight percent of people agree with me."

Cooper is everything I used to hate about the world. He makes up statistics. He has random ideas in the middle of the night and then acts on them. The only thoughts I act on in the middle of the night are "I have to pee" or very occasionally "I need to get a drink." He sees watching television with a bag of pretzels as productive. He'll drive out to film me in the middle of the night on the hunch that something is wrong. And yet it feels like he's more alive than I am, even though, of course, life is not quantifiable.

How is that possible?

Cooper smiles a lot more than I do. Maybe if life were quantifiable, smiles would be a variable in the calculation. Cooper's smiles aren't ignorance-is-bliss smiles, either; they're the type of smiles that make him look like he's telling an inside joke.

Bridget opens her window again. "How about 7.089?"

"I'd better get back up there to help her," I say. "The quiz is tomorrow."

"You should go to one of her games sometime."

Fun fact about me: I've never been to a sports event in my life. Not a professional sports event, not a Little League game, and certainly none of the high school football games that serve as communal obsessions for the entire student body. Sports are a waste of time. There are a bunch of people who run around, and then everyone goes home. What kind of contribution to humanity is that? "Organized sports aren't really my thing."

"Neutron stars aren't really mine." He has a point.

"I'll think about it."

As I'm about to go back inside to help Bridget, Cooper touches my arm. "Wait a sec. Shouldn't we talk about . . . ?" His hand drops, brushing the side of my shirt as it does. I'm very aware of my heart beating.

There's a split second during which I could play dumb and pretend I don't know what he's talking about. But I'm not dumb, pretend or otherwise. The only way out of this awkward conversation is through it. "Yes. I'm sorry about that whole thing."

"Was your dad mad?" He has a hand on the stroller's tattered blue handle, and he looks like a commercial warning against teen pregnancy.

"He wasn't thrilled."

"Is he going to kill me or something?" He winces as if he's been seriously concerned about this.

"No."

I don't tell Cooper how non-overprotective my dad was about that situation, or that he gave me an SAT prep book and we called it a night. There's a pang of hurt inside me, and I've been trying to untangle it like a tight knot. It doesn't belong there. No one wants their dad to freak out and be angry, right? Maybe I wanted to feel like he cared enough to protect me. After all, I'm his SkyBear. Why didn't he care more about some random guy kissing me? What if I had a picture of Cooper and me on my lock screen instead of a picture of Five? Something occurs to me, though it does nothing to untangle the knot of disappointment.

"He's not your biggest fan, but maybe there's a part of my dad that was relieved when I said I have a boyfriend. It's a sign that I'm turning out as a psychologically healthy teenager or something."

"You have to have a boyfriend to be psychologically healthy?"

"No. I just don't think he hated the idea." As the words come out of my mouth, their veracity strengthens. The knot pulls, and it hurts.

"You haven't ever had a boyfriend before?" Cooper stands up straighter, like this surprises him.

"No. Have you?"

Cooper laughs. "Had a boyfriend? No."

"You know what I meant."

"A girlfriend? Maybe once or twice. Or once." His eyes look past me, and I'm dying to dive into whatever memory he's reliving.

Why hasn't science yet advanced far enough to allow us to read people's minds? It would solve so many of the world's problems.

Who was she? Does she go to school with us? Did she have a phone full of pictures of him? Did she tell people that her boyfriend was sexy (because, from a purely objective, scientific observation, he is)? Was she smart? What did she look like? Why did they break up? One question comes in front of all the others like a star becoming clear through a cloud: *Why do I care?*

The answer is obvious, but I don't like it. So I brush it off and say, "Good. I didn't want the pressure of being your first."

Cooper smiles in a crooked way that shows only one dimple. "But I have to have the pressure of being your first? Do you realize how messed up it is that I have to deal with all of the fallout of getting caught making out with a guy's daughter, and I never got to kiss her in the first place?" His frown looks annoyed, but his eyes look light. Perhaps he can't decide if this is obnoxious or funny.

He has a point. I should probably thank him for taking that fall when most guys would have defended their innocence. Unfortunately, my brain somehow short-circuits because something completely different comes out of my mouth.

"You didn't try."

His eyes open wide, and his voice gets quieter. "Was I supposed to?"

"No."

"What if I had?"

"You didn't. One of the phrases I hate most in life is *what if*. The phrase itself connotes something that will never be a reality."

"No way." He takes his hand off the stroller and steps closer, sneaking a glance toward the garage to make sure his mom isn't coming out. "This conversation is absolutely worth our time. What if I had?"

I think back to last night—the stars overhead, stringing the microphone through my hoodie, talking about my mom over a five-pack of grape sodas . . . What if he had? When I try to picture it, it's easy—like remembering a dream that you had last night that only now occurred to you. He would have leaned over, and he would have tasted sweet from the soda. Would we have kissed standing up? Maybe when he put in the microphone pack? Would we have kissed sitting down after we talked about Charli? The possibilities roll through my head like a highlight reel for a movie I would, under normal circumstances, say was very stupid.

It feels like my heart is suddenly pumping fire through my veins. I hate what-ifs. But this fire isn't hatred. It's a new kind of fire.

What if he had?

His eyes are locked on mine, waiting. The answer I give here will be important, like a move in chess that might decide the rest of the game. What does he want me to say? If I say I wish he had, it could mess up our whole business proposition. He doesn't want to work with a girl who's got a crush on him. But if I say I'm glad he didn't . . . that might be a lie.

"I don't know." My voice comes out small and quiet. It's not the kind of *I don't know* that means *I don't want to say*. It's the one that means *I feel genuinely lost right now*. I wrap my arms around my stomach even though it isn't cold. "You?"

He blinks and looks up, like he hasn't given it much thought (even though maybe he has). Then he watches a pigeon fly from the tree to the coop. "If I told you that it crossed my mind, would that be completely weird?" Only then does he meet my eyes, looking for something.

The fire in my veins burns hotter. "Yeah, kinda." Because that *would* have been weird. Guys don't want to kiss me. Guys want to copy my homework.

His eyes drop to the ground, and his next words come out in a rush. "I figured. It was probs because I don't spend a lot of time out in the stars. Drunk on astronomy or something. It was so dark, and the setting was romantic. It's the filmmaker in me." His eyes flick up to mine for a moment. "But you look great in the daytime, too." Down again. "Sorry. I didn't want you to think I was suggesting you were only pretty in the dark, because that would be a really jerky thing to say. I'm not that guy, you know? But that made it weirder. Listen—" He looks at me and puts his hand up like he's solemnly swearing in court. "I'm not going to do anything to mess up our arrangement. If you can ignore all dumb stuff I just said, that would be ideal. I make films, not speeches. And the thing is—"

"Coop!" his mom calls from the garage. "I could use a hand in here!"

Cooper mutters something under his breath. I'm pretty sure it's "Oh thank goodness."

But I'm engrossed. What's "the thing"?

What was he about to say?

9

"Turn your chair about ten degrees to the right," Cooper says.

We're filming in my bedroom. I've never had a guy in my bedroom, and it feels intimate even though we're surrounded by camera equipment and not dating (which my dad still doesn't know, even though the lie is a week and a half old). We've done most of our filming at locations around town: stargazing spots, school, even the library. I never study at the local library, but we passed it while driving to his dad's camera shop to borrow more equipment and fix a lens for his dad. Cooper said, "A library— brilliant!" and pulled over. There are some great shots of me surrounded by books. The whole thing had the potential to be painfully cheesy, but he showed me the playback on his camera. It was impressive. He's been completely professional at all of our shoots. We haven't talked about the conversation outside the pigeon coop, even though it's crossed my mind many times. I even wrote it down in my notebook to analyze, as if it were an anagram that I could rearrange into some logical meaning.

The conversation reminds me of potential energy: energy that is charged up within itself. We have not converted that potential energy into kinetic: the energy that puts things into motion. I'm pretty sure that's the best option, but it's not the kind of certainty that I have about our sun being made of mostly hydrogen and helium. It's the kind of certainty I have about the logistics of string theory—there's a piece that feels like it will never make sense.

Cooper couldn't come to my house for filming until I was sure my dad would be gone; he has a seminar speaker touring his lab tonight, so he won't be home until late. I don't want to have the conversation that would follow him discovering Cooper in my bedroom.

Now I'm at my desk with a stack of astronomy textbooks lined up neatly at the back of it. My mom's dissertation is in my lap—it's like she finally has a formal role in this film that's been about her all along.

Cooper bends behind the camera. "And . . . rolling."

"During my time at the International Space Station, I propose using the current technology at the station to do a study of neutron stars and their potential capabilities in celestial navigation. My proposal would be to use the NICER to observe rapidly rotating neutron stars, also known as pulsars. The stars rotate so fast that they make a household blender look slow. The light emitted from these stars can be used as a beacon to locate a celestial body in relation to other things in space, sort of like a lighthouse. My research would provide scientists and technologists with a unique opportunity to make advances in deep space navigation. If done correctly, this research could yield a system sort of like a GPS, where we would be able to navigate places beyond our solar system."

Cooper looks up from his camera. "Do you ever use space to tell the future? I'm an Aquarius."

I mentally lock my eyeballs into place so they won't roll. "Astrology is for hippies and dreamers and is an insult to everything the scientific community stands for."

Cooper is unfazed. He leans against my bookshelf and crosses his arms. "Is that so? Well, your scientific community is an insult to my hippie dreams. What's your sign?"

Eyeballs still locked. Stare straight ahead. Without realizing it, I've locked my jaw, too. I speak through my barely parted teeth. "I have no idea."

He laughs. "That's crap. There is no way that someone obsessed with astronomy hasn't looked at what the hippie dreamers think the stars say about her. Come on. What's your sign?"

He's right. Under my bed are four astrology books full of highlights and annotations. I'm not proud of it. *Guilty pleasure* is the technical term, I think. Like how, before the internet, teenage boys used to hide *Playboy* magazines under their mattresses. It's not that I actually believe any of it (mostly). How cool would it be if the stars dictated things that happen on earth? After all, they've run my life since I was eight years old. It's not like I read my horoscope in *Cosmopolitan* or anything. Unless there's a long line at the grocery store. Or if I'm in a waiting room. Things like that. Which obviously don't count.

I sigh, giving up. My eyes roll. "I'm a Sagittarius."

"I knew it!" Cooper looks triumphant and points at me like I've confessed to some horrible crime. The camera pointing straight at me adds to the effect. Like this can and will be used against me in a court of law.

I laugh even though I try not to. "You knew that I know my sign or knew that I'm a Sagittarius?"

Cooper narrows his eyes as he thinks about this. "I meant that you know your sign. But now that you mention it, both. Because you're such a classic Sag. Adventurous, brutally honest. It's textbook."

He's right. I do fit the (completely fabricated with no basis in science) profile of a Sagittarius. Come to think of it, he fits the (once again, 100 percent fictional) profile of an Aquarius. He's the water bearer—goes with the flow, lets his emotions carry him. And if I believed in that nonsense at all (which I don't), this might be the point at which it occurs to me that Sagittarius and Aquarius are two romantically compatible signs.

"You know what they say about a Sagittarius and an Aquarius?" He looks like he wants to smile about this, but the smile is hiding behind his eyes.

"I wouldn't have the faintest idea."

We're in a stare-down. Is he going to call me out on this again? Because admitting knowing my sign is one thing. Admitting knowing that our signs are compatible is a different level—both because it betrays how much I know about astrology and because there would be the question mark hanging between us about whether or not the stars got that one right. These moments are the ones that make me wonder about that conversation by the strollers and what would have happened if that discussion had gone differently.

But I hate what-ifs.

"Add it to your research." The smile behind his eyes hasn't left.

Does he know I know? I wish he would call me out. Because I do want to hear what he thinks about what the stars say. What the astrology books say is stupid, but what he says matters. If he said that the stars got this one right, I would agree even if I didn't want to. Falling into a crush is like catching a deadly virus—you don't know it's happened to you, but once you see the symptoms, it's already too late. It's not like I asked for this, but here it is. I think he feels it, too. But if we talked about it, there wouldn't be any going back. It's hard to see what forward looks like without going there, and ruining my chances at NASA for a *guy* would make my mom roll over in her grave. The risk isn't worth the reward.

There's a rustling in Five's cage. Cooper takes his camera off the stand and films her, narrating in nature-documentary style. He puts on a fake British accent. "Ah, a laboratory rat in her natural habitat. Note the shuffling of bedding. And look—she is about to prey on a helpless seed. No, no, she skips it. The seed lives another day in the wilds of domestication."

Five breathes heavily and makes a coughing noise.

I put my hand in front of the camera and push him away. "Cooper, back up. You're freaking her out." She doesn't need any extra stress. I add some more Gatorade to her water bottle.

He laughs and puts the camera back on the stand. "Fine. Anything else you want to say about your research? What does it mean to you?"

"I told you." I hold up the dissertation like Exhibit A. "I want to finish my mom's research. Deep space travel could be at stake."

"Right, but . . ." Cooper looks at the ceiling like he's trying to figure out how to rephrase the question. "How would your life change if you were able to finish it?"

"What kind of question is that? NASA doesn't care about that."

"Maybe not. But I'm curious. Answer it for me? Not for the video?" He steps away so he's not looking through the camera anymore, just standing and talking to me.

No one has ever asked me that question. "I guess . . . I could move on? In an odd way, I would know she would have been proud of me?"

"You don't think she would be already?"

"I don't know," I say. "She never gave me, like, a grading rubric or anything. I'd feel better if I proved it for sure."

Cooper puts his fingertips to his temples, like my incessant references to school give him a headache. "Skyler. Not everything in life has a grading rubric."

"I know! It's one of my major gripes about human existence. If there were a grading rubric, I'd know exactly what to do."

"And how boring would that be? You've gotta keep things spicy." He looks around my room, trying to find something to illustrate his point. "Here! Perfect." He grabs Beaker Troll and throws it at me. "Connect that to neutron stars."

"There is no connection between this troll and neutron stars."

"Exactly!" He throws his arms up like I have nailed his point. "And that's where the fun happens."

"I don't get it." I stare at the troll in my hand. She stares back with her creepy, unblinking eyes.

Cooper purses his lips, like I'm such a slow student. "Here." He holds his hands out for me to toss the troll back, which I do. "This troll," he starts, "is very ugly."

"Right."

"But it's a . . . family heirloom?" He raises his eyebrows.

"I got it from my neighbor Julie. She's obsessed with them."

"Ah." His face relaxes like he found the track he's going to take. "So this troll"—he holds it in front of him like I've never seen it before—"is an object of pleasure. Of joy. Of, as you said yourself, obsession."

"I guess."

"And for you, neutron stars represent that sense of joy and pleasure and obsession. So this troll is so much more than a troll. It's a *representation*. It could be a star, a volleyball, or a camera for that matter. It could be anything. We as humans are connected by a common thread of seeking out joy, and on that thread are all sorts of beads. Your bead is a neutron star. Hers is a troll. And that, my friend, is how you connect a troll and a neutron star." He stands the troll confidently on my astronomy books and takes a bow.

I clap, mostly because he bowed.

He sits on my bed. "Life doesn't make sense, okay? It's a bunch of randomly connected stuff. There are no textbooks or grading rubrics. You can count on the fact that life won't always throw you what you were expecting. Rejection happens. People die. Siblings ruin—" He stops, catching himself from saying something. He shakes his head. "Whatever. The point is this: The part where you make your own sense of it all? That's humanity."

What was he going to say? What did his sibling ruin? I open my mouth to ask, but he cuts me off and points to the dissertation cover.

"What do you think she'd say if she was here right now?"

I study the book as if the answer were written in the gold lettering. I think of my poor MIT prospects, my long shot at the Teen in Space internship, and Charli. But then I think of Cooper and Bridget and all the things that have changed in the past two weeks.

"When I was little, I was scared of the dark," I say. "My mom bought me one of those night-lights that project star shapes on the ceiling. She snuggled in next to me in my tiny bed, held my hand, and said, 'Don't be afraid of the dark, SkyLight. It's when you're in the dark that the stars come out.' At the time, I only thought of the night-light. But now . . ." I trail off, deep in thought. "Anyway, that's what she might say."

Cooper's quiet for a minute before looking at me. "For what it's worth, I think she'd be extremely proud of you."

"Thanks." It's nice of him to say that, even though he has no idea.

He looks like he wants to reach for my hand, but my desk chair is too far away. "I've never met anyone like you. I meet people who make me do a hundred film takes because their hair was out of place or one of their false eyelashes wasn't positioned correctly. My entire hobby relies on making things look better than they are. But everything about you is so real." He returns to the camera, like he's more comfortable around it. "It's unsettling. And incredible."

I try to temper warmth with reason. "You realize what you're feeling isn't reality, right?" He needs to understand. I need to understand. "It's just chemicals. It's not me. It's chemicals. Dopamine and serotonin and stuff."

He smiles like that's the exact type of thing he would have expected me to say. "Humans aren't textbook pages. The sooner you learn that, the better. Until then, your fake boyfriend will be over here shooting more video." He starts fiddling with some of the focus controls.

The front door opens downstairs, and my heart stops. "Knock, knock!" a familiar southern twang calls. "Who's home?"

Cooper and I look at each other, panicked.

"Hide in the closet!" I hiss.

"Hide in the closet?" he shoots back. "How are you going to explain all of the film equipment set up in here? Who even is that?"

"My dad's new, awful girlfriend. I'll keep her downstairs." I stand up, ready to run for the door.

Her bouncy footsteps are traipsing up the stairs before I have time to think.

"Skyler? Are you home?"

"Uh, yeah," I call. "Just a second."

Cooper grabs my arm. "What's the plan?"

"I'll tell her I'm naked? Then she won't come in?"

"We haven't even kissed, remember?" He smirks even though this is no time to smile.

"Maybe I just got out of the shower?"

"Then why am I here? Are we filming a porno?"

Charli knocks on the door but then opens it before waiting for an answer. "Skyler? Oh! Hi. You must be Cooper." She holds out her hand for him to shake. "I have heard things about you, not all of them good." She winks and turns back to me. "I know your dad's got that meeting tonight, so I told him I left my purse here so he'd give me the key. I'm making y'all a nice dinner. Sneaky-sneaky, right? He's gonna love it." She points to the camera equipment. "What're y'all doin'? You turning vlogger on me?"

Cooper makes a strangled laugh and then looks at me, waiting to hear what story I'm going to go with this time.

"Um, yes," I say slowly, the idea forming in my mind only slightly quicker than it comes of my mouth. "It's an astronomy vlog. We're filming the launch video for it right now, so it's kind of intense work. But it's a surprise, so don't tell my dad."

Somewhere along the line, I have turned into a compulsive liar.

"Why would you keep it a surprise? Your dad will be so proud of you. He could speak in it! You could do a whole episode on him. Like, 'microbes in space' or something."

"No. It's a surprise. It's really, really important that it's a surprise, okay?"

"Can I take you shopping? I'd love to give you a makeover. It would be great for your online presence. All of these lights can totally wash out your skin tone."

"Thanks, but no. I'm fine. The footage we've gotten looks good so far."

"I'm not going to make you look like a doll or anything. Just like your exact self—only better." She rubs her hands together like she's already getting warmed up for all of this fun.

"Seriously, I'm good. Now, if you'll excuse us, we should probably get back to filming."

Her hands slow their rubbing and finally fall to her sides. She swallows. "Okay. I see."

She puts her hand on the doorknob, and we wait for her to walk out. She pauses, and it's almost like I see a lightbulb go off over her head. Something just clicked.

She turns back to us. "The problem about me is that I can be so terrible at keeping secrets."

Is she blackmailing me?

Cooper picked up on it, too. He does a nervous cough. "If we were to let you help with the video . . . would you be better at keeping it a secret?"

"Probably." She nods with wide, innocent eyes. "Because then it would be my secret, too. And I'm always better at keeping my own secrets." She pauses, letting that sink in.

There's a silence thick with unsaid words, and who knows if I'm reading them correctly? That's the problem with invisible words. You have to take your best shot and hope it works out.

None of us says anything else until Charli breaks the standoff. "So. Shopping, Sky? Thursday?"

It's possible that I have underestimated *Kisses from Charli*.

10

I think I'm allergic to malls. They're the opposite of logic and reason. Case in point: Charli is at a Sephora makeup counter right now inside Macy's. Harsh lights reflect off sale signs and advertisements for everything from eyeshadow to socks. Two girls in front of me are looking at a display of shoes. All the footwear is displayed like priceless museum artifacts. They even have their own lights on them.

"Oh my gosh, I *need* these," one girl says. She picks up a pair of blue heels with rhinestones surrounding the opening. "They'll match that shirt I have." She slips her foot into one of the shoes, and the rhinestones sparkle against her dark brown skin.

What is the purpose of rhinestones? Who invented these, and why hasn't clothing evolution rendered them appropriately extinct by now? They should be a historical footnote like hoop skirts and corsets.

"You totally need those," her friend nods. "One hundred percent. And look—they're only eighty-nine ninety-nine!"

Ninety dollars? For a pair of shoes? That could buy a decent pair of binoculars or nine beakers or four hundred fifty 10 ml test tubes.

"Thanks," Charli says to the woman at the makeup counter. The woman hands over a bag of cosmetics, and I eye it warily. This did not go well for me last time.

"I've got all the makeup we need," Charli says. "What's your favorite clothing store?"

"Amazon?"

She looks at my outfit like she's trying to properly appraise my style. She's wearing bright blue pants, a light tan shirt, a brown jacket, and a yellow scarf. I'm wearing a black T-shirt, jeans, and my tennis shoes. Her hair is curled and pulled back in a perfect brunette ponytail. Mine is . . . Well, I brushed it.

I can almost see her mind whirring through a database of stores and inventories. "Anthropologie," she finally says. "We'll start there."

Anthropology? The study of human cultures and development? Sounds like the kind of store where I could take refuge in a mall.

As we're walking out of Macy's, a small voice says, "Excuse me? Are you Charli from *Kisses from Charli*?" It's Blue Shoes and her sidekick, Eighty-Nine Ninety-Nine.

Charli smiles brightly. "I sure am, girlie! That shirt is so cute on you."

Blue Shoes smiles like Charli just bought her a bucket full of rhinestones. "Really? Thanks so much! I got it last year on sale. I was worried it might be out of season this year, but if you say so, then it must still be good. I'll wear it all the time now! Maybe every day! But I won't do that for real, since you said we shouldn't repeat outfits more than once a week."

Eighty-Nine Ninety-Nine speaks up. "Can we take a selfie with you?" It's like her face is a heart-eyed emoji.

"Of course!" Charli poses with the girls. They ask for her autograph, and they fumble around for pen and paper. Blue Shoes goes and buys the shoes to get a receipt so they'll have something for Charli to sign. Charli circles the part where the receipt lists the shoes, writes "Charli approved!" next to the circle, and then puts a smiley face, a heart, and her signature.

Even though I don't want my dad to date Charli, I have to admit that it feels cool to be with her. If I did an anthropological study of this mall, she'd represent royalty.

"Ready?" She smiles at me and sweeps out of Macy's into the mall, leaving Blue Shoes and Eighty-Nine Ninety-Nine to broadcast their celebrity run-in on Instagram. They're probably saying that Charli is just as sweet and beautiful in person as she is in her videos. #NoFilter.

I make a mental list of boundaries as we walk toward the clothing stores. I will play along and wear the clothes she wants me to, but I'm drawing the line when it comes to rhinestones, bows, or ruffles. I won't do it. Oh, and sequins. I will not do sequins.

"What's your favorite color?" Charli asks.

Without thinking, I say, "Purple."

Twenty minutes later, I'm standing in front of a full-length mirror and listening to Charli analyze my outfit with the same level of scrutiny that I've used to appraise some microscope slides.

"The deep purple shade of this top looks good with your soft brown hair. The high neckline enhances your bust area while simultaneously drawing attention to your neck, which is elegantly proportioned. We want attention there. This slight ruching through the middle shows off your slim waist. Do you know how many personal trainers make thousands of dollars helping women achieve a waist like yours? The gray pants accent the purple, and the silver belt looks feminine without being too girlie. The plum shoes complete the look, flats instead of heels because I think those are in closer alignment with your personality. On most people, I would recommend silver earrings or a small silver necklace to match the belt, but you could get away with silver sunglasses." She reaches for a pair on a rack nearby and then puts them on my head like they're a tiara. "Perfect."

I don't hate it. She originally described this purple as "the color the sky gets after dusk and before night really sets in," and she's right. This outfit fits me. It's not frilly, there aren't any sequins, and it looks . . . good. It's like in addition to matching the top with the pants, she considered matching everything to my personality. No sparkle, no excessive jewelry, no high heels. She tried to match *me*.

"We don't have to take any of it," she says as I study myself in the mirror. "This is your journey. You get creative control."

"It's not terrible." This isn't like one of those makeover shows where I'm going to start crying and commit to changing my life entirely to dress like this now, but I wouldn't mind having these clothes. It could be beneficial to have a go-to outfit when I need to look fashionable. Maybe for college interviews or something.

Maybe the local news will want to interview me after I am chosen for the NASA internship.

Will Cooper like it? Not that I should care.

I think he would.

Charli looks at me through the mirror. "Is that a yes?"

I pull the sunglasses from the top of my head down to cover my eyes. NASA's not going to know what hit them. "Yes."

My plan is to put this on my dad's credit card. After all, he hasn't taken me shopping since . . . ever. Charli insists that she wants to buy it as an investment in my vlog startup. Is she trying to make me feel guilty about lying? Is she doing this to try to get me to like her? Humans are like geometric shapes: we all have our angles.

The food court is loud and busy. Yet another reason the mall is a place to be avoided. A peek at my watch tells me it's only five minutes until I can logically say, "My dad's out of work now, so I'd better be heading back." We order dinner, and I wonder how fast I can eat without seeming rude.

A piece of lettuce falls from my turkey sub. Charli's "sub" is all the fillings, no bread, no dressing, in a salad bowl. Her phone rings, the ringtone a bouncy pop song about believing in yourself. She pulls it out of her purse and looks at the caller ID. "Is it okay if I take this real quick?"

"Of course." We're not exactly at a five-star restaurant.

"Shelly! Hi! Can I hit you back a little later? I'm out to dinner with a friend at the moment." Charli mouths, "Sorry," and smiles at me. "Yeah? Okay. Thanks, girl."

Charli and I are not friends. Then again, what are we? If someone who doesn't know Charli called me right now, what would I say? "I'm in the food court—yes, the food court at the *mall*—and I'm out with this vlogger who may or may not be blackmailing me, but either way, I don't like her. She seems to be a kind and generous person, but she's really vapid. Tough to like someone like that, you know? So yeah, not friends. We're . . . in a weird situation."

Charli puts her phone back in her Louis Vuitton. "Sorry about that. One of my sisters from Columbia."

Wait a minute. "Columbia the university or Colombia the country?" It's not immediately clear which one would be more surprising.

Charli laughs. "The university. I was a double major in visual arts and business. Master's in strategic communication."

She has a master's degree? From *Columbia*?

It's as if I walked in to find Five reading the complete works of Shakespeare. It doesn't make any sense. This is the woman who played *cute* in a Scrabble game. Most people in the world are enigmas to me, but she's like a Rubik's cube. Every turn makes her more complicated.

To be fair to her, I guess, *cute* was a triple word score. She took the lead with that play.

"Sky?" I turn around to see Bridget waving at me. She's walking toward a table with one of her volleyball friends, but she comes over to say hello. She's wearing Spandex shorts, probably from volleyball practice. She's sweaty but somehow makes it look glamorous. "Don't take this the wrong way, but this is the last place I expected to see you."

"Me, too."

Charli smiles, looking at me and then back at Bridget. "Funny how people can be surprising, isn't it?"

"I got an eighty-five on my chem quiz yesterday!" Bridget says. She's bouncing on her toes, clearly still on a post-success high. "We got it back today."

"Nice!" It feels like a win for me, too. My statistical analysis of our last study session projected a grade of approximately 78 to 83. I may need to take another look at my algorithm.

Bridget introduces herself to Charli, which is a relief because explaining how I know her would have been awkward. Something in the way Bridget introduces herself makes me think that she already knows.

"Sky's been a huge help to me in studying for chemistry," Bridget continues. "I wouldn't be playing volleyball without her, and we've got a tournament on Saturday."

She's right—she probably wouldn't be playing without me. Even if the time I've spent with her is time distracting from working on the NASA video, it seems worth it in that moment. I haven't changed the whole world (yet), but I helped Bridget's world (a little).

"Are you going to the tournament?" Charli asks me. She takes another bite of her dressing-free salad.

Who eats salad without dressing? That's messed up.

"No. I don't do sports."

"But your friend does." Charli points her straw at Bridget before taking a sip of her water.

What is with her throwing this *friend* word around so much? Bridget and I aren't friends. I'm the tutor, and she's the student. Her brother and I are making a video. These are all business transactions. Friends include feelings and time-wasting and emotional attachments that fall apart and distract you from what's important. When you think about it, friends are a liability. Sure, I go to some QuizBowl pregame parties (pizza and trivia—we live on the edge). I sit with my QuizBowl team at lunch. But a friend? A real, true friend? Not interested.

"You should come," Bridget says. "We play from eight until around four at the Courthouse. Coop's coming." She smiles and raises her eyebrows, as if this will make a difference on whether or not I want to go to the tournament.

"You've gotta go support her," Charli says, "especially if you're the reason she can play."

"I don't know . . ."

Charli dabs her mouth with her napkin. "Bridget, have you heard about the project Cooper and Skyler are working on? It's super fabulous. But it's a secret, so make sure you don't tell."

"Okay, I'll go." I don't know what's going on here, but we are *not* talking about my "vlog." I plaster a quasi-convincing smile on my face. "Love to."

"Great." Charli stabs a piece of lettuce with her fork and flashes a smile at Bridget, "Good luck, girlie!"

The next day, a package from Amazon shows up at my door. There's a gift receipt inside that says, "Any good personal shopper would make sure you get something from your favorite store. This seems very you. ☺" It's a black T-shirt. On the front is the silhouette of someone looking through a telescope at a field of bright stars. The caption says, I NEED MY SPACE.

11

First a mall, and now a volleyball game? This is one of the most bizarre weeks of my life. The sheer normalcy of it is completely foreign. The last time I was normal was in third grade. Then I was suddenly "the girl whose mom died." Elementary school students aren't subtle. Every time a new kid came to our class, there were whispered explanations and students pointing my way. For the annual Mother's Day tea, the teacher always "adopted" me for the day. As if you can be a mother by sharing a cup of tea. Finally, my dad let me stay home that day instead.

In middle school, I tried to be invisible for so long that people stopped noticing me. The whispers about me stopped. My class-mates were too caught up in makeup and dating and playing team sports. The loss of their wave of sympathy dropped me in the middle of an ocean, alone. It gave me more time to spend with my mom, even though the only substantial words I had from her were the ones in her 150-page doctoral dissertation. I read them again and again, filling notebooks with words I didn't know but that I would someday understand. My dad explained some of them. Google explained others. My life became single-minded: answer the questions that her dissertation left behind. Its publication would be like a letter back to my mom, my best friend, in response to the one that she left me.

"Popcorn?" Cooper offers some dry, concession-stand popcorn in its small, white paper bag. It doesn't appear appetizing, but judging from everyone else eating it, it seems like part of the cultural experience.

"Sure." I try a handful, and it's like eating well-flavored chunks of Styrofoam.

The red lights on the scoreboard change from 23 to 24.

"Game point, right?" I am getting the hang of this. Game play is to 25, best three out of five games wins. The point is to get the volleyball off your side, and the most stylish way to do so is in a bump-set-spike formation. A solid bump-set-spike that hits the floor causes the team to erupt in cheers so intense that I feel like someone should remind them this is just a game. But I've seen Bridget's bedroom many times now. It's not just a game, despite my inability to figure out why not.

I snag another piece of Styrofoam popcorn. There has got to be a carcinogen lurking somewhere in these ingredients, but it doesn't really matter in that moment. Life is never guaranteed.

The players' Spandex shorts are so tight and so short that the girls are constantly pulling them out of their butt cracks. That cannot be the most practical choice for this activity.

My phone buzzes with a text. It's my dad:

In-N-Out after the game?

I say, Sure. I can save the broccoli beef recipe for tomorrow.

Then another text buzzes through.

Planning to go w/ Charli. That fine?

It's not super fine, but I also can't back out now. That would seem immature. If I could survive that awkward lasagna dinner, burgers at my favorite fast-food place should be doable. I almost text back that I'm going to invite Cooper, but instead I pocket my phone.

Bridget's up to serve. Cooper cheers loudly, and his sister smiles through her deep breaths. She gets to the back line of the court and does her usual pre-serve routine. Even I know it now. Bounce the ball three times. One, two, three. Hold the ball straight out in front of her. Breathe in fast, breathe out slow. The whole crowd silences. Players on the other side sway slightly in crouched positions, eyes locked on the ball. Bridget bends her knees slightly, puts the throw up, takes two steps, and *bam*.

The hit echoes through the silent gym.

The ball sails toward the back line. An opposing player dives for it, but it hits just out of her reach. The line judge calls it in. Game over.

"YES!"

Cooper is almost as excited as the rest of the team. We both stand, and he grabs my arm.

"Did you see that perfect serve? That's what I'm talking about! You go, Bridge!"

His hand grips my arm tightly, in a strong but not unpleasant way. Should I put my hand on top of his? Hug him? Grab his arm, too? My brain feels a little fuzzy as I try to dissect this situation. He lets go. Bummer.

The girls are wishing each other the obligatory "Good game" and regrouping before they take on their next opponent. As Bridget walks near the bleachers, I notice a shiny pink line snaking down her thigh. For a second I think it's a stretch mark, but it isn't. It's deeper and more pronounced. It's a scar.

"What happened to Bridget's leg?" I ask.

Cooper's face clouds over. Was it rude to ask about the scar? It doesn't look like a fresh wound, but the pain on Cooper's face looks fresh enough.

"There was an accident," he says.

"Oh." I'm not usually one to pick up on awkwardness, but even I can tell that I've somehow offended him. "Sorry."

He studies the popcorn to avoid looking at me. "It's fine." He eats another piece.

This is a terrible time to be in between games, because a blank court holds nothing to distract us from the heaviness that sits between us now. He eats another piece of popcorn.

"Do they play again soon?" I ask.

"Ten minutes or so." He nods to the scoreboard where a clock is counting down.

I had already seen it; I just didn't have anything else to say.

The crowd chatters around us, but I stare at my jeans because I'm not sure where else to look. Finally I stand up and say, "I'm going to get a drink."

"What?" he asks, like I snapped him out of a dream.

"Drink," I say, making a drinking motion with my hand in case he couldn't hear me over the people talking.

"Sure," he says, shrugging. He stands up to go with me, even though I planned to go alone.

At the concession stand, I order a Mountain Dew.

Cooper asks if they have grape soda, and the high schooler working the counter says, "Coop. Man. We literally never have grape soda."

Cooper says he knows, but he's going to keep asking anyway. He settles for a Pepsi. He asks if I want to get some air, which I do. We walk outside and sit against the tan bricks of the school. They're warm from the afternoon sun. The crowd inside cheers as the players come back to the court, but something tells me we're not going to be back in there for the first few points of the game. Cooper still looks in a trance, so I wait for him to speak. I'm almost 25 percent of the way through my Mountain Dew before he does.

"Sixth grade was the first year that Bridge's school had a girls' volleyball team. She tried out, made the team, and loved it." He takes a long swig of his Pepsi and stares straight ahead, like he's telling his story to the wind. "We were on our way home from her first game— she'd served two aces and spiked two kill shots. Her coach said she had a 'lot of promise' and told her she was an official starter. We raced to the car when it was time to leave. I beat her, meaning I should have gotten shotgun, but she said she should get it because it was her 'special day.' She always tried to make every day her 'special day.'"

He stops and smiles for a split second, like he's remembering someone who's been gone for a long time. Then the smile vanishes.

"It wasn't worth the fight, so I said fine. I messed around on my phone in the back seat watching videos. Back then, my big plan was to be a YouTube star." He rolls his eyes. Then he takes another drink and looks out toward the parking lot. "I found this video of an alligator who was friends with a turtle. It was so dumb. But the turtle rode on the alligator's back, so I thought it was cool. I was an idiot. I showed Bridget, and it made her laugh. Then I showed my dad. He glanced down but then looked back at the road. I said, 'No, hold on, it's almost to the funny part.' Just like that—'it's almost to the funny part.' And when the video got to the funny part, my dad ran into a semitruck."

I choke on my Mountain Dew.

He continues, unfazed. "Yeah. It pulled out in front of us, and my dad didn't see it because he was looking at my phone. Bridget's shin hit the dash, and it shoved her leg backward into her pelvis. Her femur broke. They did surgery, and they told her she'd never play volleyball again. She'd be lucky to walk without a limp."

"She doesn't have a limp at all." It seems to me that this story has a happy ending. There's no reason to be so upset about it.

"She walks well because she did so much rehab and therapy on that leg. She worked her butt off. The local news covered the first day she walked back onto a volleyball court."

"See? It's inspirational. She's a success."

Cooper is picking at the grass near us. "Think about how good she would be if I hadn't wrecked her leg. What if she could have been an Olympian or something?"

"You didn't wreck her leg."

"I absolutely did." His eyes burn into mine. "If I'd been sitting in the front seat, this wouldn't have happened. If I hadn't watched that video, the scar wouldn't be there."

I want to tell him that he's being ridiculous—that of course it wasn't his fault. There's even a piece of me that wants to say he's being selfish. How dare he feel sad about an accident in which everyone survived? He takes a deep breath but then tightens his jaw, like he's holding his breath to keep everything inside. He starts talking to his Pepsi.

"My mom started flipping strollers to pay the hospital bills. But the bills piled up, and do you know how many strollers my mom would have to sell to pay off all the outstanding bills? Twenty thousand. Twenty thousand stupid strollers. For a mistake I made."

I picture Mrs. Evans selling stroller after stroller into infinity. Replacing diaper stains with new upholstery and painting shiny metal bars so new families can carry their perfect babies while she cared for her broken one. Maybe Bridget took her first post-accident steps at the same time some of those babies walked for the first time. Maybe the parents all cried.

A new image comes to mind: Cooper watching his sister go to rehab, watching her take those first steps, watching his parents scramble to pay bills. He would have been twelve at the time. That's too much for a middle schooler to handle.

"It wasn't your fault, Coop."

Cooper keeps a tight face. He looks up at the clouds like they're super interesting. "Anyway, that's the scar. I'll spend the rest of my life protecting her, and it still won't fix the past. My family has been through so much because of me, so I basically exist to make up for it. Everything I do has to be for them."

"Come on," I say. "You can't do that to yourself."

"Can't I?" His eyes are challenging. "Has your dad invented a time machine in his fancy lab?"

"No." I hold my cup tighter and shake the ice around.

"Okay then," he says, like that settles that.

A blast of air-conditioning hits me as I walk through the door of In-N-Out, and I'm greeted by the familiar white-and-red color scheme. Someone behind the counter yells about fries, and machines buzz and beep as they prepare saturated fat and cholesterol for human consumption.

My dad sees me first and waves from the booth where he and Charli are sitting. Maybe it was a mistake to come here. I'm glad he's happy, but she still makes me nervous.

My dad and I get cheeseburgers, fries, and milkshakes. Charli gets a burger on a lettuce bun, no mustard or mayo, and a diet lemonade. I never knew there was such a thing as diet lemonade. My dad and I sit on the same side of the shiny red booth. The booth matches Charli's lipstick.

"So what's new?" I ask with all the friendliness I can muster. It's not a lot. This is weird.

"I'm studying an antibiotic-resistant strain of strep," my dad says with equal parts excitement and concern. "They've already seen some human cases in Thailand."

"Don't bring that work home with you!" says Charli. "Am I right?"

Dad laughs. "Charli's been working on something special, too," he says. He nudges her shoulder from across the booth, which is awkward.

She puts down her lettuce burger as if she's making a big announcement. "There are so many major conferences in the Las Vegas Valley," she says modestly, "but maybe you've heard of Vlogalicious?"

I choke on my laugh but try to make it sound more like coughing.

"Are you okay?" My dad hits my back.

"Yeah." I wipe my face. "Fine. No, I haven't heard of it. Sorry." Not sorry.

"No worries. I brought a brochure!" She pulls one out of her handbag. The purse is beige with some designer logo on it.

The brochure is a splash of loud colors with the word VLOGA-LICIOUS! written across the top in silver sparkly letters. The dates are coming up, and the brochure promises that this conference will help me do lots of things. Increase my platform! Build my viewership! Choose the fashions people REALLY want to see!

There are so many exclamation points it feels like the brochure is yelling at me.

"I'm speaking at it, if you'd like to come," she says.

"She's the keynote." My dad looks proud. "You'll come with me, won't you, SkyBear?"

Picturing my dad alone at the Vlogalicious conference makes me want to cry and laugh at the same time. "I'm pretty sure I'm busy that day," I say.

"Doing what?"

Filming, probably. But I can't say that. "Studying?"

My dad laughs. "You study so hard. It will be good to take a day off and have fun." He sees my skeptical look and amends. "It could be fun, maybe. Or at least educational. How much do we know about fashion?"

"How much do we need to know?"

"Please come?" Charli blinks twice—does that count as batting your eyelashes? It feels like she's batting her eyelashes. "It would mean so much to me."

Since when do we owe this woman favors? My dad saved her life. I went to *the mall* with her. What more do we have to do?

They're both staring at me expectantly. Is this why they invited me to dinner? Because I won't say no in person? Those sneaks. "Fine."

"Goody!" Charli claps her hands and eats one of my dad's fries.

It's a quiet drive home. I even turn off NPR because I need the silence to figure out what I'm thinking. It's good to do things for your family. Going to Vlogalicious so my dad doesn't have to go alone is a good thing (I think). Cooper dedicating his entire life to his family for a mistake he made as a kid is a bad thing (I think). Where's the line? And—most pressing on my mind right now— where does "dedicating your life to your mom's research" fall?

When I turn the corner onto my road, our neighbor Julie's daughter, Lindsey, who I've seen at school, is on the sidewalk holding hands with some guy. The sunlight reflects off her smooth shoulders, and he's huge in an all-state-athlete way. As I get closer to them, the guy kisses her cheek. They turn and walk toward her house, and I never get a good look at his face. Even so, he looks familiar. Where have I seen that guy before?

A sense of dread washes over me when I remember where I've seen him—that looks just like Andrew. Bridget's Andrew. His side profile matched the photo she'd shown me. The body type was spot-on.

It couldn't be him, right? He wouldn't. Who would cheat on Bridget? She's beautiful, she's athletic, she's popular. She's not super book smart, but hey, that's okay.

I strain my neck trying to get a better look. The guy is wearing a football jersey, and it's definitely from our school. They disappear inside before I can positively identify him. I consider telling Bridget, but I don't want to alarm her for no reason.

I spend the next twenty minutes trying to convince myself that it probably wasn't him, and I don't feel very convinced.

12

Okay, so this is how contouring is supposed to work. Charli is gleeful, and my skin looks like . . . well, like Charli's. She's used a toolbox full of makeup on me. No joke—she carries her makeup around in a toolbox. A normal, green metal toolbox.

She closes the lid and says, "You're ready. Let's get you down to set." I'm not sure if my dad's lab is exactly a "set," but Cooper is down there making it function as one. If my dad finds this out, he's going to kill me. Maybe all three of us. Could I be the cause of Dad and Charli's first fight? Even though I'm not sure I like her, I don't want to be the reason they get in a fight.

If he comes home, I have no idea what we'll say when he asks why we're in there. I've gone through a number of excuses in my head, but none work. I've never been allowed in his lab without him. When I was a kid it was because he couldn't trust me around toxic chemicals, and the rule stuck. I tried explaining this to Charli, but she winked at me and said she'd take care of it.

What does that mean? Does she have a plan? Because she'd better have a plan. And if that plan includes making out with my dad or something, then it's for the best that she doesn't tell me about it. There's no need for me to vomit on the set and make a bad problem worse.

"Go check if Cooper's ready," she says while pulling a Chubby Stick out of her purse. When I say *Chubby Stick*, I don't mean a stick that has a larger-than-average diameter. There's an actual line of makeup called Chubby Stick. There's blush, lip stuff, eye stuff—they've got it all. And what I want to know is this: What crack team of advertising execs sat around a table and thought, "Yeah! Chubby Stick! That's the best possible name for this product!"? Charli slathers some Chubby on her lips. She's not even going to be on camera, but I bet it's habit more than anything. What would she look like without makeup? I appraise her through the mirror, and I conclude that she would be attractive. When did women decide we needed to enhance ourselves with gunk?

I look again at myself and try to hate the makeup. It's like a chemically induced lie. But I have to admit I look good. Charli somehow turned my boring, stick-straight hair into something that looks like it would be swishing in a viral video about hair-care. It hangs in loose curls that swirl away from my face, and it's bigger than usual. Charli complimented the "volume," which made me happy because now my hair is sort of a math problem. I'm wearing the outfit Charli bought me at Anthropologie, and I wish I were at school. Would people even recognize me? I don't look like myself, but I look familiar . . .

I look like my mom, and I'm not sure if I love it or hate it.

I still have my dad's thin lips and his weird ears. But with my lips fully lined and my hair covering my ears, the differences aren't as stark as they usually are. She used to wear her hair curled. Her eyes always looked large and bright. I never wondered about her wearing makeup or not, but statistically I suppose there's a good chance she did. I widen my eyes to try to see her in them. Would we have been that pair in the mall where people think we're sisters instead of mother and daughter? If she could see me right now, all grown up from the nine-year-old she left behind, would she be proud? I blink a couple of times—all this eyeliner is probably causing some chemical reaction that makes my eyes water.

"Everything okay?" asks Charli. "Did some get in your eye?" She whips out a packet of makeup remover wipes and leaves them on the counter. How much crap does she have in her purse? "Here's a wipe if you need it."

I blink a few more times, but the reaction seems to have subsided. "I'm good, thanks. I'll go see if Coop's ready." After one last glance in the mirror, I head for the hallway.

Charli clears her throat. She waves me back in and whispers, "Come here," with urgency, as if she's got national secrets to tell me.

She looks into the hall to make sure Cooper's not coming upstairs. Then she turns to me and whispers, "Girlie, you gotta handle the VPLs before you go on camera."

"VPLs?"

She turns pink like she just used magic to put Chubby Stick on her cheeks without touching them. "Visible panty lines. I can see your underwear line through your pants. Usually I wouldn't say anything, but there was this one episode of *Kisses from Charli* where I had VPLs going on. I got sooo many comments about it, I was mortified. People from all over the country started mailing me thongs, which was *the* most embarrassing thing. It was really sweet because my fans were looking out for me, but so many packages showed up from Victoria's Secret that my mailman probably thought I was starting an escort service."

"You want me to wear a thong?"

"Unless you want people to write comments on your page like 'All I could see were your granny panties,' then yes."

"Your fans aren't very nice."

"People in general aren't very nice."

"What if I don't have a thong?"

She looks incredulous. "You don't own a single thong? How about some Spanx? Shapewear of any kind?"

"No. Thongs raise your risk for getting a urinary tract infection." Why would people wear a clothing item that raises their risk of disease? It's like not flossing or not taking a daily vitamin—are people stupid?

Charli sighs and looks at the ceiling like she can't believe I brought up urinary tract infections. Or perhaps she's stunned I don't own a thong. Then her eyes light up, and she does a little gasp like she just had the best idea. "I might have one in my car," she says.

"Why do you have—" I start. "Wait, never mind. Definitely don't want to know."

She crosses her arms. "Don't be weird. It's in my FEK."

"Your what?"

"FEK. Fashion emergency kit. Did you not watch my episode about that?"

My eyebrows jump to my newly beautified hairline.

She waves off my surprise. "Never mind. Of course you didn't. It's got Shout wipes, foldable flats, a blister stick, a handheld steamer—"

She's speaking English, right? "I know what literally none of that is."

"Do you know what a thong is?"

"Yes."

"Okay. Well, it's also got a thong. In case of emergency VPLs." She gestures to my pants like this is the perfect occasion to illustrate the necessity of an FEK.

After mirror surveillance, I decide the underwear lines aren't that bad. Sure, I can see them, but it's not a secret that I wear underwear. We all wear underwear. I turn back to Charli. "This is not an emergency, and I'm not wearing your thong."

She sighs. "Then you need to get some Spanx or something. This is a solvable problem."

I put my hands on my hips. "I don't think this is a serious problem. Let's leave it alone."

"Do you have any Spandex shorts? That could work."

"Fine. I'll go check. It's not like the viewers should be worried about my butt anyway."

Through the mirror's reflection, I see Cooper walk through the doorway behind me. Shoot. My face flames. He's trying not to laugh, and in this moment I hate Charli. Cooper puts his hand in front of his mouth and tries to hide his laugh. "Checking to see if you're ready. Looks like you're, uh, almost there?"

I whirl around to face him, because if my back's to him, then he'll see my VPLs (which never mattered before now, but I don't want my granny panties to be all he can see). Then I realize that now my butt is visible in the mirror, and there is nowhere I can turn to get my butt away from him. Arrrgh!

Cooper has put his hand down from his mouth, and he's straight-up staring at me. His eyes are huge, and his head is tilted slightly to the side.

"This isn't what it sounds like," I say. "I only need to go change because, uh, I gotta go change." Sometimes the best idea is to get out of the situation.

He catches my arm as I walk by him. He leans in close and whispers through my curls, "You look amazing." His breath is warm on my neck, and I'm not sure if it's the words or the breath that causes shivers.

I glance over my shoulder to see if Charli heard him. She's rummaging through her purse again, but she's smiling through closed lips.

Cooper has carefully arranged his equipment around all of my dad's lab stuff. There's a camera next to a centrifuge. An umbrella light next to a stack of agar plates. He left a boom mic next to an incubator.

My dad is seriously going to kill me.

"Why are we doing this again?" I ask. "It's impossible to star-gaze in a basement."

"It's about your image," Charli says for the hundredth time. "This place looks science-y. You're talking about science." She rolls a portable whiteboard to the center of the camera's focus. "Good, Cooper?"

He looks through the viewfinder and gives a thumbs-up. "Everything looks great." He's looking at me.

The plan is for me to draw some diagrams that explain neutron stars, and then Cooper can speed it up to look like I'm writing fast. I'll have a voiceover in the background, either from things we film today or pieces we already have.

Charli also insists that while I've "got my beauty on," we have to get some footage of me looking through a microscope. This makes even less sense because I use telescopes, not microscopes, but there's no arguing with her. She's on a mission. My online presence is going to be "fantabulous," and my fans will flock to my "brains-meets-beauty" image. I almost feel bad that this video isn't going to go on YouTube.

But only almost. After all, she weaseled her way into this.

I write "Neutron Stars" at the top of the board and underline it as if I'm a professor giving an important lecture. Charli, standing behind the camera, claps her hands silently like I'm brilliant at this.

"When a star collapses," I begin, "the rotation rate increases as a result of conservation of angular momentum."

Charli puts her hands in front of her and presses downward.

I silently mouth, "What?" and hold my hands up in an I-don't-know motion.

Cooper laughs. "You know I can see you and not just hear you, right? That got recorded."

"Ugh. Now I have to start over."

"You weren't very far," Charli says. "I was telling you to take it down a notch. Slow down your talking, and make the science easier to understand."

"I'm pretty sure the people at NASA are going to know what I'm talking about."

"How do you know NASA people are going to see your vlog? You never know who might sign on! You have to be ready for any audience."

Cooper's panicked eyes alert me to my mistake.

"Right." I nod too enthusiastically. "Of course. You never know. Good advice. Let's start over."

"I'm still rolling," says Cooper. "Start when you're ready."

Where do I start on dumbing this down? I look to Charli for advice. She's moving her pointer fingers in a star shape and mouthing, "Explain a star."

Oh my. NASA is going to think I'm an idiot. Cooper can edit this out later.

I draw a star on the board. Not a real star, but the five-pointed thing you find in kids' shape books that in reality looks nothing like a star.

"This," I begin, "is a star. It's a shoddy representation of one, anyway. A neutron star happens when there's a big star"—I draw a huge one next to my first one—"and it explodes." I pick up my red marker and scribble all over the big star, showing that it has clearly exploded. I giggle and look toward Cooper and Charli, expecting them to laugh at how elementary I have made this. Cooper's face is hidden behind the camera, and Charli is doing a very enthusiastic silent clap.

I spend the next half hour struggling through various explanations of neutron stars, some scientific and some not so much. Cooper also gets the footage of me at a microscope.

"What am I supposed to be looking at?" I ask. "There's nothing on this slide."

"Here." Charli plucks out one of her eyelashes. "I looked at a mascaraed eyelash under a scope in chemistry once. It's freaky."

When the eyelash comes into focus, she's right. There are giant globs of black crud all over the hair. That's disgusting. When I look up, Cooper and Charli laugh at my horrified face. It's a good thing the makeup was on my eyes before I saw this slide, or I never would have let Charli come near me with it.

Finally, Charli calls, "That's a wrap," and declares that Cooper has enough basement footage. She goes upstairs to start dinner (that's one nice piece of having Charli around—I don't have to make dinner all the time anymore). Cooper and I start the arduous process of making sure the basement looks like no one's been there.

"What is this for?" Cooper asks, picking up a mortar and pestle. "It looks like a tiny bowl and puncher that ancient women used to grind grain." He holds the white ceramic piece with the rounded end down and pretends to grind into the matching white bowl.

"That's not far off," I admit. "But my dad doesn't grind a lot of grain down here. Put it down. Don't leave fingerprints."

"Don't leave fingerprints?" Cooper puts the mortar down and rubs the pestle between his hands. "My fingerprints are all over it now. Is someone going to use this as incriminating evidence against us? But we hid the body so well!" He does an evil villain laugh.

I leave my beakers and go rescue the pestle from his hand. His hand is warm and soft, and I wish I had a reason for mine to linger. "Cooper William," I say. "You're going to break something."

Cooper tilts his head and narrows his eyes. "William? That's not my middle name."

"Sure it is," I say as I put the mortar and pestle back on the shelf to his right, trying to remember the exact angle so nothing will look out of place. He hasn't moved since I took the pestle out of his hand, and I'm standing close enough to him to smell his woodsy cologne. Neither of us steps away.

He laughs nervously, like I've made an embarrassing mistake. "No, seriously. My middle name is Dash."

Never would have guessed that.

"I needed a middle name for effect," I say. "People always listen when you use a middle name. Also, your middle name is *Dash*?"

"You know, like *dashing*. Means 'dapper' and 'suave.'" He grins.

"Whatever. You're named after a reindeer."

"That's Dasher."

"I bet Santa calls him Dash."

We are engaged in the practice known as flirting. Even though I am new at this, I have always considered myself a quick learner. The air between us seems alive, like it's fizzling with electricity. I pick up a box of microscope slides and put them on the shelf, even though they don't go there. To reach the empty space on the shelf, I cut the space between us in half. He doesn't step back.

He looks at the slides and then back at me. "Why William?"

"Dunno. It just fit." I survey Cooper's face, trying to figure out why he looks like a William. "Maybe it's your earring. You look like a pirate."

"A pirate?"

"Not a zombie one, if it makes you feel better."

Cooper laughs. "Glad to hear I look better than the undead." He picks up a graduated cylinder and puts it on the other side of the shelf, stepping toward me. It doesn't go there. He has to nudge two Erlenmeyer flasks to make room for it.

"Don't say I never gave you a compliment," I say.

He's so close that I can see where the gold of his eyes fades into green. There's no equipment left on the shelf to pick up, so I pick up the bottle of green dish soap by the sink. Now its new place is next to the microscope slides, though it doesn't make a lot of sense to keep the soap there.

Neither of us will back away. I'm standing closer to him than I ever have, and my heart is beating so fast that my symptoms would be indicative of acute tachycardia. Is his heart beating fast, too? His chest rises and lowers with his breath, and I wonder if the skin under his gray T-shirt is as soft as his hands.

With nothing left on the counter at all, Cooper reaches for the dish soap on the shelf. "This should go . . . by the sink," he says, putting it on the side of the sink closest to me. He speaks slowly, like he's having trouble putting a sentence together. He can't even take a full step now, but he moves closer anyway. We're inches apart.

"I . . . uh . . ." I'm out of things to say. As a matter of fact, I have now stopped breathing. Have his eyelashes always been so long?

Before I can find another item to move, Cooper kisses me. It's sweet and light, and I close my eyes because I want to remember exactly how his lips feel on mine. I want to remember the rustic, citrus smell of his skin, the melting of everything inside me, and the absolute perfection of the moment.

From now on, I will never judge anyone for closing their eyes while kissing.

He takes a sudden step back, scratching his jawline. "Listen, I promised I would keep this all business. But come on. You feel it, too. I know you do. Forget the chemicals, okay? If you think about it, our entire body is one big pile of chemicals. You can spend your whole life fighting them, or you can embrace them. Especially chemicals that feel like this"—he motions between the two of us—"because, wow, those are—"

I never hear what it is that they are, because I destroy the space between us and start making out with Cooper in my dad's chemistry lab.

The world gets fuzzy. My focus zeroes in on Cooper: his mouth, his hands, his arms, his hair. In that moment, nothing in the universe exists besides him and me.

I accidentally knock a beaker to the floor, and it shatters. We barely pause.

I can't even think. Maybe I'll never think again—let's just keep doing this forever.

Forever is cut short by the basement door opening. Unlike the beaker, this sound stops us. I expect to hear Charli's dainty steps on the stairs, but the steps are heavy . . . like someone's testing each stair to see how much weight it can hold.

13

My dad's view of us is obscured until he's about halfway down the stairs. There's only enough time for Cooper to jump away and for me to hop from the counter and frantically rearrange my hair (which, upon reflection, made us look even more guilty).

My dad stops on the bottom stair, startled to see us. There's not usually anyone in the basement. His white lab coat is stained, and his hair is sticking up on the left side. Looks like he had a long day.

"Skyler!" he exclaims. "What are you—" Then he looks toward the ceiling in annoyance. "Seriously? Were you *making out* in my lab?"

"No," I lie instinctively.

Cooper clears his throat.

"Then what are you doing down here?" His gaze shifts to the floor. "You broke a beaker?"

Shoot. What are we doing down here? Filming a vlog? No, that's the lie we told Charli. Working on an application? Even worse—that's the truth.

A few weeks ago, I told him we were making out when we weren't, and now I'm telling him we weren't when we were. My lies are getting confusing. I should put them in an organized binder. With flow charts.

It's like Cooper can sense that I'm lost. He reaches up to scratch his temple and whispers, "Go with making out," behind his hand.

I massage my palm with my thumb. "Yes, well, we, um . . ."

Why is this so hard to admit? It wasn't a problem at all when it was a lie.

I'm hoping my dad will get the gist and bail me out, but he doesn't. He crosses his arms, waiting for my explanation. The harsh lights reflect in the top of his glasses.

"Okay, we were making out." My cheeks flame.

My dad's eyes narrow in suspicion. "Really?"

This is rich. Now he doesn't believe me.

His eyes sweep over my outfit and study my makeup and hair. Does he see the same thing I did when I looked in the mirror? Do I look like her? He tilts his head and then shakes it, like he thinks he's seeing things. "You're . . . dressed up. What's the occasion?"

"Making out!" Now I feel defensive. Why couldn't I be making out? Is that so unbelievable? My dad uncrosses his arms. "Why would you come to my lab to make out?"

"Uh . . ." I look to Cooper for help.

"For the chemistry?" Cooper offers. He laughs at his joke, then quickly rearranges his face to look chastised. "Sorry. It was too easy."

Does he have to say everything that comes into his mind?

"I'm missing something," my dad says. He steps into the lab and looks around, like there will be evidence of what we're doing. Luckily, we cleaned up.

"Jack!" A panicked voice floats down the stairs. "Where are you?"

"In the basement," he calls up.

"Ack!" Charli's heels click above us as she runs to the basement stairs. "Don't go down there!"

A little late, Charli.

Now my dad looks even more suspicious. "Why not?" He looks at the stairs and then back to me.

Charli flings the basement door open and rushes down so quickly that she trips and has to catch herself on the banister. My dad goes to help her, but she's to the bottom of the stairs in a snap. "Sky," she says. "I actually, um, found the thing!"

"What thing?" my dad asks.

"The *thing*," she says. "I needed Sky and Cooper to check down here for something, but I already found it." She smiles at me, but she's a bad liar. The smile comes out looking more like a bared-teeth grimace.

This was Charli's plan? If so, it was a terrible plan.

"What did you need from my lab?" I can't tell if my dad is more annoyed or curious.

Charli's mouth is slightly open while she thinks. "I . . . can't tell you."

"Why not?"

"It's a surprise."

"Was it a beaker?"

Charli looks confused. "No." She shoots me a wary look. "Maybe?"

My dad sighs. "Can someone please tell me what's going on?"

The three of us look at one another in thick silence, none of us willing to sell anyone else out.

Finally, after a painful silence, my dad says, "Can I talk to Skyler alone?"

Cooper and Charli both shoot me nervous glances, but they head upstairs.

When we're alone, my dad crosses his arms again. "SkyBear. What's the deal?"

I'm tempted to tell him the whole truth. Even if he gets mad, at least I won't have to sneak around anymore. This isn't what we do. At what point is keeping the secret worse than the secret itself? There should be tables to consult about this. My secret has got to be nearing critical mass.

My pause must be too long, because my dad fills the empty space for me. "It feels like I don't know you anymore."

He walks toward me. For a second I think he's going to hug me. I even move to hug him back, but he bends down and starts picking up the broken shards of glass. I hurry to help him. He warns me to be careful, as if I haven't been picking up broken glassware for years. We transfer the pieces to a plastic sharps container.

"Things will make sense soon," I say. "Can't you just trust me?"

His mouth sets in a grim line. Anger, sadness, and fear mix in his blue eyes as he meets mine. "For the first time ever, no. I don't think I can."

It feels like he punched me in the stomach. If we don't have each other, what do we have left? Even though he's the one who said the words, it looks like they hurt him, too.

He grabs a blue whisk broom to sweep up more glass. His body sags. "I don't know what's so important that you've got Cooper and Charli both willing to cover for you. I'm your dad, for goodness' sake. Who in all of Darwinian evolution loves you more than I do?" He throws the glass away with more force than necessary.

"I'll explain," I promise. "Eventually."

When he does find out (hopefully when I get this thing), what will he do? I'm eighteen, so he can't stop me from going. He'll forgive me, right? Surely I'm not sacrificing what I had with him for something my mom will never know about.

My dad has one brother—Phil. My dad and Phil used to be close, but a few years ago they got in this huge fight when my dad missed Phil's wedding. He was on the brink of a discovery in his research about bioluminescent bacteria, and he couldn't trust anyone to watch his cultures at the critical end stage.

In my dad's defense, it was a *very critical stage*. And it was Phil's third wedding. Phil came over a few days later, livid. He yelled about how my dad is obsessed with his work, selfish, and that he's completely missing out on the rest of life. My dad said that Phil was egotistical and had no appreciation for the importance of scientific inquiry. They still call each other on

Christmas and birthdays, but things between them have never been the same. Also, the bioluminescent bacteria research didn't even pan out.

It wasn't worth it.

This is different, right? He'd never let a fight ruin a relationship with me. We're family.

Well, Uncle Phil was family, too.

A cold feeling washes over me. When I started this project, I was sure my dad's eventual anger would be a yell-and-then-get-over-it kind of thing. Now he doesn't trust me, and we hardly ever see each other. Even when we're both home, I'm always careful around him. The easiness that we once had is gone, replaced by a calculated tension. It's like this secret has been a cancer on our relationship. Once the secret's out, will our relationship recover? Or will it be too far gone?

Is it worth the risk?

He leans against the black epoxy-resin lab counter and takes his glasses off to clean them. I want to hug him and have him tell me everything will be okay. He used to do that all the time when I was scared. But I can't now.

I can't even hug my dad. What's happened to us?

He puts the glasses back on his face. "Here." He pulls a piece of paper out of his lab coat pocket. It's folded into crisp fourths. "I came home early to see if you wanted to go to this with me. Feels like I never see you anymore."

The paper is a printout of an email. It's an announcement for a lecture tonight titled "Analysis of Lactate Dehydrogenase Activities and Isoenzyme Patterns." Some families go to the movies or to sports games, but we've always gone to lectures. It's what we do.

"Sure," I say, swallowing. "Looks fun."

"I think I'm getting a migraine," he says. "I need to take some ibuprofen and lie down. We'll catch the next one." He heads upstairs, leaving me in the lab alone.

The paper feels heavier than it should. I made the wrong choice. If it costs my dad, then NASA isn't worth it.

We can still finish the video, I reason with myself. I don't have to *submit* the application. Cooper can still use his work. But how will I explain my decision to Cooper? And what will Charli think when there isn't a vlog? Also, if I have an entire application and don't submit it, the uncertainty of wondering what might have happened will be unbearable. I can't submit the application, but I can't pull the plug on the project, either.

What have I done?

14

If you made a list of "Places You Will Never See Skyler Davidson," you could have safely put Vlogalicious on there. It's a two-day conference for fashion vloggers, and I can't think of many places that are a bigger waste of time. Jail, maybe.

YET HERE I AM.

Charli invited Cooper the night that we filmed in the basement. I told Cooper he didn't have to come, but I was glad when he said he would. Also, due to our new relationship developments, we don't even have to fake liking each other.

My dad gives our printed tickets to a lady wearing a furry teal vest and short purple shorts. What the heck sort of animal is supposed to have teal fur? Her eye makeup is the exact color of her shorts blended with the color of the vest. It's impressive and also bizarre.

"I feel underdressed." My dad makes a fake nervous face. He's wearing khakis and a plaid short-sleeved polo. He had a tie on with it earlier, but I told him that ties don't go with short sleeves. This is something Charli taught me, and it was probably for exactly this type of situation.

Why is she with him again?

My dad and I haven't talked about that night in the basement. Since I'm still not willing to tell him what's going on, there isn't much to say. We're friendly and light, but it feels fragile.

I haven't told Cooper about my second thoughts on the project. After all, he'll still need it for his own application. There's no reason to explain that I might not use his footage, especially when I haven't yet made up my mind.

"Looks like the eighties are back," my dad says, nodding to a group of teenagers wearing highlighter green, yellow, and orange leggings. "I should have brought my Rubik's cube."

I'm wearing black dress pants with a dark gray collared shirt. It's the same outfit I wear for college visits. Cooper is wearing a white T-shirt with a jean jacket. Black pants. He's the only one of us that looks like he belongs here. His smallest camera bag is slung over his shoulder. "A true cameraman always has a camera," he has told me multiple times.

"Did you solve the cube?" Cooper asks my dad. He tries to be jokey and casual, but it's hard to come back from my dad catching us doing who-knows-what in his basement lab. Things still feel a bit odd, as if we're strangers acting like family. I'm not sure if my dad was thrilled that Charli invited Cooper today, but he's tolerating it.

CHRISTINE WEBB

Despite the awkwardness, my dad and I look at each other and smile. "Did I finish it?" he says. "I was the president of the Rubik's Cube Club. I could finish it in thirty seconds."

"Your school had a Rubik's Cube Club?"

I grab his shoulders. Any excuse to touch him is a good excuse. "You're missing the point, Cooper. THIRTY SECONDS."

He tries to look appropriately amazed.

I drop my hands back to my sides. "My fastest ever was thirty-seven." I was doing really well that time until my dad came in and asked if I wanted Pringles. It completely threw off my focus. We still debate whether or not he did that on purpose.

Charli's speech starts in about fifteen minutes, so we have time to spare. We get in line for the cinnamon almonds, both because they smell amazing and because we look strange enough without also standing around and gawking at people.

While in line, the girl behind me taps my shoulder. She's wearing a sleeveless orange turtleneck and light blue pants with a gold belt. Her hair is a beautiful mess of black curls. "I love your shoes," she says. "Are they Gucci?"

"Um, no. But thanks." My black flats are from Target. I start fishing for the money I'll need for the almonds. She taps me again.

"Sorry to bug you, but I have to say—your makeup is gorgeous. So natural. Who do you use?"

"Um, me?"

She laughs. "No, I mean what brand? Like, what designer of makeup?"

"I don't wear any."

"No!" She puts her hand to her chest like I've admitted to being an alien. "You're kidding."

"Gorgeous, right?" Cooper puts his arm around me. I lean into him as if I could soak up his body. He kisses my hair. "Can you believe she wakes up looking like that?"

"How many times have you seen her wake up?" my dad asks. He's half joking, but only half.

Cooper drops his arm. "Never. You're right. Maybe she looks awful in the morning."

"She doesn't." Now my dad puts his arm around me. "And I'm the one who made her, so I should know."

It's like the tension is as bright and visible as Orange Turtleneck's outfit.

She gives me a sympathetic look before turning to my dad. "You're surely not old enough to be her dad?"

He smiles proudly. "Teenage pregnancy is a rampant epidemic in society today."

My dad was thirty-one when they had me.

"Hey, y'all!" We're rescued by a familiar twang. Charli gives my dad a hug and smiles at us. "Thanks for coming!" She's wearing a dark green sheath dress (this is a term I learned two days ago) that hugs her in all the right places. Her hair is down and curled, and her high heels are pale green. The bottoms of the shoes are red, though. Maybe a color pop? Who knows.

"We wouldn't miss it," my dad says. "I always say that a day of learning anything is better than a day of not learning at all."

He does say that. It's doubtful whether he truly meant for it to apply to "Building Your Social Media Platform at the Same

Rate You Build Your Shoe Collection," but that's Charli's lecture topic.

My shoe collection grows at a rate of about one pair per year, so my social media platform only needs one new follower a year to accomplish her objective. I could manage that. No reason to, but I could.

"Oh my gosh," Orange Turtleneck says. "You're Charli!"

"Sure am!" Charli is always friendly when her fans recognize her. If that happened to me, I feel like I would say, "What? Who? LOOK! A METEOR!" and then run away before they could talk to me anymore.

Orange Turtleneck looks from Charli to my dad. "And you two are . . ."

"I know, right? Am I lucky or what?" Charli plants a kiss on my dad's cheek, leaving a lipstick smudge. Even though I should be grossed out by this, it's kind of cute. Charli is so clearly out of my dad's league, and yet she thinks she's the lucky one. And really, she is. I'm so proud of my dad, and everyone should be able to see how amazing he is. It's just that not many supermodels see past the Einstein hair, thick glasses, and plaid polos.

"This man took care of me when I had that awful toe thing. I almost died."

"I saw your episode about that! 'Perilous Pedicures'!"

Charli nods. "Gotta be careful out there, girlie. Can you imagine how embarrassing it would have been if I died of a pedicure? And this genius saved my life. Not only that, but he walked with me every step of the way. No pun intended." She laughs at her joke.

"You're a hero," Orange Turtleneck says to my dad. "The entire fashion community thanks you."

"It was nothing," my dad says, because what are you supposed to say when someone calls you a hero? "Just doing my job."

Charli gives my dad's shoulders a squeeze. "I've gotta get backstage, but I wanted to come say hi. Catch me after!" She waves at us and scurries off. How does she move so fast in shoes so tall?

When we sit down, I pull my notebook out of my backpack. "Seriously?" Cooper asks. "You're taking notes?"

"It's a lecture," I say. "It's what you do."

My dad has hauls out his Chromebook. "There's always more to learn, Cooper."

"Hold up." Cooper shakes his head. "You're not working on other things? You're taking notes on this presentation?"

My dad and I look at each other, confused, and then back to Cooper. "Yes," we say in unison.

"Ah! This is too good. This is exactly why I always have a camera." He pulls the bag around to his lap. "Pretend like you're taking notes."

"The talk hasn't started yet," I point out.

"Fake it. Write the title or something. I have to get this." He jumps out of his seat and excuse-me's himself out of the aisle. Then he excuse-me's himself through to an empty seat about five aisles in front of us. "Go," he mouths.

My dad and I look at each other again, and then my dad starts typing. I start writing. "Shoes and Social Media," I write at the top of the page. My dad types, "Cooper looks like a weirdo right now."

I stifle a laugh and write, "Lady next to him is giving him some serious stink eye."

My dad types again. "Why is he videoing us?"

"No clue," I respond. Almost true. "We stand out in this crowd." Definitely true.

"Is this seat taken?" a woman asks me, pointing to Cooper's seat. I tell her that it is, sorry. This place is filling up fast. It can fit hundreds if not thousands of people, and it looks like it will be sold out.

Someone motions for Cooper to sit down, and he finishes getting the footage he wants. He's on his way back to us when a guy in the row behind us taps him on the shoulder. "Stop it right now. I am in love with your bag."

"Thanks," Cooper says. "It's a Sony."

"Sony's making satchels? I had no idea. You're so cutting-edge."

"I try to stay current," Cooper says. He smiles. "They're at Norman Camera on the corner of Gibson and Sixth if you want to get one."

"I'm texting that to myself immediately," the admirer says, pulling out an iPhone with a red zebra-print case. "Thanks."

Cooper makes it back to his seat. "Did you hear that?" he asks. "I'm cutting-edge. You should feel lucky to be seen with me."

"I do," I say. Cooper asks me to pass the almonds.

The lights dim, and an announcer comes out to introduce Charli. Her résumé is impressive. She's presented in thirty-five countries, her vlog was named the fastest-growing vlog of last year, she was on *Good Morning America* (really?), and she has a book coming out next year about finding the best color palettes for your skin tone (I didn't know that, either).

When Charli comes to the stage, the crowd roars. Sure, they're here for the whole conference, but in this moment, it seems like they really all came just to see her.

She waits for them to quiet down and then begins. "Thanks for coming out today. Y'all look *fabulous*."

My dad types his first lecture note: "I look fabulous."

As I watch Charli up on that stage, preaching to a congregation of her fashion followers, even though I want to be repulsed (after all, this is fashion we're talking about), I am impressed. Charli tells the story of her vlog, from when her only follower was her Aunt Kacey, all the way to where she is now. There was a lot of work involved. There was a business plan. Marketing. Drive. Perseverance. Where I had seen mindlessness, there were years of careful calculation. My throat feels thick, and I swallow the shame. Maybe this is how my dad sees Charli. She's driven, motivated, and successful. Perhaps I should have given her a chance. Would that have changed the way things are between my dad and me now? A couple of weeks ago, I would have called my dad my best friend. It's amazing how quickly things can unravel. It makes me wonder about the relationship we had in the first place. Was it that fragile? Are all relationships that fragile? That's kind of scary when you think about it—like how a space shuttle that goes only a couple of degrees off course will be doomed. It didn't seem like the NASA video or the conflict over Charli would be too damaging, but here we are.

By the end of the lecture, my dad has three pages of notes. I have two. Good thing I'm not typing my notes, because writing takes only one hand. It leaves my other one to hold Cooper's. My dad gives our hands a death glare toward the end of the presentation, and I drop Cooper's. Not because I'm embarrassed, obviously. It's more because, um . . . I don't know. It feels like what I should do to keep the peace. Cooper looks hurt. I didn't mean to hurt him. I go to reach for his hand again, but then I tuck some hair behind my ear at the last second instead because the whole thing is just too weird. Count on me to make things weird between me and Cooper *and* me and my dad. I'm a disaster.

Charli leaves the stage to a standing ovation. My dad is clapping louder than anyone else. I hope he'll be clapping that loud for me one day.

Surely he'll be proud of me when I get back from the International Space Station, right? And I can open my lecture with, "Funny story—my dad didn't even want me to go on this mission. I had to secretly apply for the internship behind his back. But now we laugh about it."

Why do I feel like no amount of passing time will make the lie I've told my dad funny?

When we get back from the conference, Cooper has to accompany his mom on some Craigslist deal. ("Do you want me to get murdered over a Baby Jogger, Cooper Dash? Do you?") Charli is staying at the conference for some fan event. My dad and I order a pizza and put on a documentary about nebulae.

My dad chews a bite of mushroom. I don't know which one of us should talk first. I wish I could talk to him about how I felt at Vlogalicious, how maybe we've gotten off course from the positive relationship we had. I want to apologize for everything and fix it somehow. Or maybe he wants to say he's sorry for saying he doesn't trust me and doesn't know who I am anymore. I want to have those deep conversations. I even feel almost ready for it. He takes a deep breath like he's ready to speak, and I hold mine. What's he going to say?

"If you could invite any scientist to have dinner with us tonight, who would you pick?"

Oh. Okay. I guess we're going with "act normal." But surely he doesn't think old routines can fix fresh wounds, especially ones as deep as "I don't know you anymore"?

We've had the scientist-for-dinner conversation a million times. The rules are that you can't pick a scientist who's been picked before. A few years ago we added the rule that you could pick scientists at different points in their lives. Example: Einstein after discovering the theory of general relativity versus Einstein back when he was working at the patent office evaluating weird inventions like gravel sorters. After all, they were practically two different people. People change.

Is this what's happening to us? A gradual growing apart that happens because people change? That can't be it.

"Hmmm." I take a bite of ham and pineapple. I could call him out on avoiding the real issues, but it's not worth it. Pretending everything is fine sounds easier. "I pick Hertzsprung."

"Of Hertzsprung-Russell? Why not Russell?"

"Because Ejnar Hertzsprung discovered the relationship between star luminosity and temperature in 1911. It took Henry

Norris Russell until 1913. His name shouldn't even be on the H-R diagram, really. He's sort of a tagalong."

"Fine. Then I'm inviting Russell. So they can still be together."

"What if they don't like each other?"

"They do." He says this with the authority of someone who knows them well, even though they've been dead for years. "Hey, look!" He motions to the TV with his pizza. "The star is about to blow up." It feels good—like a version of old times, before Charli, before Cooper, and before NASA. A weird version, like a pixelated one that doesn't look quite like the real thing, but at least it's recognizable.

Maybe it's time to come clean. Then I'll work with as many known variables as possible when deciding whether or not to submit my application. I take a deep breath and put down my pizza slice. I open my mouth to speak, but my dad's cell phone rings.

He looks at the screen. "Hospital," he says. "Gotta take this." He goes to the kitchen to take the call, and I finish my slice of pizza alone.

By the time he comes back, I've decided that there's no reason to start a fight. Why ruin a good day? After all, if I apply and don't get the internship, then there's no issue. We only have an issue if I apply and get chosen, and that's something I can deal with at that time. The thought of a few borrowed weeks before addressing this cheers me up, but the cheer doesn't go all the way through me.

When I go to bed, Five's food looks exactly like I left it this morning. "Five?"

As soon as she doesn't pop her head out of her hut, my stomach drops. Whenever I'm home, Five jumps out of her hut and climbs the side of the cage, eager to come out and play. She's been a little slower about it for the past couple of days.

"Five?" I say it a little louder, the single syllable getting caught in my chest somewhere.

I open the cage with shaking hands. "Are you in there, girl?" Maybe she got out. Perhaps she's munching the crackers I left on my nightstand.

My hand is shaking as I pick up the hut. There she is, curled in a ball. It would be so easy to believe she's sleeping. She's not struggling to breathe anymore—she isn't breathing at all. There will be no more sneezes. Her nose is tucked in her small paws, and her eyes are closed. Her ears are flat against her head, no longer listening for me to walk into the room.

15

Cooper offers to take the day off from working on the video because of Five, but we don't have the time. It's due in a week. Plus, who's ever heard of taking the day off for a rat? Ludicrous. She was just a rat. He says that at least we have to call it an "editing day" and spend the time at his house rather than shooting on scene somewhere. At this point, we should have almost all of the footage we need. That's fine; I don't have much energy today anyway. My stomach hurts, and multiple times, I've felt like crying. It must be PMS. The female reproductive system is truly an inconvenience.

"Hey." Cooper pulls me into a hug as soon as I walk through his door. "We made something for you. It's outside." He heads to the back door without bothering to shut the front one. I shut it and trudge behind him.

He gets to the back of his yard near some bushes, and it takes me a second to see what he's looking at. There's a small mound of disturbed earth under the bush, and there's one of those number-shaped birthday candles. It's a five.

"Wait," I say, disbelieving. "Is that . . . ?"

"Charli let me in to get her after you left for school."

All of my other rats have been thrown away, disposed of unceremoniously like the lab rats they were. And sure, that was hard to do sometimes, but anything else would have felt ridiculous. It's on the tip of my tongue to tell Cooper that this is over the top and that I'm going home. She was only a rat.

Yet somehow, standing here under the harsh Nevada sun and seeing that small pile of dirt, it doesn't feel ridiculous. Maybe it's because Cooper did it instead of me.

Maybe it's because she was never just a specimen.

"I have the eulogy!" Bridget calls from the house. She comes out carrying a piece of paper in one hand and Snickers in the other. Chewy plods along behind them.

"Sorry about the dogs," Cooper whispers. "Bridget insisted that Five would want representation from the animal kingdom. This whole thing was her idea. A good one, too."

Oh my. The burial plot was one thing, but this appears to be a full-out funeral. This is simultaneously the kindest and strangest thing anyone has ever done for me. Then again, these are the progeny of parents who flip strollers. I shouldn't be too surprised.

A light breeze rustles through the leaves on the bush. Bridget is wearing black leggings and a black shirt. A black bow holds her ponytail in place. "I hereby call this funeral to order," she says soberly.

That's not how funerals start, but they also don't usually include dogs or birthday candles.

"Why are you doing this?" I ask. "You never even met Five."

"It's what friends do," Bridget says, like now I'm the stupid one. Somewhere along the line, Cooper and Bridget have become my friends. I'm not sure where it happened—I don't recall signing up for this—but it did. Cooper reaches for my hand. I have fallen squarely in the middle of everything I hate about high school, yet I hate nothing about it.

Bridget unfolds a piece of paper and clears her throat before she begins reading. "We are gathered here today, in the presence of God and these witnesses"—Bridget motions to Chewy and Snickers—"to remember the life of a wonderful rat. Five brought joy to many people. She brought disgust only to people like Chelsea, who's awful anyway."

I giggle through my suddenly blurred vision.

"Five was a pioneer in astronomy and is probably one of the only rodents to have ever gone formally stargazing. She was smart, she was adorable, and she was a true friend. She is an example to all of us of loyalty and commitment. Her relationship with Skyler Davidson was an inspiration to everyone who knew them. She was the . . ." Bridget trails off and holds the paper out to Cooper. "What does this say?"

Cooper's face turns bright red. "Goose to Sky's Maverick."

"The Goose to Sky's Maverick. Let us all observe a moment of silence to remember this wonderful creature."

We stand in a small semicircle with me in the middle. Chewy lies down and puts his jowly head between his paws. Even Snickers seems to have picked up on the somber tone and puts his tongue all the way in his closed mouth.

As we stand in silence, I remember the many fun times Five and I had together. She liked to be out when I did homework. I trained her to turn pages—she would pick up the corner of one page and run across the length of the book until the page was turned. The problem was that she could never do it on command, so she would randomly decide when I was finished reading that page and would turn it. It became a sort of race: Could I read the whole page before Five decided that I was finished with it?

One time I left a bag of sunflower seeds too close to her cage. She pulled it close and chewed through the corner. By the time I got back to my room, her entire cage was littered with sunflower seed shells. When I saw her, she froze. She was holding a seed between her paws, and she looked up at me like I caught her robbing a bank. Then she shoved the seed in her mouth, ran into her hut, and looked out at me as if to say, "Seed? What seed? I see no seeds!" She even pushed up bedding to blockade the door as if I wouldn't have any idea where to find her.

It's like a highlight reel runs through my head, but then I look again at the small mound. Before I can stop myself, tears have escaped my eyes and are sliding down my cheeks. I hug my middle and grit my teeth. I have tried so hard to stay detached, to remember that she wasn't a pet. But it turns out that she was a pet all along, and I missed it.

I never said I loved her. Never told her she was a good girl. We never played for the sake of playing. *She never even had a real name.* She deserved all those things, and now it's too late.

My ribs are tight, and the tears fall faster. I want to talk to Five, to apologize, but I'll never see her again.

Cooper is the one to finally break the silence. "What element was she?" He has always found my elemental classifications highly amusing, but his eyes don't show any hint of teasing now.

"She didn't have an element." I wipe away my tears. "She was a rat."

"Come on, think about it. She had an element."

Bridget pats Snickers and whispers, "What?"

"I'll explain later," Cooper says. "We're all elements. You're rubidium."

"Ah." Bridget nods so enthusiastically that her ponytail bounces. It's what she does when I'm tutoring her and explain something poorly. She looks at me encouragingly. "What element was Five?"

The breeze blows my hair, and I tuck it behind my ear while I think. "Yttrium," I decide. "Because it's used in LEDs. It helps light things up. Some people think it has magical properties—the people who believe in crystal healings and energies and stuff, you know? And then other people like me say that they're silly for believing in that. Just like no one understood why I thought a rat made a good friend. But she did. Even if that's stupid." More tears fall. "Sorry."

"Why are you sorry?" Bridget puts Snickers down and puts her arm around me. "This is a loss. It's okay to be sad."

"Being sad doesn't help anything. It doesn't change anything." Human emotion serves no scientific purpose. If I could turn myself into a robot who never had to cry again, I would do it.

"It doesn't matter if it changes anything. How you feel matters," she says. "The only way out of it is through it."

She sounds like some self-help guru, but it doesn't matter. I let her put her arm around me.

"Hold on. We forgot something." Cooper jogs into the house and comes out with a bouquet of lilies. He lays them on top of the tiny mound, which could be covered by one flower. "May she rest in peace."

Perhaps I lost one friend, but I have been left with some pretty great ones.

Bridget puts her hand straight out in front of her. Is she going to recite a blessing over the grave or something? She looks at Cooper and me expectantly, but we're confused. "Hands!" she finally says. "All in!"

We stand in a triangle around the lilies and put our hands in the middle. "To Five on three," Bridget says. "I mean, when I count to three we say, 'To Five.' It's confusing with all the numbers."

Turns out you can cry and laugh at the same time.

Bridget counts to three, and then we say, "To Five," and raise our hands out of the circle like we're breaking a time-out. It's all she knows, and there's no manual on how to end a rat funeral.

After the ceremony, Cooper goes to the basement to edit some video while I help Bridget with tutoring. Stoichiometry today—she struggles hard. I look out the window while she's trying a problem for the third time, and the flowers stand out in the yard. Even though Five's gone, it felt good to honor her. Maybe Bridget is a lot smarter than I thought.

Is her way better? Are any of our ways better?

We've been working for about twenty minutes when Cooper runs up the stairs. "I've got to run to the shop. My dad's got some expensive Nikons to fix by tomorrow, and he can't figure them out."

Bridget rolls her eyes. "Does he even *try* anymore? You're always there." She thinks for a moment. "Hey, take Sky! Chemistry can wait for a little while." Bridget tries to look sacrificial and kind, but she also drops her pencil on her desk as if it's made of hot iron.

"We still have eleven problems in the problem set," I say. "Do you want to understand stoichiometry or not?"

"Honestly, no." Bridget looks relieved that I asked. "Phew, glad to get that off my chest." She picks up her phone. "I need to update the dogs' Insta anyway."

"Your dogs have Instagram accounts?"

"They share one, but I update for them. They have over a thousand followers." She clicks a few things. "Here, look at yesterday's post." She holds the phone out. It's a picture of Snickers balancing on Chewy's back in Bridget's room. The filter makes the colors more intense than they really are—so much purple and gold—and Chewy's droopy eyes look annoyed. Snickers looks alarmed.

"I captioned it 'Giddy-up!'" Bridget shakes her head at her own cleverness. "Today, I'll post something somber. Maybe an RIP near Five's grave. That cool with you?" She looks at me expectantly, waiting for me to give consent for my dead rat to be mentioned on social media.

"Sure?"

"Great." She almost runs out of the room, probably concerned that I was about to explain that stoichiometry is more important than her dogs' social media presence (which it is).

With Bridget gone, Cooper and I are alone in her room. The temperature rises about five degrees, which it seems to do when I'm alone with Cooper.

"Do you want to go to the shop?" Cooper asks. "It shouldn't take me long."

There are more productive things I could do than watch Cooper fix a shutter, but doing unproductive things with Cooper sounds more satisfying than being productive anywhere else. Plus, being home would be weird. Five's cage is still there and empty. When I told my dad that Five died, he tried to give me his condolences, but it was a little awkward: "Sorry, SkyBear. She was a good specimen. I'll find you another one."

I don't think he understood that I don't want another one. Five was irreplaceable somehow. She was a friend more than a rat. I see that now, but I don't think he does. I should probably explain it eventually, but going with Cooper sounds easier than yet another tough conversation with my dad.

Cooper's dad is joking with a customer when we walk in, but he makes eye contact with Cooper and gives him a quick wink. His laugh fills the store, and the slight wrinkles on his face prove that smiling is a well-worn position for his skin. He points to something on his computer and then to the wall across from him, showing the customer an example of the custom framing option.

Norman Camera is a small, square-shaped store. There's a glass counter that hugs two sides in an L-shape with an impressive number of cameras and lenses packed into the space beneath it, like someone played Tetris with all of the pieces until they fit into the display. Some lenses are small, and some are comically large—longer than my arm. Does anyone carry around lenses that big? They look more like telescopes.

One wall of the store includes shelves of accessories. There are decorative frames, lens cleaners, and those chintzy signs that say things like NANA'S KITCHEN or WE DON'T SWIM IN YOUR TOILET, PLEASE DON'T PEE IN OUR POOL.

"We can have that to you next week," Cooper's dad says, typing something into his computer. "Print on metal for all three of the photos, twelve-by-twenty panoramic?" He turns the screen so the customer can preview the images. While the customer is looking at the screen, Cooper's dad mouths, "In the back," to us and points to the door at the back wall.

We head through the back door into a small room that has a cement floor and off-white walls. There are a couple of tables holding cameras, video cameras, lenses, and other equipment in various states of disrepair. There are three chairs, a few partially full Gatorade bottles, and a discarded pair of reading glasses.

"This is the one he was talking about," Cooper says, picking up a lens. He inspects it before sitting down to work. He tries to explain what he's doing, but it's technical. I settle for sitting across from him and flipping through a book of photography proofs.

Cooper's dad comes in about five minutes later. "Welcome to my workshop!" He pats Cooper on the shoulder, which seems a bit perilous considering that Cooper is using tiny instruments to take apart the guts of a camera. As if this has happened before, Cooper quickly holds the tools up so they won't get bumped to the wrong spot.

"Hi, Mr. Evans," I say.

He looks over his shoulder, alarmed. "Oh wait, me? You're talking to *me*? Oh no, I'm not Mr. Evans. I'm Norman. Can I interest you in a Gatorade, Skyler?"

For a second I think he's going to offer me one of the half-empty ones, but he opens a mini-fridge under a back table. It's filled with Gatorades in a rainbow of flavors.

"No thanks."

"Comin' atcha, Coop." Norman throws a lemon-lime at him, and Cooper barely looks up from his camera. He catches it and twists off the top in one swift motion, tossing the orange cap on the table. There are seven orange caps on the table.

Cooper's relationship with his dad seems seamless, like they've been through all these motions a million times. Did my dad and I ever operate like that? We certainly don't now. I'm a little jealous of Cooper.

Norman puts the reading glasses on and opens a grape Gatorade. Cap number eight joins the club. "Now, Skyler, do you know how to fix a tripod?"

"Uh, no."

"Then this oughta be fun." He picks up a two-legged tripod from the corner and tosses it to me. Then he goes to the opposite corner and picks up the third leg. "Geronimo!" He throws it javelin-style, and Cooper looks up from his camera.

"Dad, come on. There are thousands of dollars of equipment in here. How are you going to explain to a customer that you broke their lens with a tripod leg?"

"Good thing your friend can catch." Norman gives me a thumbs-up. "Tools are there." He motions to a side table littered with screwdrivers of all sizes, wrenches, and a bunch of tools I don't recognize. Then he sits down and picks up a camera. "Coop, did you get that flash mount fixed yesterday?"

"Yeah," he says absentmindedly, still working on the shutter. "It's on shelf five."

Norman starts fiddling with a camcorder. There's a brief pause, and then he turns to me. "Are you going to get a tool, or are you planning to fix that tripod with magic?"

"Wait, you actually want me to fix this?" I hold up the two-legged piece in one hand and the stray leg in the other. Norman's personality is bold and bright—he strikes me as the element neon.

"Dad, you can't ask her to fix stuff. We stopped by to fix this one shutter. I'll be done in a minute."

"It's a *tripod*. Not rocket science."

Rocket science would have been easier.

An hour later, Norman is out front with a customer. I'm attempting to fix a second tripod. "How does he have so much stuff to fix?"

"He's terrible at fixing things, that's how." Cooper sighs. "Sorry. I'm almost done." He holds up a film camera and clicks a few things before frowning and putting it down again. "He said there was only a shutter this time, but it's never one thing. I should know better by now." His jaw clenches.

Norman owns a camera store. How can he be terrible at fixing cameras?

He barrels back into the workshop. "Do you have that Cannon from last week?"

"Shelf three," Cooper says without looking up.

"Man, forgot that guy was coming in today." Norman walks over to some shelves and picks a camera up off the third one. "This guy," he says, patting Cooper's shoulder again while he looks at me. Cooper reflexively holds his tools up from the camera. "He's a better fix-it than I am. Don't know where the store would be without this kid." He opens the door and announces to the customer, "Good as the day you bought it!"

"You fix everything?" I ask.

"No," Cooper says. "My dad fixes some of it. Sort of. He's good at tripods."

It only took me thirty minutes to learn how to fix a tripod.

We work in silence for a few minutes before Norman comes back again.

"They don't make cameras like they used to," Norman says. "You give me any fifteen-year-old camera, and I'm a whiz. Today's stuff? I've been a little busy building my photography empire to keep up." He shrugs. His tiny store is hardly an empire, but his pride in it is endearing. "That's why this kid"—he points to Cooper—"is my secret weapon."

"And Tim will be just as good," Cooper reminds him.

"Right." Norman studies Cooper for a second before turning back to the umbrella. "Good old Tim."

"Tim's thinking of taking over for me when I go to film school," Cooper explains. "He's one of Dad's friends from college, and he's great at current technology."

The vibe in the room is suddenly uncomfortable between them, like maybe Cooper and his dad have disagreed on Tim before. My throat tightens as it dawns on me: Cooper is necessary to running this shop. He wants to go to film school, but his dad will sink without him.

Surely they'll find a way to work it out? Cooper can't give up on his dreams of film school to work in a dinky camera shop, right? Even as I tell myself this, I wonder if it's true. I'm positive Cooper wouldn't leave his family in a lurch, and his dad doesn't seem motivated to replace him.

Cooper's stuck here.

The jealous feeling I had earlier is gone. I want to hug Cooper and yell at his dad to hire that Tim guy already, but I do neither of those things. I go back to fiddling with a tripod and think of my own dad. Until I told him about the NASA Teen in Space internship, he'd always been supportive of my dreams. Maybe I've taken that for granted.

Maybe I've taken him for granted.

16

It's a few days later when the apple-pin secretary interrupts Mr. Sinclair's physics class. "Mr. Sinclair? Can I borrow Skyler Davidson?"

What did I do?

I stand up and head toward the hall, but she says, "Get your stuff. I don't think you'll be back by the end of class."

Okay seriously—what could I have done? I rack my brain, but there's nothing. Is something wrong? Is my dad okay?

As soon as the door closes behind us, the secretary says, "Cooper Evans is waiting in the office for you. Did you forget about community service today?"

Say what now?

I almost ask for clarification, but I'm smart enough to wait. If Cooper's cooked something up, I'm not going to wreck it.

When we get to the office, Cooper's looking at his watch. He smiles wide when he sees me, which shoots a jolt of something down my spine. A pleasant something.

"Thanks," Cooper says to the secretary. "Sky, we're going to be late." He's trying not to laugh.

Mrs. Ling says, "Skyler, in the future please tell your dad that while an email note is okay this time, it really is preferable that he come sign you out in person if you're leaving campus. It's for security reasons, you understand."

"Absolutely," I say, nodding.

When we're out of earshot, I grab Cooper's arm. "Are you crazy? I'm not skipping class." I hold on to his arm about 2.7 seconds longer than I need to. What is he thinking?

"We're not skipping class." Cooper looks at me like I suggested something ludicrous. "We're doing community service." We get out to the parking lot, and he clicks the button for his car to unlock.

"What kind of community service?"

"A mystery kind." He smiles. Those dimples kill me. "Get in."

"How did you hack my dad's email?" I put on my seat belt, a little stressed that I'm missing the end of a lecture on the theory of relativity.

Not that I don't already understand the theory of relativity, but still.

"I didn't." He gives me a long look. "You don't have faith in me at all, do you? You think I forged a note from your dad and, what, got you out of class so we can make out or something?"

"It wouldn't be the first time teenagers did that."

"I'm ashamed of you, Skyler Davidson," he teases. "You don't give me enough credit. But now that you mention it . . ." He turns off the ignition and leans over to kiss me.

My breath catches in my chest. This is better than the theory of relativity.

He pulls away. "But seriously . . ." He puts the key back in the ignition. "We're going to be late."

Five minutes later, we pull into the parking lot of the elementary school that we both attended. Cooper starts unpacking film equipment from his trunk. "I emailed your dad last night and asked him to sign you out, but he couldn't. Anyway, he emailed for you." Cooper hands me a tripod and then closes the trunk. "You're the guest speaker in Miss Timmer's kindergarten class today."

"Excuse me?" Small children are horrifying.

"Miss Timmer is my aunt, and she agreed to let me film you reading a book to her class. I didn't tell you earlier for a few reasons: One, I only thought of this last night. Two, it would've been easy for you to tell me no over text, which I didn't want. Three, your face right now is priceless." He gives me a quick kiss. "We need a final piece to help you look more approachable to the American public. This could be it. Let's go." His smile falls, and he starts walking before I can respond.

"But there are . . . boogers. And grimy hands." Is this why my dad agreed to this? Am I being punished by having to hang out with small children?

"What, you're a germophobe now?" Cooper doesn't look behind him.

"No, I'm a *kid*ophobe. Kids don't like me."

He stops and turns to me. "Kids are great. Viewers love footage of people with kids. Why do you think politicians put those shots in their commercials? It hits the audience right in the feels. Listen—if you don't want to do this, I can do it alone. It's a read-aloud of a book about space and then a question-and-answer time. I can answer five-year-olds' questions."

"You might get the answers wrong."

"That's a risk you'll have to take." He mimics the Q&A, using a high-pitched voice for the kindergartners. "*Mr. Cooper, how many stars are there?* Somewhere between a million and a gazillion. *Mr. Cooper, are aliens real?* Maybe. I hear they like snatching small children from their beds. *Mr. Cooper, are you a real astronaut?* Yes, yes I am. *Mr. Cooper—*"

"Fine." I laugh. "I'll do it. You'll mess them up."

Cooper wipes fake sweat from his brow. "What a relief."

The classroom is full of loud colors. It has an under-the-sea theme, complete with a friendly orange octopus on the wall with a speech bubble that says READING IS FUN! Some cartoon sea turtles are wearing party hats and standing on their back flippers so they can hold balloons next to the birthday board. That is biologically impossible.

There are multicolored fake jellyfish hanging from the ceiling, which is ridiculous. Why would any teacher want her students to have positive emotions associated with jellyfish? What if they decide to swim through a school of jellyfish one day?

Oh wait, a *school* of jellyfish? Is this supposed to be a misguided pun?

I'm contemplating this when a teacher as loud as her class-room comes to shake my hand.

"Hi! You must be Skyler."

Miss Timmer is tall, thin, and blonde. She reminds me of Teacher Barbie. Her voice even sounds like Barbie's.

"Okay, kids!" She turns to her group of twenty-five tiny humans. "Miss Skyler is here to read our story for story time today! Guess what she's going to do when she grows all the way up?"

About a dozen of them raise their hands.

"Be a princess?"

"Be a cowgirl?"

"Be a bird?"

"Help people with their 401k?" (I can guess what that kid's parents do.)

"No," Miss Timmer says. "She's going to study space!"

There's a chorus of wowed *Oooooo*s.

"And Mr. Cooper"—she motions to him—"is my nephew. He's going to make movies when he grows up."

Another round of *Oooo*s.

"You have one more minute to finish up your space pictures!" The kids start furiously coloring. Miss Timmer turns to me and drops her loud, excited teacher voice. Now she sounds like a normal human. "Hey, thanks for coming in."

"Thanks for having me?" It seems appropriate to thank her even though I didn't know I was going to do this until about two minutes ago.

Her quick transition between her kid voice and adult voice makes me think she's a gallium. Gallium is solid metal at room temperature, will melt in a human hand, and then goes back to solid as soon as it's back at room temperature. It's a crazy process to watch.

"Coop, I'm thinking I'll put them on the carpet over there. Sky can be in the rocking chair, so you'll get her face and the back of the kids' heads. Sound good?"

"Prime." Cooper starts setting up his equipment, and my hands wring involuntarily. "What am I reading?"

Miss Timmer grabs two books from her desk. "The library had a few on space, and these ones connect best to what we're studying. Pick your favorite."

The first book is called *My Friend on the Moon*. There's a picture of a small girl and a purple alien on the cover. The second one is called *Pauline's Planets*. The cover is a girl standing on a spaceship—why is she *on* a spaceship?—and zooming past a shoddy facsimile of Saturn. Oh boy.

What is the class studying? All the ways that science fiction can go horribly wrong?

"I guess I'll do this one." I hold up *Pauline's Planets*. At least this one doesn't have aliens.

A few minutes later, the kids are settled on a colorful carpet in front of the rocking chair. Each of them is sitting on a "personal space carpet square." Hopefully, that means they won't touch me.

"This book is called *Pauline's Planets*," I say tentatively. "It's by George . . ." His last name is spelled Pswaychvftski. "It's by George."

A brown-haired boy in overalls pipes up. "My grandpa's name is George!"

"Great." I clear my throat and turn to the first page. "'Pauline was bored on earth. One day, a fairy showed up and said, "I will help you, Pauline. You can have one wish." Pauline wished to see all the planets.'"

The book doesn't have aliens, but there's a fairy on page one. What are schools teaching kids these days? The fairy takes Pauline to see all the planets, and they also go to Pluto. This is too far. I put the book down.

"Okay, kids. Just so you know, Pluto isn't a planet. It has been reclassified as a dwarf planet."

A girl wearing glasses too big for her face and missing one of her bottom teeth talks without raising her hand. "If it's not a planet, why is it in the book?"

"There's also a fairy in this book. Not everything in books is real."

"Fairies aren't real?" Her eyes get huge, and she looks like she's about to cry.

Cooper waves from behind the kids and mouths, "Cut!" He draws his hand across his neck in case I didn't understand.

I swallow. "I suppose scientists may not have thoroughly researched all possibilities of past or future fairy existence."

Miss Timmer jumps in. "Maybe it's time to ask Ms. Skyler some questions. Does anyone have a question?"

"If fairies aren't real, are elves?"

"Is Santa real?"

"Are armadillos real?"

Miss Timmer stops them again. "We're only going to ask questions about space, okay? And raise your hand, please."

Almost everyone raises their hand. I call on an intelligent-looking kid. He is sitting with his hand raised calmly, not reaching in the air and waving like his life depends on me calling on him.

He takes a deep breath, like this is a tough question but he can handle the truth. "Are all planets fake? Is Earth real?"

Miss Timmer does a literal face palm. "Kids. Nothing else about what is real or fake." Half of the hands go down.

I call on another kid—an Asian girl with one hand in the air and the other sucking her thumb.

She pops her thumb out of her mouth to ask the question. "Will you be my friend?"

I try to keep my composure, but it's tough. Cooper is silently cracking up, and Miss Timmer is biting her cheeks to keep from laughing.

"Yes, I will be your friend."

"Yay!" She jumps off her carpet square and runs to give me a hug. Her slimy thumb brushes my arm. So much for personal space.

A bunch of kids start asking if they can be my friend, too. The raising of hands has been abandoned.

In an attempt to quiet them down, I say, "Everyone can be my friend if you be quiet."

"Yaaaaay!" the overalls boy whispers. He jumps up to hug me.

Now all of the kids are whisper-yelling "Yay" and running up to me. It's the creepiest thing you ever saw in your life.

Now none of us can keep from laughing. There's a dogpile of kids burying me in the rocking chair. Cooper dives behind the camera to make sure he gets this footage. Miss Timmer looks like she might stop it, but instead she grabs her iPhone to take a picture.

They're kind of cute, now that I think about it. Terrifying, but in an adorable way.

The chaos of hugs continues for about thirty seconds until the overalls kid yells, "HEY! I LOST A TOOTH!"

"He's *bleeding*!" a kid next to him exclaims.

The prospect of blood is frightening to Overalls, who bursts into tears and runs to the classroom sink mirror in order to inspect the damage. The mob follows him, horrified and intrigued by their fallen comrade.

Miss Timmer jumps to action, somehow getting the kids back in order. The teacher voice is back in full force. She's a total gallium.

I help Cooper pack up in the back of the room, and we sneak out with a wave to Miss Timmer. She nods back and smiles while enthusiastically telling the students how much fun addition is.

The sun is bright when we get outside, and our walk in the parking lot is quiet. My time in kindergarten has given me a new appreciation for silence.

"That was the perfect footage," Cooper says as he loads up the equipment. "You nailed it." His smile doesn't reach his eyes.

"My visit ended up with the book unfinished and a kid bleeding."

"It happens." Cooper shrugs. "The video is bomb." He closes his trunk so slowly that I'm not positive I hear it latch. It stays down, so it must have. "Well . . . I guess that's it."

"What do you mean?"

"We have all the footage we need." He rubs the back of his neck. "It's been fun, huh?"

Is he saying that we're not going to spend more time together? My chest tightens. The sun shifts to aggressive instead of pleasant.

"It doesn't have to change. We can still hang out, right?" The sun is behind him, and I put my hand up to shield my eyes.

"Of course." He nods and puts his hands in his pockets. "We started our deal because of the video, and I didn't know if things might be different now that it's over. Now that it's filmed, you don't need me as much." Cooper, usually so sure of himself, looks small.

"Sure I do." I kiss him, but it's nervous. "Kissing wouldn't be nearly as fun alone."

He laughs, but it's the kind you do without opening your mouth. Then he meets my eyes. "I'm scared that things are about to change."

How long has he been thinking about this? The pain in his eyes makes it clear this isn't the first time it's occurred to him.

"They won't," I assure him. "We won't let them change."

Even as I say it, something feels unsettling. Am I promising something impossible? If he's going to stay here working at Norman Camera for the rest of his life, and I'm going to go to space . . . that doesn't feel compatible. I know he has big dreams, but ever since seeing him at his dad's shop, I see Cooper's dreams for what they really are: fantasies.

My dreams are goals. I'm making them happen. That doesn't make me any better or worse than Cooper, but we're definitely on different tracks. All of this thinking gives me a headache, and it's a quiet ride back to the high school.

17

Later that week, Cooper and I go out for frozen yogurt after school. Not because we're filming anything, just because of fro-yo. Cooper doesn't even bring his film equipment.

Okay, that's a lie. But he brings only the most necessary film equipment. It's the stuff he has on him at all times in case of alien invasions or zoo breakouts. You never know what might need to be documented.

Our topics of discussion include, in no particular order:

1. The best fro-yo topping. (Me: raspberries. Him: peanut butter cups topped with marshmallow sauce.)

2. Whether or not "peanut butter cups with marshmallow sauce" is two toppings or a single

compound topping. (You can guess who voted what.)

3. Favorite filming location over the past few weeks. (Me: stargazing. Him: chem lab.)
4. The easiest and hardest camera items to fix. (Me: knows nothing. Him: knows all the things.)
5. Famous astrophysics discoveries. (Me: knows all the things. Him: knows nothing.)

For the first time, things feel awkward. There are loud silences. There are those nods people do when they act like they're into what you're saying but have no idea what's going on. What's happening to us?

This never happened when we were filming. It's not like we talked about the video all the time, either. I mentally roll through many of our conversations and wonder why we can't flow like that now. Perhaps we're psyching ourselves out. That's exactly what it is. It's like the placebo effect, but with awkwardness. We're expecting awkwardness, so we're getting it.

Just because we're finished filming is no reason things have to be weird. After all, I told him they wouldn't be. What I need to do is share something deep and personal that I wouldn't tell anyone else. That might slice through it.

"I got my period last week."

He stops with his spoon halfway to his mouth. He looks around as if wondering if anyone else heard me say that. "Thank you for sharing? Was that unexpected?"

"No. But you never know these days. Cycles can be so irregular."

Never mind. Sharing was a terrible idea.

Where did the easiness come from before? We need to find it again. Now we're both quiet, eating fro-yo. I hate the moment when fro-yo has warmed up in my mouth but I haven't swallowed it. It's a creamy, warm, gross mixture of flavors. That's what this moment feels like: familiar, but wrong.

When we finally scrape the bottoms of our fro-yo cups, Cooper suggests that I come over to take a look at the editing he's done so far.

It's like a weight lifts off me. "Yes. Definitely."

He smiles. It's a real smile—the kind with his dimples—and for a moment we're back. He's tacitly acknowledging that the awkwardness is there, so we're going back to the project. We'll figure the rest out later.

We drive separately, and the whole way over I make a mental list of topics to bring up. It's a short list. None are great. It was so much easier when I wasn't trying.

Cooper's basement looks like a sketchy day-care robber lives there. There are strollers three deep lining the back wall, and tables along the side wall holding various stroller parts: wheels, handles, fabric trim in various shades, and even lights. A bulletin board has four to six pictures of each stroller, and next to each picture is a notecard listing the buying price, necessary upgrades, and estimated selling price. The absence of sunlight in the basement makes the whole thing dark. There's a cloudy egress window close to the ceiling, but it lets in only enough light to be creepy.

This is the ambience in which Cooper apparently does his best work. He's got a desk set up in the corner with two desktop monitors as well as a space for his laptop. The bookshelf next to his desk holds camera equipment, but most of his is strewn about the floor in various stages of unpacked. One of the desk drawers is marked CREATIVITY. There's a very good chance that drawer contains more grape soda and pretzels. There are two open cans and a rolled-over pretzel bag on his desk.

He loads the clips. "I hope you'll like it. It's almost done, since I did a lot of editing as we went along. I have to add in the school stuff and a few other things, but this will give you an idea at least." He clicks play and sits back.

The video starts with a shot of me looking through the telescope. There's sad, sentimental music in the background. A voice-over—shockingly, my voice—says, *She was the kind of person who made you want to believe in luck.*

What?

The scene cuts to me at my bedroom desk, holding my mom's research. *My mom studied neutron stars before she died, and my whole life is dedicated to finishing her work.* Then the screen is filled with pictures of my mom—one from when she presented at MIT, the one from her obituary, picture after picture, like Google images puked on his computer monitor. My voice comes through again, now accompanied by sad background music: *We baked cookies every Saturday. She would always say, "Hey, Sky, you up for some kitchen chemistry?"*

My mom doesn't belong in this dingy basement. Her smile on the screen is haunting. Cooper and I never discussed including pictures of my mom. It feels violating, like he rummaged around in my past and exploited this woman he never knew. Also, what is the cookie story in there for? He wasn't supposed to be recording when I said that.

I think back to that night in the desert. Did he even care about my stories? Were his questions simply a way to get better footage for his film?

"Is this a joke?" I ask. "It's not funny." I want to run. This basement feels claustrophobic. It's stuffy in here. The video was supposed to be about science. How dare he not only record me without my knowing, but then use it against me? He seems like a stranger for the first time since we met.

Cooper pauses the video. His eyes are wide and startled. "I thought it would be a surprise."

"It is."

"But . . . not good?" He clicks off the screen, like he can tell I can't look at it anymore.

Seeing her like that is so jarring, like a sudden visit from a ghost. There are stacks of photo books in my closet, but I only get them out on certain days. Mother's Day, her birthday . . . On all the other days, it's too hard. I keep one picture on my desk to use as inspiration, but the rest are packed away. Sometimes I pick up the box just to feel the sheer weight of it, and it's heavy in every sense of the word. That's where the pictures belong. How does he not understand? I cross my arms and curl into myself.

"We never discussed pictures of my mom."

His shoulders tense. "I thought they would add an emotional component."

"My mother is not a component." How can he talk about her like she's a prop? My stomach clenches, and I'm afraid I'll throw up. He sees my mom like a paper doll—a two-dimensional figure that can be used to dress up our video.

"It will help people relate to you. I'm trying to make this movie marketable."

He has completely missed the point.

"It's not supposed to be marketable. It's supposed to be scientific."

"NASA wants someone to be the face of space travel. We both know it's a publicity thing. They need someone marketable, who will make people feel happy and sad and all emotional. Marketability is all about feelings."

My fingernails dig into my arms. "*Intergalactic space travel* is on the line. I hired you, remember? This is my film. My film, my rules."

"No offense, but this isn't your film. You can't even work a camera. Without me, there would be no video." He spins slightly in his desk chair and starts clicking around on the screen. He unrolls the pretzel bag.

"Without me, there would be nothing to make a movie about."

"Really?" He stops his chair and snickers, but not because he thought anything was funny. "You think that out of all the people in Nevada, I couldn't have found anyone else to film? It's not all about you."

"I know. It's about my mom."

He catches himself before fully rolling his eyes. "That's even worse. You can't revolve everything around someone who's . . . not here."

"She's dead. You were going to throw in my face that my mom is dead? Therefore, nothing I do for her matters?"

"You can't do something for someone who's gone. It's like you're still putting seeds in Five's cage every day, and Five will never come back to eat them."

Now he's brought up my mom's death and my dead rat in the same conversation. My fists ball, and I can barely spit words out. "I don't like this version of you."

"The version of me that has brilliant videography skills, even if you don't recognize them?"

"A lot of good they're going to do you," I seethe. The words are tumbling out before I can stop them. "Face it: you're always going to be stuck in your dad's shop. How can you not see that all over your dad's face? He's never going to hire Tim. You're it for him, and you're stuck. Brilliant skills or not, they're not ever taking you away from here." I regret the words as soon as I've said them, but I don't regret enough to apologize. They're true.

His face clouds enough that I know I've hit a nerve.

"At least I'm honest with my dad about what I want instead of sneaking around behind his back!"

My heart is pounding in a completely different way than it usually does around Cooper. "I'm going after my dreams, Coop. It's something you don't understand. Your dreams live in nebulous clouds. I'm making mine happen."

Cooper's face is red. He starts to say something, then stops himself. "What did you want? One shot of you explaining neutron stars at your desk with occasional cut ins of slides and other footage? No other narrative?"

"That was the plan."

The fact that he articulated the plan betrays the fact that he knew what it was. He went rogue without consulting me at all, like I'm one of his prom actresses who stars in the show but has no creative control. This is not how it was supposed to be. We were a team.

"That was never our plan," he says. "You said that's what *you* wanted, but you won't be chosen for an internship with it."

"You know nothing about NASA."

"You know nothing about filmmaking."

Our arms are crossed like barriers in front of our bodies. I didn't think I would ever wish for the tension we had over frozen yogurt, but I do. Hot coals have settled in my stomach, smoldering with anger, sadness, and missing the old Cooper.

"I'm not submitting that video," I say. "Make the one we planned."

"Whoa." Cooper motions to his desk full of equipment. "You don't order me around on my own equipment." As if he can't look at me anymore, he turns to his desk. He throws the pretzels into a drawer and slams it.

The thin light from the egress window dims.

"We had a deal," I say. "Stop messing it up."

He stands so that his eyes are level with mine. "I've been working my butt off, and I'm making you a video. It's better than the one you wanted."

I swallow hard. "It sucks."

His voice hushes, but it stays hard and sarcastic. "I don't like this version of you."

"Cooper!" Norman's booming voice yells down the stairs. "You there?"

Cooper does roll his eyes this time. "Yeah. Editing. What's up?"

"Do you know how to fix a Canon XA15?"

Cooper's eyes meet mine. There's a forever moment where he's deciding what to say. I want him to say, "No, no clue." I can't leave here until things are better again. A surgeon would never walk out of a hospital room with a wound still open.

He takes a sip of grape soda before yelling back.

"Yeah."

"Good," Norman yells. "A rush order called. Something about a shoot in Africa on Friday? Head over to the store with me?"

Cooper closes his eyes for a moment before answering. "Yeah."

He drains the rest of the grape soda.

Even though I know he has to help his dad, I'm angry. This video is important. This conversation is important.

"So, what now? I have to leave?" I ask. There's a part of me that wants him to say no, that I should come fix cameras with him. Maybe a tripod will be broken. Heck, I'll go buy a tripod and break it so I can have an excuse to fix it. We need to fix this situation before it calcifies and becomes impossible to rectify.

But he doesn't say that. Instead, he says, "Yes. We're done here anyway."

I'm still mad at him, but I'm also scared. Is this the track we're on now? Sure, today was awful, but it was only one day. Not a new direction.

Right?

He picks up his keys and hands me mine. As if he's reading my mind, he says, "I told you things would be different." He looks sad. "We both knew it, deep down."

"When can we finish talking?"

"Not sure. I'll text you."

Does that mean he's not sure when he'll be finished fixing the camera, or that he's not sure if he wants to keep talking? I want to ask, but he's already packed up.

On my way home, I have the rare feeling of being angry at my mom for dying. It's selfish, it's stupid, but I am. There's nothing I want more than to talk to my mom about this. My dad would never understand guy issues. Why can't he understand these things? I'm angry at Cooper, at my mom, at my dad, and at the guy who brought in that Canon X-whatever. I'm even mad at myself. I shouldn't have said those things to Cooper about being stuck in his dad's camera shop. They were too mean. When did I become so mean?

But he was mean back, really, to say those things about me sneaking around on my dad. I'm not *sneaking* around, if you look at it from the right angle . . .

No, he's right. I'm sneaking around.

And then I wonder why my dad and I don't have a good relationship. Maybe I'm being stupid. I drive too fast. Desert palms whip past my windows, and it's like I'm daring cops to give me a ticket. It would hurt less to be angry at a faceless stranger.

18

The next day, there's a DVD in the mailbox when I get home. I watch it while I make a salad to go with dinner. It's a voiceover of me explaining my mom's research and my plans for work at the space station. The only cut-ins are a few of my PowerPoint slides, some footage of me near my telescope, and a shot of me in my dad's lab. It feels very scientific and professional, which I love. It also feels a little . . . The only word I can think of is *cold*, but that's because of the tension between me and Cooper. It's a very good video. Just how we planned it.

How *I* planned it, I mean. But it was a good plan.

I upload the video to my laptop, put the file in with my résumé and my letters of recommendation, and submit the whole application package before I can question my decision. It's anticlimactic. Even though there weren't plans for the official submission moment, I guess I hoped it would be with Cooper. We'd high-five or something. Probably kiss. Celebrate our victory and hard work.

Instead, a piece of salad spills onto my laptop.

A confirmation email hits my inbox. Results will be released November 3—just over two weeks away. I clap my hands once over my head, like I'm giving myself a high five. This moment wasn't supposed to be sad.

I head up to my room when I'm finished cooking. Five's cage is empty, so I can't celebrate with her. My dad would kill me if he knew I applied at all. I tell Beaker Troll that the video has been submitted. She's wearing her blue tutu to celebrate the occasion.

I text Cooper: Thanks for the video.

He texts back a thumbs-up emoji. Not even one word. An emoji.

I pull my mom's dissertation from the bookshelf, cuddle it like a teddy bear, and crawl into bed for a nap.

Cooper avoids me at school for the rest of the week, which is easy to do since (1) our school is huge and (2) we have no friends in common. The NASA deadline passes, and he doesn't send me so much as a *good luck* text. I consider texting him to say I submitted my application, but that seems stupid. Of course he knows I submitted it. It was our life for the past month.

So is that it? Is this how breakups work? You're everything to each other, and then suddenly you're nothing? You're supposed to pretend that the moments when your life tangled with this other person's never happened at all?

The whole arrangement between Cooper and me was a business thing. We shook hands on it eons ago at the film club meeting in the band room. It was never supposed to turn into what it was, which was . . . Well, I'm not even sure what to call it. It was a small change at first, like an orbital period changing only a degree or two. But now everything's out of whack, and I can't really remember how things were before.

Bridget texted me that she doesn't need any more chemistry help, and I'm sure that has to do with Cooper. Goodness knows she didn't suddenly learn chemistry.

By Sunday night, I feel a bit desperate. Desperate people do drastic things.

"Hi, girlie!" Charli's voice is loud through my phone's speaker. "What's up?"

I've never called Charli before. This is scary and somehow super embarrassing. I almost hang up. If phones didn't tell you who's calling, I would have hung up. But now, because of stupid technology, she would know I'd called and just call me back. So I have to say something.

"Hi. Um, it's me, Skyler." *Duh.* She already knows that. I wince. "Yeah. Hey, listen. Do you want to get burritos tonight?"

"Burritos?"

"Like the Mexican food."

"I'm familiar with the concept."

She sounds confused, but I don't want to explain everything over the phone. "I want to talk to you about . . . things."

"Oh." She pauses, making whatever connections are being made in her mind. Then her voice brightens to the overly cheery level that she uses for fans and videos. "Sure, girlie! Let's do it!"

"Want to do the place near the Galleria?" Near a mall means she knows where it is.

"Sure. Six o'clock?"

"Perfect."

The Mexican place is called Los Amigos Burritos. It's a family-run restaurant owned by the abuela.

Charli is there when I arrive. She's working on her laptop like this is a Starbucks, but the entire restaurant only has five tables. Charli is drinking a Coke (diet, I'm sure) but has no food.

Her hair is half up, which is a style I haven't seen on her before. It looks good. Her lipstick matches her wine-colored tank top, and she's drinking through a straw so it doesn't get smeared.

She smiles when she sees me. She doesn't give me a hug, which I appreciate.

We order burritos, and Charli insists on paying. She puts ten dollars in the tip jar.

After we discuss the weather, Charli's blog, and school, Charli takes another sip of Diet Coke. "Want to tell me why we're here?"

No, I really don't. But I do need advice.

"A friend of mine needs help. She's not sure what to do about a guy situation."

Charli gasps. The pimply kid washing tables looks up to make sure we're okay. Charli claps her hands quickly. "How exciting! It's you and Cooper, right?"

"No. My *friend* needs the advice."

"What's your friend's name?"

Dang it. "Um."

"I knew it! Great. Okay. What's going on with Cooper?"

Ugh. I continuously underestimate this woman. No reason to keep up the lie. "We were really good friends, you know?"

"I thought you were dating." Her face is serious. It's like she's a lawyer collecting evidence to use in trial: the state of my relationship at the time of the disturbance is vitally important to our stance on the ensuing contact with the heretofore nameless defendant.

"We kind of were. I mean, I think we were."

"Was there a DTR?"

"What?"

"A 'defining the relationship' conversation? Was it explicitly stated that you were exclusive?"

Oh my gosh. She's serious. Is a DTR a thing I should have known about before? Did Cooper know about it? Is there paperwork involved? Relationships keep getting more complicated. Mental note: look up DTR later and figure out if that's real or just a Charli thing, like the FEK.

I finish chewing my tortilla chip. "We didn't have a specific conversation. Like, he didn't formally propose girlfriendhood."

"Mmm." Charli nods. "I see." Clearly that was not an acceptable answer.

"I'm pretty sure it was implied."

"Mmm." No nod at all. She disagrees.

I take a bite of my burrito to buy some time. It feels like I've broken a bunch of rules I didn't know existed, which seems unfair.

When I don't go on, Charli speaks gently. "Did he sleep with someone else?"

A piece of rice gets caught in my throat, and I start coughing. A lot. Charli offers me a drink of her Diet Coke, which is kind.

When I'm able to speak again, my face is so hot I know it has to be completely red. We'll say that's from all the coughing. "No. I mean, I didn't ask him because I haven't talked to him, but it's doubtful. We haven't had sex."

Just a few weeks ago, I was blissfully studying for the SAT. Now I'm choking on a burrito and talking to my dad's girlfriend about my sex life. Perhaps I need to examine the choices that led to this moment.

Charli's shoulders relax, and she sits back in her chair. "Whew. That's good. It's tough to bounce back if he slept with someone else. I mean, don't get me wrong. It's been done. I had a sorority sister at Columbia whose boyfriend slept with someone else, but now they're married and have three kids. So it's a thing. But it's so much easier if he didn't. Anyway, what's going on?"

"He's not texting me."

"Oh." She looks a little confused. "What does he do when you text him?"

"He responded with an emoji."

She blinks. "He always responds with emojis?"

"There was just the one time."

"You only texted him once?"

"I thought it was pretty clear that he was mad and didn't want to talk to me."

Her eyebrows shoot up. "You got that from an *emoji*?"

When she puts it like that, it sounds stupid. But I don't want to be that needy, annoying girl. I only know how to be independent. Plus, back in the basement he said *he* would text *me*. That means wait for him to come around. Right? Is there another rule I'm missing?

"We had a fight. I think. We were both really frustrated. We said some mean things. Then we got interrupted by Norman— that's his dad—and Cooper had to go fix some expensive camera. He said he'd text me later. But then I waited too long to text him, or maybe he waited too long, and now things are weird."

Charli nods like she's tracking with me now. She even picks up her untouched burrito. "Just to be clear—that's the main concern you're here to discuss?"

"Yes."

She smiles to herself and takes a bite of the burrito. She gives me a thumbs-up and, before she's even done swallowing, says, "You're fine."

I take a nervous bite.

There's wine-colored lipstick on her flour tortilla, but Charli doesn't notice. She's in business mode. "Okay. You have plenty of options. A ghosting, whether misinterpreted or intentional, can be very painful. But you've got me, and we'll handle it together."

Her words are comforting. She's like a sage older sister (and realistically, she's young enough to be my older sister). *Someone's going to help me.* My muscles relax a little bit, and I hadn't even noticed how tense they were.

Come to think of it, there are probably teen girls all over the country who would kill to have *the* Charli advising them on guy issues. And yet here she is, getting lipstick on a burrito with me. That realization feels warm, like the first sip of tea.

"My first piece of advice would be that you've got to text him. What if he thinks you're mad, and you think he's mad, and the whole thing is a big misunderstanding?"

Something tells me it's more than that, but I shrug. "Maybe."

She grabs a napkin. "Maybe he's doing it on purpose. I have no idea. But until you text him, neither of us will have any idea. At least when we know, we'll know."

For the first time, I voice the fear that's been gnawing at me all week. "But if I do text him again, and he doesn't text back . . . what does that mean?"

Charli takes a deep breath. "We figure that out then. It could mean anything. It might mean he's not into you, but it could also mean lots of other things. For all we know, he's run away and joined the circus. We have no idea."

I smile.

Charli takes a sip of her soda. "All I'm saying is that we don't know unless you try."

"What do I say?"

Charli looks thoughtful. "There are the direct and indirect routes. You could go direct and say something like, 'Hey, I miss talking to you. What's up? You okay?' or you could go indirect by asking a question about something you have in common. Maybe your vlog?"

Yeah. My "vlog."

"We're not doing that project anymore."

"Why not?"

I get really interested in dipping my chip into salsa. There's not enough salsa on it, so I dip it again. "We decided it would be too much work to keep up, so we abandoned the project."

When I venture to meet Charli's eyes, they're slightly narrowed. Chewing my chip seems very loud. Finally, she says, "That's the story you're going to stick with?"

I don't know what comes over me in that moment. Maybe it's because Charli's being so nice to me, maybe it's because I'm sick of keeping my secret, but I don't want to lie anymore. I take a deep breath. "No. There never was a vlog."

She nods once, looking a little disappointed. "I suspected as much. Why lie about it?"

"I'm trying to hide it from my dad." I explain about the NASA internship and how I want it pretty much more than anything, but my dad doesn't want me to apply for it. I explain how the lie seemed simple in my mind when I started it, but now it seems to have spiraled into some sort of relationship block with lots of other lies tied to it.

The words are tumbling out, but I don't want to stop talking because of the inevitable judgment I know I'll get from Charli. I expect her to tell me how stupid I am for ever thinking this would work or maybe what a horrible person I am for lying. What I don't expect is what she says when I finally run out of things to say.

"Your dad loves you so much."

Even though I know this (most of the time), it's still good to hear it.

Charli continues, "He would probably be more hurt by your lies than by your determination to apply to NASA."

She might be wrong there, but I'm not sure anymore.

"I'm sorry I lied to you," I say. It feels good to come clean.

Charli shrugs. "Thanks. I get it. But I really think you should tell your dad the truth. He's a good man, and he cares about you more than anything. He deserves the truth."

She's right, and I know it.

I seriously consider this. Can I tell him the truth? I mean, what's the worst thing that can happen? He'll be mad, or maybe sad (which could be worse), but then at least the mess that's between us could get a little cleared up.

What if he still tries to stop me from accepting the internship if I'm chosen? After all the work I've done? Then again, my relationship with him might be worth it.

As if Charli can read my mind, she says, "Maybe when he sees how dedicated you've been in working toward this internship, he'll reconsider his opinion."

"But maybe not."

She concedes. "Maybe not. But there's only one way to find out."

Once again, she's right. The path I'm on hasn't been going so well, so maybe it's time to try something new.

When all that's left of our dinners is chip crumbs, Charli says, "I have to be honest—I thought you wanted to come here to talk about your dad."

"My dad?"

Her confident veneer fades, like the lipstick that is now almost entirely off. She sloshes the ice in her almost-empty cup.

"You're not my biggest fan. I thought maybe you were going to try to convince me that I was, I don't know . . ." She shrugs. "Ruining your life or his life or something."

Guilt washes over me.

"You're not ruining our lives," I say.

She doesn't look that comforted. "Good." She tries to drink more of the Diet Coke, but it's gone. She blushes. "I just want a chance to show you who I am, you know?"

I need to say something, but I don't know what. I'm still not excited that she's dating my dad, but she's been very kind to help me out today. Maybe I don't hate her, but it's not like I'm ready to hit the mall with her, either.

"You're a lot better than I thought at first" is the best I can do.

"Thanks." She smiles.

There's got to be something else nice to say. "My dad seems to like you."

"He does, doesn't he?" She smiles to herself. "Do you know how rare your dad is? I have dated so many terrible men. You have no idea. They look at me and see the image I've created. The hair and the clothes and the makeup." She gestures to herself as if in this moment, she finds those things repulsive. "I've had guys tell me I look scary without makeup, because I usually go so long before I let them see me without it. They want to date *Kisses from Charli*, but not just plain old Charli."

She fishes out a chip crumb from the basket.

"Your dad had never heard of my vlog. The first time he told me I was beautiful, I wasn't wearing a single product. Not even *moisturizer*."

I try to look appropriately awed, but I come up short. "First of all, I've never used moisturizer in my life. Second of all, I bet you're beautiful without it."

Although I said it more as an observation than as a compliment, her eyes get a little glossy. "Thank you, Sky."

As soon as I get home, I type out my rehearsed text to Cooper. Charli and I decided that I'd text him, Hope that camera got fixed. I'd love to chat sometime.

There was much back-and-forth about whether or not the text should include exclamation points. Charli speaks in exclamation points, so she thought adding them was natural and cheerful. I thought they looked overeager and desperate. In the end, it's my phone. She seemed to understand but told me to let her know what happens.

I hold my breath as I hit *send*.

Three and a half long minutes go by. Then the three dots show up to let me know he's texting. They show up and then go away, then show up again. Is he putting as much thought into his text as I did into mine?

His text comes through: Talk after school tomorrow? Hallway by the film club room?

That betrays nothing about how he feels or how this conversation will go, but at least we're talking. I text back a thumbs-up emoji.

I take a deep breath. I need to steel myself for an awkward conversation with Cooper, but I also want to gear myself up to talk to my dad about the truth. I tell myself to take it one conversation at a time: I'll talk to Cooper, and then I'll talk to my dad.

And maybe, just maybe, things will start to work themselves out.

19

After lunch the next day, Kendra from my QuizBowl team catches me in the hall. "You're friends with Cooper Evans's little sister, right?"

Unsure of how to quantify what the heck is going on because even I'm not sure, I go with "Yeah. Maybe?"

"I'm pretty sure she's crying in the bathroom by the gym. She ran into a stall."

Class starts in two minutes. If I go check on Bridget, I might be tardy to class. There isn't a single tardy on my record. Not even in elementary school. I don't do tardies. One time, someone pulled the fire alarm while we were in between classes, and I still went to my next class to make sure it was okay to go outside. But if Bridget's crying, maybe she needs a friend. The second hand on the clock is racing, eating away at my decision time.

She'll be fine. I walk toward class, but it's like an invisible force slows my feet down. Then I'm stopped in the middle of the hallway, looking at the clock again.

No matter what's going on between Cooper and me, I'm still Bridget's friend. I remember her face at Five's funeral when she said, "It's what friends do." Now I'm going to be tardy.

The door echoes off the bathroom walls when it closes. The room smells of industrial cleaner, and the purple stall doors are all open except for the last one. "Bridget?" I call. "You in here?" If she's not in here and I'm tardy because of this, Kendra's going to get it.

Bridget is in there.

"Sky? Is that you?"

"Yeah."

There's a metallic click of a door unlocking. "You can come in."

Does she think the stall is her office? "Bridget, I'm not talking in a bathroom stall."

"It's the handicapped stall."

Thirty seconds until the bell. I have no shot of making it to class on time. Handicapped stall or not, though, I'm not going in there. We can talk in the public section of the bathroom like normal people. "Can we talk out here? There's a Febreze air freshener. Lavender. Your proximity to the chemically constructed essential oils will help reduce your anxiety." That's not true. The chemicals in Febreze won't do a lot aside from a psychosomatic effect. But a psychosomatic effect is still something, and I'd rather this tardy not turn into full-blown class skipping.

She sobs again. "Get in here, okay?"

I guess the person crying gets to call the shots.

Once I'm in the stall, it's clear why Bridget doesn't want to come out. Her face is a mess of smeared makeup. She looks like I did back when I tried to follow along with those makeup vloggers. She's sitting on the toilet with her legs pulled close to her chest, and she's been crying into the knees of her light-wash jeans. They've got makeup stains, too. Her hair probably used to be in a topknot, but now it's a messy bun that is far more *messy* than *bun*.

There's obviously not another seat, so I set my backpack down and lean against the wall.

Bridget doesn't wait for me to ask what's wrong. "Andrew's *cheating* on me." She gets up and points to the toilet accusingly, where her phone has sunk to the bottom of the bowl. Not sure how this is supposed to explain anything.

The bell rings. For the first time ever, class seems unimportant. Fresh guilt washes over me. So it *was* him I saw with Lindsey that day. If I had said something, could this have been avoided? Could I have protected Bridget? Cooper would kill me if he knew I let this happen. I study my fingernails so I don't have to look at her. I'm a terrible friend.

"Are you sure? Why is your phone in the toilet?"

"Because"—she gives an exasperated sob like I'm stupid for not understanding—"it's full of pictures of Annndrrrewww. And watch, it doesn't even flush." She stands up and flushes the toilet. Sure enough, the phone swirls around but doesn't go down into the pipes (which is good for our school's plumbing bill). When it doesn't go down, she starts sobbing again.

Should I rescue the phone? It seems like a waste of technology that Bridget might regret later. I could throw it in a bag of rice and hope for the best.

Then again, maybe the phone is not the point.

How do I be a supportive friend? I've failed her once, and I'm going to get it right this time. None of my QuizBowl friends have ever been cheated on, so I'm not sure what to do. Wait—there was a movie once where someone got her friend ice cream after a breakup. Or was it chocolate? Maybe chocolate ice cream?

"Would you like chocolate ice cream?"

Bridget stops crying long enough to look confused. "What?"

"Can I get you ice cream? They have some in the caf, I think."

"I don't want freaking ice cream," she sobs, more morose than angry. She grabs a wad of toilet paper and wipes her already smeared face. "I want Andrew to love me."

Okay. Think, Sky. You can't force Andrew to love her. You can't make him be a good person. She doesn't want ice cream. What's left to do?

I remember Bridget holding Snickers at Five's funeral and taking it as seriously as if it were a funeral for a person. She never even met Five, but because it was important to me, it was important to her. Maybe the same rule of friendship applies here. Just being there is worth something.

"I'm sorry," I say. "What happened?"

She sinks down the side of the wall until she's sitting on the floor with her knees in front of her. "Anna saw him making out with Lindsey at lunch."

"They were making out at lunch?"

Some people haven't evolved past basic instincts, I swear.

Bridget sniffs. "They were in Lindsey's car. Like, who makes out in a car at school? Are you kidding me? He was mauling her. Second base like it was nothing. Anna took video."

"She showed you?" Anna is even more of a drama queen than I thought.

"She showed *everyone*." Bridget gives a fresh sob and reaches for more toilet paper. "She texted it to the whole world."

I refrain from pointing out the ridiculousness of this hyperbole. Also the fact that I didn't get the text, so clearly it hasn't made it down to the lesser echelons of the social strata.

"And she said she did it to help me, because Andrew deserves for everyone to know what a jerk he is. Which I totally see where she's coming from. But how am I supposed to show my face now? I thought he loved meeeee." She sinks even lower into the floor and is now curled in the fetal position. "Lindsey sucks. Andrew sucks. My life sucks." She reaches behind her and feels for more toilet paper. Finding it, she pulls more down.

So many germs on that floor. My dad would be having a coronary. I'm close to having one myself.

"Come on, Bridge." I squat and pull her up to a sitting position, but then give up on sanitation and sit with her.

She leans her head against my shoulder. "Did he ever love me?"

"I'm sure he did. Guys are idiots." I don't know if that's true, but it feels like the right thing to say here. She cries for a while, and I just sit. My calculus teacher is going to be livid, but I don't mention it. This is more important than integrals. Also, I can do integrals in my sleep.

"Do you want to know the worst part?" Bridget sits up and switches to sitting cross-legged, turning toward me. "I think he did it on purpose."

I'm quiet, mostly because I'm confused about how anyone would think that he accidentally found himself in Lindsey's car with his tongue in her mouth.

Bridget seems to sense my confusion. "Getting caught, I mean. What if he wanted to break up with me, and he didn't know how? Maybe this is his way of saying he doesn't want to be with me anymore?"

"Then he doesn't know what he had." I put my hand on her back. "You're amazing. Any guy would be lucky to date you. He'll regret this later for sure, and it will be too late."

She scowls. "You're saying that because that's what everyone's supposed to say when this happens."

"None of my research or previous life experience has told me how to handle this situation, I assure you."

Bridget laughs in a way that doesn't quite make it to her eyes, but it's at least a laugh. "I believe you."

Suddenly, there's a commotion in the gym. At first, I can't tell what the people are yelling, but then I can: "FIGHT! FIGHT! FIGHT!"

We both whip our heads toward the door as if we can see what's going on through the walls.

Bridget gasps. "Cooper and Andrew have fifth-period gym together! You don't think . . ."

Oh no.

I don't know Andrew, but I know Cooper. And if he's seen that video, then that's who's fighting.

Bridget and I burst out of the bathroom stall, leaving everything behind. We run to the gym and see Mr. Jones vainly blowing his whistle. It's difficult to see through the cluster of students at first. Then I see Andrew throw a punch and hit Cooper on the right side of his face. It feels like a ghost of the punch hits me, too.

"Stop it!" Bridget screams. She runs into the crowd. "Andrew! Stop! Cooper!"

I'm frozen near the back of the cluster. Some people are still chanting. Some are trying to break them up while avoiding punches. Andrew slugs Cooper in the stomach. Cooper tries to fight back, but it's clear that he's losing. Should I run for help? Should I try to break them up? There's nothing I can do. Andrew's huge.

It feels like time has stopped. Another punch lands on Cooper's nose, which starts gushing blood. He throws a punch back and hits Andrew's shoulder, but it's tough for Cooper to see while he's trying to defend his head with his other arm. Finally, after an eternity, some of Andrew's friends get ahold of him.

"Football, dude," I hear one of them yell. "He's not worth getting benched."

At that moment, our principal, Mr. Grant, runs in. "What is going on?" he demands.

Mr. Jones looks relieved, and the crowd parts to allow Mr. Grant through. Cooper is bleeding and whimpering while holding his nose and trying to stop the rush of blood. His shirt is stained and only getting worse. Andrew looks angry but completely unscathed. Bridget is sobbing while some girl (a volleyball player?) hugs her.

Mr. Grant orders the two guys to his office. When Cooper passes through the crowd, his eyes meet mine. If possible, he then looks even worse, like me seeing him added another injury to the ones he has. He turns away before I can offer any encouragement, not that I would have known what to do anyway.

Science is easy. People are hard.

Everyone goes back to whatever they were doing in gym. I sneak out the side door before Mr. Jones can ask why I've decided to join his fifth-period gym class. It seems like whoever was holding Bridget is going to take care of her now, so I scoop up my backpack from the bathroom and head to calculus.

I brace myself for the wrath of my teacher when I walk in, but she only tilts her head. She asks where I was, and I tell her the bathroom. She says okay and goes back to writing on the whiteboard.

What? No tardy slip?

The clock tells me I'm only a few minutes late, but they were some very long minutes. I sit down and avoid the curious glances of my classmates. A couple of them check their phones. Are they getting texts about the fight? How quickly does this news make it through school?

It's impossible to focus on integrals when I know Cooper is hurt. After an excruciating fifteen or so minutes, I raise my hand.

Mrs. Batts stops talking about finding a complicated integral. "Yes, Skyler?"

"May I use the bathroom?"

"Didn't you just come from there?"

Shoot. I say the first thing that comes to mind: "I forgot something." The class snickers. I can't fault them. What does one forget in the bathroom? Telepathy isn't real, but I try to send a message to my teacher through the air molecules: "YOU HAVE

TO LET ME GO." I bite my lips and widen my eyes, trying to look desperate. It's not contrived.

She raises her eyebrows, but my complete lack of shenanigans at any point in the past works in my favor. "Hurry back."

The empty halls make it easy to run to the office.

Cooper is sitting on the same navy chairs where I was when Five came to class with me. He's holding an ice pack to his eye, and he's wearing a school gym shirt that's too big for him. It makes him look small. Mrs. Ling isn't at her desk, and the door to Mr. Grant's office is closed.

"Cooper!" I rush in and kneel in front of him. "Are you okay? What happened?" Stupid question. I want to kiss him, but his lip is busted. "You look awful."

"Great." Most people think frowns are something that a mouth does, but Cooper has found a way to frown with his entire face.

"I'm sorry. I didn't mean it like that. I just . . ." His jeans are rough beneath my hands. "Are you going to be suspended? Will this go on your record?"

His good eye narrows. "Seriously?"

My hands freeze in place on his legs. "What?"

"All you care about is your permanent record. No, my nose isn't broken, thanks for asking. They're not going to call an ambulance, thanks for asking. Yes, I knew Andrew would kick my butt, thanks for asking. Bridget is more important than getting suspended, okay?"

"I know. I'm sorry." I rub my hands on his thighs again, so happy to be touching him even if he's still mad at me. "I'm sorry about everything, okay? Can't we fix it? Start over and pretend like none of this happened?"

He winces as he pulls the ice from his eye. I pull back and swallow, trying not to gasp. His eye socket is purple and swollen. He'll need a doctor's attention. More bills. I want to go punch Andrew myself.

"It's fine," I say desperately. "It's not that bad." Not sure if I'm talking about his eye or about our relationship. Possibly both, and I'm for sure lying about one.

"You got your video," he says. His voice is missing the warmth he always had when we talked. His eyes (well, eye) don't have the sparkle he used to have when he looked at me. It's as if I'm a stranger. Worse than a stranger, because he's friendly to everyone he meets.

"I know. I got the video. But it wasn't just about the video ... was it?"

"We don't have anything else in common."

"Of course we do!" We have . . . Crap. What do we have in common? "I like pretzels! And you like pretzels!"

What am I doing? I'm a scientist. I know a terrible, desperate argument when I see it.

There's no compassion in his eyes. "There isn't anything. The project's done."

"That doesn't mean we have to be over. Look at my dad and Charli. What do they have in common, huh? Nothing. And they're awesome together."

"You hate them together. You said it's a scientific anomaly that is an insult to evolution."

"Maybe I want to be a scientific anomaly, too." I move my hands from his thighs to holding his hand. "Screw evolution."

Who am I anymore? What am I saying?

It's weird to hold hands with someone who isn't holding mine. His hand is limp as if nothing is touching it at all. He looks at me again, and a flicker of sadness passes through the iciness. "Skyler . . ."

He never uses my full name. My lungs freeze like I've breathed in his ice.

Cooper lets out a breath. "I've given this more thought than I care to admit, okay?"

"Right." I nod and try vainly to get him to hold my hands again. "Me, too. See? We can't stop thinking about each other. That's a good sign."

"It has to be over," he says. "There's nothing to wait for. We're on different tracks. You said it yourself. And yeah, it was a pretty crappy thing to say to my face, but we both know you were right."

I swallow, unsure of how to respond.

Cooper continues, "Graduation's right around the corner. Then what? You're NASA. I'm Norman Camera."

"You'll be in Utah becoming an amazing filmmaker. We'll be chasing dreams together. So what if our dreams are different? You can still go for yours. I was wrong, Cooper. You're not stuck here."

Cooper puts the ice back up to his eye. "I rescinded my film school application."

I must have misunderstood him through the gashed lip. "Excuse me?"

"That night after you left, my dad and I got in a fight. I told him I didn't want to fix cameras all the time and that Tim should start sooner. Turns out there is no Tim."

No Tim at all? As in, he never existed or he's not coming to take over the position? Neither option is great. I open my mouth to speak, but Cooper cuts me off.

"The money that my parents were going to use to hire a second guy got spent. Bridget's medical bills and stroller investments and who knows what else. My dad has no plan for what to do when I'm gone. He was hoping to bring in more money before I found out, but here we are."

Wait. Just like that, the dream dies? Cooper has worked so hard—it can't all be wasted. "He'll find some way to let you go to college, right?"

"That's not how real life works. You and I both know that the shop will go under without me. So I'm going to stay—at least for a year or two until Dad has enough money to hire someone else. It's the only logical option."

It's hard to watch him clinging to a way out, even if I desperately want it to work for him. Maybe his parents will be financially in a place for him to get out a year or two down the road, but realistically . . . probably not. And we both know it. Still, I refuse to admit defeat.

"Since when have you ever cared what's logical, Coop? Come on. You're the least logical person I know." Seeing his face scrunch up, I hastily add, "That's a compliment. It's one of my favorite things about you."

"I have to start making logical choices now. So far, they all suck."

"Fighting Andrew wasn't logical."

He glares at me. "I'm not perfect, okay? Come on, Sky. I'm trying hard here, and you're making it harder. Will you just leave me alone? Please?"

Does he mean right now? Or forever?

Mrs. Ling walks in and looks startled to see me with Cooper. She shifts the files she's holding, which get momentarily caught on her apple pin. (Yet a different one. This one has a worm in it.) "Can I help you?"

"No," I say, which is true in more ways than one. "I was checking on Cooper."

"Do you have a hall pass?"

"Mrs. Batts told me I could go to the bathroom."

Mrs. Ling puts a hand on her denim-skirted hip. "Does this look like the bathroom?"

"Right." I squeeze Cooper's hands and try to convey everything I'm feeling in one last glance. He doesn't meet my eyes. That doesn't seem like a good sign. Are we really over for good? Separated that easily by life circumstances? Will I get the chance to talk to him again, to maybe change his mind? My insides feel heavy, but I don't know what else to say. "I'll head back to class." I rush out of the door before she can hand me a tardy slip.

20

The next several days pass excruciatingly slowly. After talking to Cooper went so poorly, I kind of lost the nerve to confess to my dad. I keep trying to work it up again, but there's never a great time to tell your dad, "Sorry, I've been lying to you for weeks, and I did something you expressly told me not to do." So now things are still weird with my dad, and they're silent with Cooper. I feel more alone than I've felt in a long time.

When my mom died, everyone assured me that I simply had to wait until my life adjusted to the "new normal." I hate that phrase because there's nothing normal about growing up without a mom. Also, life never stabilizes. It might be stable for a second, but it's like an unstable isotope. There's always a particle bouncing here or there, trying to stabilize, and the whole thing ends up radioactive.

At lunch one day, one of my QuizBowl teammates asks why I never hang out with Cooper anymore. I say we broke up. She looks uncomfortable, thinks for a second, and then offers to get me some ice cream. I tell her it's not like that.

I try to stabilize into this new routine: one marked by loneliness, studying to retake the SAT (less than two weeks away), and halfheartedly dominating at QuizBowl matches. Charli comes to one with my dad, wearing a short-sleeved gray-plaid suit and a black fedora. None of my QuizBowl friends recognize her, but a few raise their eyebrows at the fact that my dad brought a date. I tell them it's a long story.

But, as always, there's a stray particle that keeps the whole thing unstable. Right now, it's my NASA application. As much as I want to win, 1 percent of me hopes that I lose. If I lose, the particle falls into place. Things can move forward. I'll take the SAT, I'll do better this time, and I can complete my application to MIT. Even if I don't get into MIT, I'll get in somewhere. I can go to college and grad school and track my way up the astrophysics food chain like my mom did. Sure, I'll miss the NICER camera, but I can do . . . something else. I don't know what yet. Something smart. My dad will be proud, and he'll never have to know any of this happened. Or I can confess, say I'm sorry, and we can move forward because the application is no longer an issue. Maybe, if enough time goes by, I can forget about it.

However.

If I win, I'll have to tell him everything. We'll argue about whether or not I can accept the internship. I'll accept it anyway, and it will be a whole mess. The mess will be worth it, for my mom and all, but still. It will be a mess. The video will be shown all over the country, and every time I see the video, I'll be thinking about the boy behind the camera.

Maybe it's closer to a 2 percent hope that I lose, 2.5 percent max.

Then one Instragram post changes everything.

We live in a strange world where one simple post—a few hundred characters—can change an entire life.

I'm lying on my bed at 4:56 p.m. when I see it. I know the exact time because I log in to Instagram, and I have a notification that I have 456 new followers. Weird, and it's 4:56. What an odd coincidence.

But wait—456 new followers! Where did they come from? Yesterday, I had seven followers. Six were QuizBowl teammates, and one I'm pretty sure was a bot.

There are also notifications of people tagging me in their posts. The first message isn't even in English. German? Polish, maybe? Am I signed in as myself? Yes. How could I have accidentally signed in as someone else?

I scroll through the notifications until one makes my heart leap and crash at the same time: *@NASA tagged you in a post.*

@NASA TAGGED ME IN A POST.

@NASA—THE ONE AND ONLY @NASA—TAGGED ME IN A POST.

My hands are shaking as I click. Why is NASA tagging me? Results don't come out for a week. Six days, six hours, and four minutes, to be exact.

Oh my gosh.

NASA tagged me because I made it to the top ten. They never said they were going to announce a top ten. What would Cooper say about this? Has he seen it?

Has my dad seen it?

OH MY GOSH. HAS MY DAD SEEN IT?

My dad doesn't have an Instagram, so surely he hasn't. It's probably private between me, NASA, and my 456 new friends.

No wait, 460 new friends.

461.

This may be a problem.

Should I text him? Call him? Give him a heads-up somehow? What would I even say? "Uh, hi, Dad. Funny story . . ." Why didn't I confess when I had the chance? Charli was right. I should have said something. Now NASA is going to beat me to it. Sometimes I feel like a large part of my life could be described by the facepalm emoji.

I'm screwed. Beaker Troll's face looks like she's laughing at me. "Put some clothes on," I hiss in retaliation. "You look ridiculous."

My phone lights up with a text from Charli. It's a screenshot of the NASA post. Her caption is three exclamation points. Is that a good thing? Or is she also concerned that my dad doesn't know yet? It's hard to interpret naked punctuation.

Okay. Think. I am a 4.0 student. Astrophysics is easy for me. I can handle an Instagram post. There is a clear answer here. It's like an equation. I just have to think hard enough, figure out the correct algorithm . . .

462 followers.

I slam my laptop shut like I can stop myself from going viral. Viral—what a gross word. Like I'm sick. If that were true, I could douse the whole laptop in hand sanitizer and stop this thing from spreading. But this post is on the move, and I can do nothing to stop it.

I put my hands to my temples. How am I going to explain this to my dad? Should I text Charli back? Will Cooper see this? It's more a matter of: *When* will Cooper see this? Will he be happy for me? Upset? WHAT IS HAPPENING?

My chest feels tight. Maybe I'm having a heart attack. I look around my room, not wanting to look at my computer but not knowing where else to look. Then my gaze lands on a familiar black book, and something occurs to me: I am in *the* top ten.

Then suddenly I'm crying. It's overwhelming to be so excited and terrified at the same time, and about so many different things.

My dad's going to kill me. My mom would be hugging me.

Cooper and I did it! Cooper and I aren't speaking.

I might get to go to space. *I might have to go to space.*

The particle has gone rogue, and this isotope has become radioactive. Things are about to blow up. As a matter of fact, they're already blowing up around me. Charli knows. Therefore, my dad probably knows. Cooper's gotta know. Regardless of whether or not I make it out of the top ten, there's a lot I'm going to have to handle. Soon. Now.

My phone rings. It's Bridget. She must've gotten a new phone already. Crap. Ignore call.

Wait, did I hit *ignore* too fast? I should have let it go to voice-mail so that she wouldn't know I'm sitting right here. Hopefully, she thinks my phone's dead or something.

Ten seconds later, she's calling again. Oh my gosh. Phone on silent. I should flush it like she tried to do with her old one.

Once I hear the garage door open, the phone is the least of my worries. My dad's home early.

Should I wait for him to come up to my room or meet the situation head-on?

I go downstairs so that it doesn't look like I'm hiding out, although I would be hiding if there were any chance I could get away from this inevitable confrontation.

I'll be getting a glass of water when he walks in. Maybe I can play this off as nonchalant. And maybe I can be the one to tell him the news. It's still not going to go great, but it will be best if he hears it from me. It only posted a few hours ago. News travels fast, but maybe I can be a little bit faster.

He walks in, shirt untucked, and one look at his stormy face confirms my fears.

He knows.

"So," he starts. "I got a very interesting text from my boss today."

"You did?" It's suddenly like I'm five years old, when I broke a rack of test tubes and didn't want him to know about it. I blamed it on his lab rats. I was five and scared—logic eluded me. Now, however, there's no one to blame but myself.

"Yes." He throws his keys onto the counter with more force than necessary, then walks over to a barstool and sits. His arms are crossed. "Would you please explain to me, Skyler Renae, why my boss congratulated me on your great accomplishment with NASA?"

I wince. He heard from his boss? That's even worse than if he heard it from Charli.

"I'm really sorry, Dad." I don't bother to fill up my glass with water. I set it on the counter, empty, but grip it. "I was going to tell you. Charli told me to tell you, and I should have listened to her, but now it's too late, and can we just pretend—"

"Charli knew before I did?" My dad's face gets stormier.

"Um . . . no?" I think about how to backtrack out of that one, but I'm in too deep. "Yes." I sigh. "I'm really sorry. I'm sorry for all of it."

His eyes narrow, and he shrugs in a way that keeps all his muscles tense. "Are you actually sorry?"

I know the correct answer is yes. But his question gives me pause. Am I sorry? If I could rewind this entire thing—if I could go back to the first post I saw about the Teen in Space internship and force myself to keep scrolling—would I do it?

Cooper's face flashes in front of me—meeting him in the band room, filming out under the stars, kissing him in the basement, and even seeing his broken and swollen skin the school office. The good times and the bad—would I erase them?

Five would be in a landfill somewhere instead of a loving grave. Bridget wouldn't have ever been my friend. She probably wouldn't be eligible for volleyball. I may never have even understood what a friend was, as much as it hurts to lose one.

That's all not to mention this chance—not just the chance of a lifetime, but the chance of two lifetimes. This is for my mom as much as it is for me, and I'm only nine people away from clinching the victory for both of us.

My answer slices through the kitchen silence. "No."

"No?" His eyebrows shoot up. Neither of us expected me to say that.

"No," I repeat, my resolve hardening. "Not really. I mean, I'm sorry that I didn't tell you sooner. But for applying to NASA? No, I'm not sorry." I feel a little shaky, and I hold my breath. What is he going to do? I don't think I've ever told my dad no before, and especially not on something this big. We've always been a team—us against the world. Now it's like I just quit and started playing some other game. What happens now?

He places an elbow on the countertop and leans forward, a calculated move that feigns interest. "Would you care to explain why you are not sorry that you went directly against what we agreed on regarding the NASA internship, and why you lied to me, snuck around behind my back, and then let me find out from my boss? Please explain."

His jaw is clenched, and I wish he'd yell. It's like we're in a Cold War standoff. Neither of us is willing to explode, but the potential energy is enough to blow us both off the map. I'm still holding my breath, and the ball's in my court. I have to say something.

"I'm not sorry because, even if I don't get the internship, it's better than if I never took the chance at all."

"If you go, you could die. If you die, you would kill me. Is that what you want? To kill me?"

"I might not be picked."

"You're the smartest girl in the whole United States. Possibly the world. Of course you'll be picked." His voice is angry, not prideful. "You have your mother's brain. You even look like her."

So he's noticed, too.

He slams his hand on the counter. "I couldn't keep her safe. Why won't you let me keep you safe? I have one job in life, okay? One. And you're going behind my back and wrecking it."

My grip on the glass is so tight I'm worried I might break it. I slam it into the sink. "Are you trying to keep me safe or trying to keep me from becoming an adult?"

"Safe. Only safe. Go to college. Go do all the grown-up things you want. I don't care. But don't go to space."

He throws his hands up and paces the kitchen. It's a small enough kitchen that he ends up turning around a lot. He's practically pacing in a circle. He starts talking again, and I'm not sure if it's to me or to himself.

"I have to be the only dad in the history of dads who has had an argument with his daughter about going to space. There is no parenting book for this. I've read all the parenting books. They tell me what to do if you're drinking underage, if you're failing classes, if you're smoking pot—" He stops pacing momentarily and looks hopeful. "Are you smoking pot?"

"What? No."

He throws his hands up in exasperation. "Ugh! See? No directions for this. None. There is not a single chapter in any of the books that gives parents a clue of what to do if their daughter decides to go to space."

"Fine. I'll write one. Chapter 237: 'When your daughter wants to go to space, you let her. The end.'"

He stops pacing and glares at me. He is not amused. "So I can lose you to some space disaster? No thank you."

"The world has advanced in technology since then."

"Did someone invent technology to make you get over the loss of a family member? Because I swear to you, I would have been all over that years before now." He's being sarcastic, but his eyes are fiery.

"Mom would want me to go."

He laughs and starts pacing again. "No she wouldn't."

"Yes she would."

He stops and looks angry. "You knew her for eight years. I knew her for twenty. Don't tell me what she would have wanted."

"She would have wanted to go herself. But she can't, and I'm the next best thing we've got. Don't wreck her chance."

"This isn't her chance. Her chances are over, Sky. She lived a life she loved. She loved her work, but she loved her family more."

Finally, something we agree on. "You're right. She would have done anything for us, and that includes putting her personal fears aside and allowing us to follow our dreams. She probably would have helped me with the application video instead of holing up in her lab so completely that she didn't even realize I was filming it."

"You're smart!" He points at me like he's accusing me of something terrible. "Is it my fault that you're smart enough to be sneaky? You're blaming me for the fact that you're a good liar? I don't feel like I know you anymore."

"That's because you don't. You haven't known me for a long time. News flash: while you were in your lab, I grew up. I learned how to cook, and I took care of cleaning the house and doing all the things that a parent is supposed to do. Where were you? Studying your freaking microbes. Sure, we can eat pizza and talk about science. Do you know my dreams or what fears keep me awake at night?"

"You dream of going to MIT."

"How's that going for me?" Tears fill my eyes. "I don't have the SAT scores or the extracurriculars. Am I allowed to have noncollegiate dreams? What if I dream of, like, having an exotic pet? Or writing a book? How about if I want to visit the pyramids?"

"Do you want to do any of those things?"

"No. But that's not the point. You've never asked. I've never had the chance to tell you. Our lives are science. Real life? Like, out-there life?" I gesture to the window. "It's more than science. There's a whole bunch of other stuff, like volleyball and vlogs and pigeons and . . . stuff."

He looks at me like I'm speaking a foreign language and then shakes his head. "What?"

"Never mind. The point is that I got so much from applying to this internship. Even if I don't get it, I'm not sorry for applying. If I do get it, I'm going. Because I grew up while you weren't looking. And while you might be right that mom would have been nervous to let me go, you know she would never have passed up the opportunity to go herself. Don't try to keep me grounded. You know it wouldn't have worked on her."

He's quiet, which means I'm right.

"I wish you would be excited for me."

"I'm not." He crosses his arms, and his eyes are steel.

"Why are you being selfish?"

Selfish. That's what Uncle Phil called him when my dad missed Uncle Phil's wedding.

Dad looks genuinely confused. "You can't talk to me like that. I'm your father."

"You stopped parenting me years ago, so I'm not sure why I suddenly owe you all this respect. What's for dinner tonight?"

His confusion increases. "What does that have to do with anything?"

"Because it's chicken pot pie, which I made, which is in the oven, and you didn't even know it because you don't pay attention to anything around here."

As if on cue, the timer dings. My dad jumps.

"Enjoy your dinner, Dad."

My dad asks where I'm going as I head up the stairs, and I tell him I'm not hungry.

I lie on my bed and stare at the painted constellations on my ceiling, wondering if I'll have a much closer view of them soon. But my advancement into the top ten feels hollow. The space between my dad and me feels larger than the space between earth and the ISS. What if it doesn't go away?

I pick up my phone and scroll through my texts, telling myself I'm just bored. These are *bored* tears. People cry from boredom all the time. That's all this is.

Lying to myself is getting difficult. I used to be unaware I was doing it, like when I believed that Five was only a specimen. Now I can tell when I'm wrong, but I still try to talk myself out of the truths I can't face.

I click on the text conversation with Bridget. My last text from her was a week ago, saying thanks for helping her in the bathroom. I responded, NP. What are friends for? She sent back a kissy emoji with a heart. Then I click on my last conversation with Cooper, which hurts to even open. The last text is one from me that says, I'm not ready to give up on us.

He never texted back.

I type How've you been? but then delete it. I type I made the top 10—thanks for your help but then delete it. I type I miss you, but I delete that, too. Maybe he's right. Maybe our being together doesn't make any sense.

Nothing does anymore.

21

It's 1:00 a.m. when I decide to do a Walgreens run. We're out of ibuprofen, and my head is killing me. My dad's sleeping, but I leave a note on the counter. Everyone knows that it doesn't count as sneaking out if you leave a note on the counter. Plus, even if he does see it as sneaking out, I'm sure one of his parenting books would cover that.

Also, I'm pretty sure he couldn't get madder at me. I might as well do what I want.

In the Walgreens parking lot, I pull out my phone again. I type You up? to Cooper but then delete it. It's 1:00 a.m. Of course he isn't up. Even if he is, what would I say?

This type-and-delete method has become commonplace over the past week.

The pharmacy has extra-strength ibuprofen, and I pick up

a huge bottle because I have a feeling I will need a lot. My dad probably will, too. How do other families handle that awkward moment when a kid isn't a kid anymore? On the one hand, I don't feel ready to be grown-up and to be making my own decisions, but on the other hand, it feels like I've been there for a long time.

On the way to the checkout counter, I pass the wall of formerly mysterious cosmetics. Should I pick up another lip shimmer? I'm almost out of the sample size that Charli got me from the mall. Then again, who cares if my lips are shimmery? It's not like anyone cares about my lips anymore.

Still, I pick up one of the tiny tubes. I'm not sure if the sadness is more from the fact that I now know what this is and how to pick a good color or from the fact that I no longer have a reason to buy it.

The name of this one is Pop Fizz. It reminds me of grape soda.

Reading the ingredients gives me a familiar comfort in recognizing the chemical compounds. It's amazing how simple rearrangements of elements can create anything from ibuprofen to lip shimmer. You've got H_2O—water—and with one more tiny oxygen tagalong you get H_2O_2—hydrogen peroxide, which can kill you.

Wait a minute.

This must be how Isaac Newton felt when that apple landed on his head and he discovered gravity. Elements come together in a million different ways to form molecules. People have a million different traits and experiences that make up who they are. We aren't elements at all—we're *molecules*.

This is either brilliant or it's 1:00 a.m., and I'm too tired to know that it isn't. Either way, there's one person who needs to know about my discovery. Perhaps it would change things.

I squish Pop Fizz back among the other lip shimmers, then take it out again at the last second. It can't hurt to have some extra lip shimmer, right? And it was the impetus for my discovery. It's Newton's apple. But shimmery.

The checkout line is clear, but I linger by the candy. There's a college-age guy with a six-pack and some Oreos, and it looks like he might want to check out soon. Sure enough, about a minute later he walks to the counter.

Score.

I get in line behind him, and since I'm clearly in line and therefore justified, I grab the *Cosmo* from the rack and check my horoscope. BECAUSE I'M IN LINE. It's fine.

Sagittarius . . . Sagittarius . . . okay, here I am. It says, "Take a risk on the twenty-fifth. The handsome stranger might end up being exactly who you're hoping he is."

My watch tells me it's the twenty-seventh, not the twenty-fifth. And Cooper's not a stranger. But if you round up twenty-five, you could get to twenty-seven, right? And things are definitely strange between me and Cooper, which could make him sort of a stranger.

"Miss?" The cashier looks at me expectantly. Six-Pack and Oreos has already left the store. Oops.

You know what? Forget *Cosmo*. It doesn't even matter, and astrology isn't real. I'm going to Cooper's first thing in the morning.

The rest of the night crawls by, both because my headache is quite stubborn and also because I'm trying to plan my trip to Cooper's. Nothing I mentally rehearse is great, but I have to talk to him. I have to tell him what I discovered and see if it will make a difference.

By six o'clock, my headache has subsided but my anxiety has not. I figure it's best to go there and get this over with. He usually gets up early-ish. This is probably fine.

That's what I think until I get to his driveway. It is too early to be socially appropriate to knock on the door, especially when we haven't talked all week. I can't throw rocks at his window like in movies. Driving over to someone's house in the early hours of the morning is theoretically romantic, but in reality, I sort of feel like a stalker.

I sit in his driveway, alternating between putting my car in reverse and in park. How do I make this romantic and not creepy? This could push him away, or it could be the kind of grand-gesture, spur-of-the-moment, go-with-your-gut thing that he would love. I'm playing the odds.

Odds say stay.

No, reverse.

Park.

Reverse.

If only there were a way to make sure this was romantic and not weird. In movies, there's always inspirational music and birds flying overhead in these situations.

That gives me an idea.

I put the car in park, definitely this time, and sneak out. The pigeon coop sits behind Cooper's house, and I don't want to be spotted before I have my pigeon props. After all, 97 percent of people would think these white pigeons are doves, so the romance must be transferable.

When I open the coop, the pigeons stare at me with their beady, half-opened eyes. "Good morning," I say, trying to convince them that this is a good time to fly.

I look around for a net or some other way to grab the pigeons. Then I feel dumb—they're not butterflies. I hold my finger out to one, hoping it will hop on like a parakeet. It continues staring at me.

How am I supposed to carry and release a bunch of pigeons?

Maybe I'll settle for one pigeon. It's the thought that counts, right?

There's one in the corner that's sleeping or possibly dead. Hopefully, it's sleeping. I carefully put both hands around its tiny body and then grab.

Ack! Not dead. Very not dead. Wiggly and squawky and pecking my hand.

I run back to my car saying "Ohmygoshohmygoshohmygosh" the whole way. I'm carrying a bird. I squeeze harder, but then I loosen my grip because what if I kill the thing? I'm trying to win Cooper back with as few casualties as possible.

I stand outside Cooper's first-floor bedroom window with the bird. Um, now what? This plan was not well formulated. It was a very Cooper-esque plan. I look around and then shove the bird in my hoodie pocket. It doesn't like that.

"There, there." I whisper as I pat my stomach. "Calm down." It doesn't.

Now I need some inspirational music, but I need to play it quietly so I don't wake up Cooper's family. I pull out my phone and search for something romantic and inspirational.

I'm still scrolling when Cooper's blinds open. His eyes are half-open like those of the pigeons from the coop, but they get wide when he sees me. He opens his window. "Sky? What are you doing here?"

He's kind of glaring at me. It isn't the starry I-love-you look I was hoping to see.

"I miss you." I'm tearing up, but it could be because I'm tired or because the bird is pecking me or because this makes no sense and I don't even care. "And I realized something."

"So you're standing outside my window like a creeper?"

I see his computer on in the background. He's editing video. "You were up early anyway."

"You weren't exactly invited." He crosses his arms. My mouth feels dry.

"I know, but my realization was too long to text. Here's the thing, Cooper—we're not elements. We're compounds."

"Excuse me?" He looks confused but not intrigued.

"I never got around to telling you, but your element is gold. Because you're so go-with-the-flow. And also, um, aesthetically pleasing." I wince at my own words. "But you're more than gold. You're *gold bromide*. None of us are made of just one element, or there would only be a hundred and eighteen different types of people on earth. That's ridiculous. But if we're compounds, there are billions of options. That makes more sense. You combine gold and bromine—gold because you're so malleable, but bromine because you're also strong in the face of hard things. Did you know bromine compounds are added to pajamas to make them flame retardant? No one wants people running around on fire. Plus, bromine is added to some types of citrus sodas—like Mountain Dew—to be an emulsifier that keeps the oils from forming a separate layer. You keep everything together, Coop. I see how you do that in your family. You're gold bromide—get it? We can't be restricted to one element, so the possibilities are endless. It's about taking the time to discover each other for who we really are. There are no set tracks."

For a second, I think Cooper is checking me out, but he's staring at my hoodie pocket. "What's in your shirt?"

"Oh yeah. This is the other part. Because I did the speech, and I was supposed to have background music, but I couldn't find it in time, and now for the finale." I pull the very peeved pigeon from my hoodie pocket and throw her into the air. She's supposed to fly over our heads romantically. Instead, she falls to the ground and quickly waddles over to a bush. Also, there's poop in my hoodie. Ew.

I reach to pick up the pigeon again, but it doesn't care much for me. It waddles farther into the bush and then hops up onto a small branch. I'd have to army crawl under there to get it. "Do I need to, um . . . ?"

Cooper sighs. "I'll get it. Go home, Sky."

It feels like his words have punched me. Go home? Logically, of course he would say that. What did I expect, that he would invite me to crawl through his window where we would make out on his bed?

Not that I would have said no.

"Are you listening to yourself?" Cooper hasn't smiled this whole time. "I only understood about half of what you said. It sounds like you're going through some great personal growth or something, but this"—he points between the two of us—"is never going to make sense. I don't understand you, in so many senses of the phrase." His eyes are sad instead of angry, but it still hurts.

"You could learn," I offer. "I want to learn about you."

"Sometimes in life, it doesn't matter what we want."

I'm encouraged by the word *we*.

"What do you want, Cooper? If you could have anything, what do you want?"

He stares at me. I see a flicker of longing, but it's possible that I'm making that up because I want to see it. I stare back, all my cards on the table now. The pigeon coos and hops to another branch, but neither of us look at it.

Then he breaks the stare down. He slams his hands on his windowsill and looks down. "I want you to win."

"Win what?" For a split second, I don't know what he's talking about.

His green eyes meet mine again, and they're softer. "Congrats on the top ten."

Right. When did that become unimportant? How did I forget about it, even for a second? "Your idea for the movie could have worked, too," I offer.

This is supposed to be an olive branch, but it is the wrong thing to say. Why do I always say the wrong thing? He tenses up again, and the softness flees from his eyes. He stands up straight.

"I didn't mean it like that," I say. "You had really good ideas, and I want you to know—"

"I know. I get it. I'm happy for you." But now he doesn't sound like Cooper. He sounds formal, like we're scientific rivals and he's congratulating me on a discovery. Whatever "it" is that he thinks he gets, he doesn't. Where did the soft eyes go? The second where I almost saw the real him? Please, Cooper, come back. My ribs feel like they're trying to squish my lungs.

I pull in a piece of flyaway hair. "No, wait. That was supposed to be—"

"Doesn't matter. Hope you go all the way with it." He rubs his arms as a breeze rustles past us. It plays with his hair. Lucky wind. "I'd better get back to work." He points to his computer.

"Right." Neither of us moves. This is the part where I should go home, but our eyes are locked. If only I had the technology to read what's happening in the brain behind those beautiful eyes. Can I kiss him? His lips were always so soft. My stomach clenches. I picture myself leaning over and kissing him before leaving. I'd walk away, he'd call my name, and he'd say that he misses me and that we can make this work. He'd kiss me, deep and strong, and hold me like he never wants to let go again. It happens in all the movies.

The pigeon hops to another branch. We break from staring each other to look at it. This isn't the movies. This is Cooper's house, and I stole one of his pigeons and stood outside his window on my phone until he found me. My throat feels thick. I'm lucky no one called the police on me. A sudden wave of humiliation hits, and I want to throw up (which would be the perfect cherry on top of this horrific situation).

"I'm sorry." I cover my face with my hands, but they smell like pigeon so I slam them to my jeans instead. It's like if I rub hard enough, I could brush off this whole mess.

"No prob. Good luck, okay? I'll see you around."

He's lying.

My eyes burn, and I have to leave before I cry or puke. Both seem probable.

"Bye." I walk backward for a few steps, trying to memorize his face because I may never be alone with him again. Then I turn and all but run back to my car.

22

After school, I drive home to find a fire truck, an ambulance, and a police car outside my house. There has only been one other day that a police car pulled up to my house. That day flashes in front of my eyes almost as clearly as if it were happening again: third-grade me watched from my bedroom window as my dad crumpled on the front stoop. I hid in my closet until he found me, both of us crying, fifteen minutes later. Heat surges through every part of my body. No. Whatever these vehicles mean today . . . no.

Today was already an awful day at school, one of being congratulated by people who don't care about me on something they don't understand. A freshman came up to me and asked if I would be willing to take a message from him to the aliens. Social activity has never been my strong suit, so the day was a complete mess. Being popular has never seemed appealing, even in temporary form. The last time I got that much attention was after my mom died. Now, in the moment that I'm trying to bring her back to life in an odd sort of way, all eyes are on me again. Eyes are never good.

Unless they're Cooper's.

Bridget didn't congratulate me. Maybe she's mad because I didn't take her calls yesterday? It hurt me even though it shouldn't have, and then I was angry at myself for being hurt. Imagine putting all the emotions in a blender: hope, excitement, happiness, anger, humiliation, and sadness. Then hit puree. Then drink that smoothie. That was my day. I had been convinced that it couldn't get worse, but I now understand that I was wrong. None of the rest of today matters. The only thing I'm drinking now is a shot of pure panic.

I can't park in my driveway because it's blocked by the emergency vehicles. Neighbors are out on their lawns gawking. Julie is taking pictures with her ancient phone. I pull off into the lawn, park at a diagonal, and leap out.

A police officer is standing outside his car and tapping away on an iPad. What is he documenting? The sun glints off the metal on his badge, and there are shadows caused by the razor-sharp pleats in his pants.

"Excuse me, officer? Excuse me? I live here. What happened? Where's my dad?" I'm embarrassed that there are tears in my eyes even before I know what happened. I'm not drinking one shot of panic now. I'm getting drunk on it. My legs are weak. I might not be able to walk. My heart is slamming my ribs. I try to hold steady, but my hands are shaking. Everything is shaking. My eyes scan the people outside, all of them now faceless because I don't see the face I'm trying to find.

The officer puts his iPad on the top of his car. "Everything's going to be fine."

That is exactly what people say when everything is not fine.

My body goes from hot to cold like I walked into a shower of liquid nitrogen. What happened to my dad? Am I going to be an orphan? I don't believe in God, but in that moment I beg him or the ether or whatever out there is listening to please let my dad be okay. I don't care about anything else. Please let him be okay.

The lights on the trucks are on, but the sirens are off. Smoke is coming from my house. "Is my dad in there?" I'm about to run in. I don't care if I die. I'm not living without both of my parents. Surely the universe wouldn't be that cruel.

The officer's voice cuts through my panic.

"Listen. Look at me."

He puts a hand on my shoulder, maybe because he could see I was going to run. I look back and forth between him and my house.

"Look at me," he says again, with more authority. Then I look at him, bracing for the worst. As if there's really any way to brace yourself for terrible news.

"Your dad is fine."

I let my breath out, only then realizing I'd been holding it. Adrenaline and relief mix in a way that leaves me shaky and weak. "He is?"

"Yes, he's fine. He's over there." The officer points to the fire truck. "The fire is under control now, and the damage is minimal."

I'm sure it's inappropriate to hug a member of law enforcement, and I've never wanted to until that moment. But hugging him would take away time from getting to my dad, so I run to the fire truck instead.

At first I don't see him, but then there he is: sitting on the curb, head in his hands, looking small in the flurry of vehicles and personnel swarming around our house. It's like everyone has a job to do, and my dad's playing the part of "dejected victim."

"Dad!" I drop to the curb and hug him in a way that feels more like a tackle. His white coat is singed and covered in char. He smells like smoke. When he puts his arms around me, it's like I'm five years old again and counting on him to keep me safe from nuclear fallout. I had a nightmare about it for years after reading a book about Fukushima, and I would run to my parents' room in the middle of the night, sobbing. My mom would try to explain the science behind why I was safe from nuclear fallout, but my dad wouldn't say anything. He would just hold me. And really, that was what I needed.

When he finally lets go, I see his face properly for the first time. Even though he isn't crying, there are tracks through the soot on his cheeks. The hair on his left side is singed (which isn't the first time that has happened, but there haven't been fire trucks before). Even though he has let go, he keeps a hand on my knee like he doesn't want to part from me completely.

He focuses like he's about to say something of vital importance. My stomach gets nervous again.

"What's your favorite color?"

I blink. "What?" How much smoke did he inhale?

"Your favorite color. I need to know what it is."

"Purple."

He holds a closed fist to his mouth like this is exactly what he feared. The tears threaten to come back.

"Not purple?" I offer. "I can pick a different one. Blue? Green? What color do you want?"

"Your favorite color used to be black because the night sky was black."

"Right. When I was a little kid."

"When did your favorite color stop being black?"

"At Mom's funeral." I remember the exact moment. I was staring at my black shoes—the shiny ones that I hated because they gave me blisters. My black tights were itchy, and no one had washed my black dress, which smelled like the musty back of my closet. It was wrinkled, but my whole life felt wrinkled. My great-aunt had plunked a black headband on my head because it was "cute" and would "look good in pictures," as if it were normal to take cute pictures at a funeral. The headband was too tight. All anyone wore that day was black, and it didn't remind me of the night sky at all. So in that moment, staring at my shoes, I did the only thing I knew how to do in protest: I demoted black from my favorite color to least favorite.

"I'm sorry," he says.

"For what?"

"I should have known your favorite color."

Even though my mind is swirling at galactic speeds, I can't find how that is relevant to this situation. "No, really, it doesn't matter. Like, at all." How did the fire start? Is he really okay? The

244

ambulance is still there, but it looks like the EMTs are packing up. Perhaps they shouldn't be leaving so fast.

"What kind of dad doesn't know his daughter's favorite color? Charli told me it was purple, and I said she was wrong." He presents this information like it's evidence of terrible parenting.

"Okay?" I'm still not tracking. "Dad, are you all right? What happened?"

"Oh, that." He glances back at the house like he'd forgotten about it. "There was a fire."

I laugh a little even though the situation is the farthest thing from funny. "Could you get a bit more specific?"

"The kitchen's a little damaged, but I've been meaning to upgrade stuff in there anyway."

"No you haven't." My dad doesn't upgrade anything except lab equipment.

He runs a hand through his singed hair. "Last year, I made a note to myself to get batteries for the smoke detector."

"We had no batteries in our smoke detector?"

"I needed them for an experiment."

That is so classic for my dad. "Of course you did."

"I was making pasta today. After we . . . talked, I thought about the fact that you really do most of the housework. That's a lot to put on a kid. And then, the more I thought about it, I realized you're not even a kid anymore. But you're not gone yet, so I wanted to do something to show you I am going to try harder. I can't coach a Little League team or anything, but I want to be a good dad."

"Dad, I've never been on a Little League team. I hate sports."

"Right. And you don't dance, so I can't show up at a dance recital to show my support. I'm not an exciting, fun dad. I'm a boring, distant dad. But I want to make up for that."

He takes off his glasses and wipes them with his lab coat, but I can't imagine that'll help.

"I tried to cook dinner," he continues. "It was going to be ready when you got home. Pasta primavera, because you used to love that. But then I got focused on some developments in the liver study I'm doing in the basement, and I forgot."

He puts the glasses back on his face.

"Then I smelled smoke, and by the time I got upstairs, there was smoke all over the place. Not sure if the pasta caught on fire or maybe the paper towels I left by the stove or what, but . . ." He waves his hand like the rest is self-explanatory.

I take off his glasses and wipe them on my clean shirt. "It's okay. You're fine. It's no big deal."

"I don't care about the kitchen. What I care about is the fact that I got so absorbed in my work that I ignored the rest of my life. Today it was pasta. But for years it's been you. And I didn't even know it, because you've been such a good kid. It was easier to focus on my work. Real life is harder than science."

"I know." I hand the glasses back. "It is." Cooper's face flashes into my mind, but I try to push it away. Things were easier when all I cared about was science, but maybe life isn't about finding what's easiest. Discoveries come in many forms.

"I had no smoke detectors in life to tell me how much of a mess I was making. Or maybe there were signs, I don't know. I probably wouldn't have noticed. But yesterday, Charli was talking about you. Charli knew your favorite color, and Charli knew you went to a volleyball game, and Charli was the one who told me you and Cooper broke up. She told me about your vlog cover story, which you never used on me because I didn't notice anything." Every time he says *Charli*, he winces like her name hurts. "And all that time, I've been at the hospital or in the basement dissecting livers." He wrinkles his nose like this is disgusting (which it is, but his disgust isn't for the same reason other people would find it gross). "I'm so sorry."

"Dad, it's fine. Your work is important."

"It's not, though." His grip on my knee tightens. "Nothing is more important than you. I'm going to do better."

It's awkward to have a parent apologize, so I just say, "Okay. Thanks."

"Maybe dinner was not a great place to start." He gives a thin laugh, and I smile. "How about this instead?" He sits up and takes a deep breath. "I want you to accept the NASA internship when they choose you."

"You do?"

"Yes. Because you're right; it *is* selfish of me to think I can keep you a little girl forever. You've changed. I forced you to grow up before you were ready, so the least I can do is allow you to be an adult. I was in so much pain when your mom died that I tried to protect both of us from everything dangerous or painful ever since. That's not fair. You deserve to live the life you want to build."

It's like the wall built between us is being torn down brick by brick. The relief I feel extends even deeper than when I found out my dad was okay. Not only is my dad okay, but maybe *we're* going to be okay. Maybe things won't be like they were before, but the new version of us could be even better.

"Thanks, Dad." I take a deep breath for the first time since turning onto our road.

"But when you finish your mom's research, I want you to know that I won't be one microgram prouder of you than I already am. Because whether you go to space or just cook dinner a lot better than I do, you're the best thing that ever happened to me. And I know you've always said you're silicon, but I think you're iron. Because it's what makes steel, and you've got strength unlike anyone I've ever seen. At the same time, iron is so easy to take for granted. It's in our door handles and our forks and in our blood, for goodness' sake. You're as monumental as the Eiffel Tower and as important as my blood. You're iron."

I smile. "No boring, distant dad would say something like that."

He laughs ruefully. "Then I don't know what kind I am."

"I've always considered you the mad-scientist type. And you're rocking the vibe today."

He squints, considering this. "What do mad-scientist dads do?"

"I'm not sure. Would you prefer I take up ballet so you can have a stereotype to follow?"

He nods and feigns relief. "Would you, please? Because a ballet recital would be more convenient for my schedule than a rocket launch."

"Okay." I stand up and brush off my jeans. I spin and attempt one of those jumping-splits things ballet dancers do, then shrug. "Sorry, I have no natural talent."

"Then rocket launch it is." My dad smiles. "Your mom would be so proud of you."

This seems like the kind of thing a single dad would say many times throughout a daughter's life, but it's the first time my dad has ever said it. It stops me in my tracks. "You really think so?" Mostly I want to hear him say it again.

"Of course I do."

He stands up and gives me a hug. It feels safe, like everything is going to be okay. Dad hugs have a way of feeling like that, and I realize he hasn't hugged me in a long time. I hug him back, squeezing tight and trying to hold on to the feeling that we'll be all right.

23

National Aeronautics and Space
Administration
300 E Street SW
Washington, DC 20024-3210

Ms. Skyler Davidson,

Thank you for your application to our Teen in
Space internship program.

There were over 1,200 applicants for the
single research slot. You were among the top
ten candidates, an achievement of which you
should be proud.

However, we chose another student to
become the intern, based on the
combination of academics, recommendations,
and an engaging video presentation.

We wish you all the best in your endeavors
and hope you continue your research.

Sincerely,
The NASA Teen in Space Program Coordinators

My mom's dissertation is covered in tears, and I don't care. I'm sitting on my bed hugging my knees with the book between my knees and my chest. It's over. After all of my work, it's over. Am I an idiot for thinking I could do this? There's a piece of me that really believed I would get this internship. After all, I always win the science fair. My GPA is a 4.0. But plenty of high schoolers graduate with an A average every June. Our parents spend years telling us we're special, but when it comes right down to it, most of us aren't. Most of us are just normal teenagers. And as cheesy as it sounds, I thought I was special. The NASA position would have confirmed it. You don't become the youngest person in the history of the world to go to the International Space Station unless you're special.

But I'm not. I'm a statistic. I'm one of the 1,200+ people the real intern can brag about beating. I'm a name in a paper shredder somewhere. Perhaps the letters on my name have even been torn apart. This wouldn't have happened to my mom. If this program had been around when she was my age, she would have been chosen.

"I'm sorry," I whisper to the book again. "I tried."

I rest my forehead heavily on the top of the book even though it will leave red marks. It doesn't matter. Nothing matters. My SAT prep book mocks me from my desk even though I'm not looking at it. The test is on Saturday, and I'm not ready. It's my last chance to get a higher score, and I haven't studied hard enough. Where am I going to go to college if not MIT? It's always been MIT.

There's a notebook on my nightstand where I jotted ideas about what I would take with me to space. I had crafted answers to the questions magazines and news outlets would have asked me. It all seems stupid now. For my whole life, I thought I was smart. If I'm not, then I don't know who I am.

Five would make things a tiny bit better. I should have cleaned out her cage long before now, but I've been so busy that there wasn't time. Or maybe I wasn't ready to face that she's really gone. How weak can I possibly be?

There's no way to pull myself into a tighter ball than I am right now. It's like I'm trying to compress myself into nothingness. My dad can't help me. Cooper and I haven't spoken since that morning at his house. Even if I could talk to my mom, I bet she wouldn't understand. She was extraordinary.

I wipe my nose on my jeans. Tears on my mom's dissertation is one thing. Snot would be too much. I put my head down again, because who cares if I get snot in my hair?

There's a soft knock on my door.

I shove the dissertation under my bed and rub my face with a Kleenex. Good thing there's no mascara to run. "I'm a little busy," I say.

"Are you sure?" It's Charli.

Gosh, she is nosy. I hate her. I hate everyone. I hate myself.

"Yeah." I sniff, trying to compose myself. "Super busy."

"Okay." She sounds unconvinced. I hold my breath, waiting to hear her footsteps walk away. They don't.

"Can I tell you something real quick, girlie?" Her voice is quiet, barely loud enough for me to hear.

"I guess."

"Whatever you're going through in there, I'm sorry you're going through it."

It's quiet again. No footsteps.

She continues her one-sided conversation. "You don't have to tell me anything. But can I bring you tea? Or chocolate? Or something?"

"No." That comes out sounding pouty, and I don't want to sound juvenile. "Thanks, but I'm fine. Just busy."

"Do you want me to get your dad? He's running a lab in the basement, but I'm sure he'd come up."

I'm suddenly so angry I can hardly stand it. I launch out of bed and whip the door open. "I don't care what you do, okay? You're probably only going to be in our lives for a second. And there's no reason for us to pretend otherwise. I thought maybe we could be friends, but we can't. My mom should be here today. I really need her right now. Instead it's just . . . you. Please go away."

My hand covers my mouth even before tears pool in her eyes. Where did all of that come from? I'm so angry and she was . . .

there. Like someone caught in the rush of an exploding volcano. Enough of what I said *is* true that I can see my daggers have hit their mark. I try to mentally justify that I *did* tell her I was busy. She should have walked away sooner. This is . . . her fault?

No. If possible, I only hate myself more.

"Oh." She steps back like I hit her. "I'm sorry. I'll go." And then the footsteps I wanted to hear earlier do echo down the hardwood floors of our hallway.

Slamming the door feels like it would be childish, so I close it softly before running back to my bed. I pick up my mom's dissertation to throw it at the wall—this book has ruined my life. I even pull it back behind my head, so much potential energy built up that it would surely make a satisfying crash.

I can't do it.

No amount of anger can make me throw this book.

Why am I so controlled by a book?

I grip the book in front of me, knuckles white. My teeth are clenched in my closed mouth, and my nostrils flare while I try to channel all of my hatred into this book. Instead, I rearrange my fingertips so that, instead of my nails, the pads of my fingers are gripping the book. No sense in leaving fingernail marks on my sacred text.

This book is not my mother. The tears that have burned my eyes start falling, and I let them fall on the book. It's a hardbound—it can handle it. Like my mom. She could handle anything.

Why have I treated this book like it's the last remaining piece of my mom's soul? It's not. She's not coming back. Even if I could have gotten to space, finished this research, and put my own hardbound book next to this one, it wouldn't have brought her back any more than if I made a chocolate chip cookie with one butterscotch chip. Somehow, she seems gone even more now. The veil between us is hardened. No matter what happens, I won't be able to part it.

This scares me almost as much as realizing I'm not as special as I thought. The combination of both at once makes me dizzy. I shove the book in my closet and fall on my bed. My tears have stopped, and I stare wide-eyed at the ceiling. It looks foreign. Without space, and without my mom, what do I have left?

My phone pings.

I don't care.

It pings again.

I turn the sound all the way down—go away, world—but I notice the text is from Charli.

Sorry to bug you . . . Cooper's here. Tell him you're busy?

Yes, I type back. Then I delete it and type No. Then I delete that, too, and put my phone down. Let my silence be the answer.

But Cooper's here. My heart flutters in a way that doesn't hurt. He's right downstairs, here at my house, and I could talk to him.

What if I lash out at him like I did at Charli? I'm clearly not in a state to talk to anyone.

But he's only downstairs. Closer than any of my neighbors. I look to Beaker Troll for advice. She's smiling. Stupid, optimistic Beaker Troll.

If forensic experts analyzed Beaker Troll, I wonder if they'd find Cooper's fingerprints still on her. The oils our fingerprints leave behind have been known to last a number of days or even years, depending on several factors.

I wait for my brain to start cycling through the science of fingerprints. There's enough to distract me for at least a little while. Science is comforting, like a lullaby that's always in my brain.

But instead of accessing my mental database of fingerprint information, my mind swirls to Cooper and the day he used Beaker Troll to show me how life is about connecting the seemingly unconnected. He'd seemed so sure that day, like he had the secrets to life all figured out.

That was before the cold Cooper, the fighting Cooper, and the morning-never-to-be-remembered Cooper.

Are those versions of Sky and Cooper as gone as my mom?

If they're that gone, then why is he here?

It's not like this day could get worse. He knows the Teen in Space results by now. The intern's name is already up on NASA's site. I unfollowed them on Instagram, even though I'll probably refollow them tomorrow.

"Skyler?" Charli peeks her head around my door as I sit up. "I'm so sorry."

Her eyes are red, and I bite my lip.

"Cooper's here, and he already saw your car, so . . ." She holds her hands up apologetically. "I said you don't want to talk right now, but he insisted. He wants to see you. We agreed that if you say no right now, he'll leave."

Before I can overthink it, my mouth says, "Okay." It's like it momentarily disconnected from my brain, but I'm not stopping it.

I sneak a glance in the mirror but wish I hadn't. I'm a mess.

"All you need—" Charli holds up one finger and then puts it down like she remembered she's not supposed to talk to me.

"I'm sorry," I say. "Those things . . . I didn't mean them."

"It's fine." She waves her perfectly manicured fingernails like she's already brushed the comments off, but we both know she hasn't. Her eyes fill with fresh tears.

"What were you going to say?" I ask.

"Nothing. I'll get Cooper."

"Wait, please." My voice softens. "What were you going to say? You have a ten-second fix. I know it."

She wipes her eyes. "I was going to say that all you need is a hairbrush and a tiny dab of lip shimmer. You're gorgeous, girlie." She nods authoritatively and whispers, "But they always love the lip shimmer."

She does a half smile and puts her finger to her lips like we have a secret. I do my best to smile back.

As Charli goes to get Cooper, I run a brush through my hair. Is the lip shimmer too much? Nah. I might as well go for it.

Cooper appears at my doorway. He's wearing loose jeans and a film club hoodie. His hands are in the pocket. His hair is mussed, like maybe he ran his fingers through it in that way he does when he's nervous.

Oh, like what he did just now.

His eyes aren't sparkling, but they aren't cold. They look a little lost. I'm sure mine are the same. Look—something we have in common.

"Hey." His one-word introduction cuts the thick silence. He closes the door slowly behind him and stands right in front of it.

Does he expect me to respond to *hey*? He's the one who showed up unannounced, so he should be the one to open the conversation. I certainly did when I said all that stuff about . . . well, the stuff. I try to suppress that memory and get back on track with thinking about the science of fingerprint oils.

His fingerprints are here, now. On his soft hands.

Brain, stop it. You're science-ing all wrong.

He swallows. "Uh, I know we haven't, um . . ."

I fold my arms in an attempt to appear defensive when really I feel small.

"Bridget's missing." Cooper's eyes brim with tears, like it hurts him to even say it.

My arms drop to my sides, losing their defensive posture. "What?"

"You heard me." A hint of impatience creeps into his voice. "She's . . . gone. I hoped maybe she came here." He looks around my room as if Bridget is going to pop out from behind my desk chair.

"No, sorry."

He sighs. "I knew it was a long shot. I was wondering if maybe, um, you could help me look for her? The thing is, you're the smartest person I know. You'll think of things I won't. And I know we're not, erm, *close* anymore, but Bridget was kind of your friend, too, right? So maybe you'd care to make sure she's okay? Or maybe not. Maybe this whole thing is stupid. It's just so stressful, and I couldn't think of where else to go, but—"

"I'm in," I interrupt. "I'm one hundred percent in. Let's find her."

"Great." Cooper's shoulders sag in relief. "Thanks. Let's go." He turns and walks out my door like we don't have a moment to lose (and maybe we don't).

I have so many questions, but I guess they'll have to wait for the car ride to . . . wherever Cooper plans to go next. I want to know about Bridget's disappearance and all the details they've collected so far. That's taking up probably 95 percent of my brain space. But if I'm being honest, 5 percent is taken up with me wondering about what this means for Cooper and me. If he's still turning to me in times of trouble, is there a chance for us? Or will things go back to cold and hostile as soon as we find Bridget?

I'm afraid to know the answers, so I don't ask the questions. Plus, it's awfully selfish of me to even think of that when Bridget is missing. Our number one priority needs to be Bridget. But she's going to be fine, right? She has to be fine. There's no other option.

Cooper's face is pale, and I know he's considered the other option.

Mine blanches a little, too, as I get into the car. He's counting on me to help, but I'm only smart about certain things. It's not like Bridget is missing in space. Still, it's Cooper. He needs me, and I'm here for him. NASA seems almost (but only almost) insignificant in the face of this bigger problem.

Even though I know superstitions are dumb, I cross my fingers and hope for good news.

24

It's past two in the morning, and Bridget still isn't back.

Although the search-party thread is now riddled with texts in various stages of caps lock and emojis, none of it is organized. Everyone is panicking. When I first agreed to help, Cooper and I drove back to his house together.

It was mayhem all evening.

I kept trying to logic through this: Maybe she went out with a friend and lost her phone. Perhaps she was training somewhere else? All of my arguments were thin, and they became even more emaciated as the evening went on. Now they are pretty much dead. Something is wrong.

Our biggest breakthrough came at seven o'clock, when Bridget's coach called and informed Mrs. Evans that he'd discovered Bridget was ineligible to play in the finals. Her chemistry grade had dropped below a seventy. He called the chemistry teacher and the principal after getting the email and argued for a half an hour, but neither would budge. "School policy," they kept saying. "Rules are rules."

Bridget must have known. When she found out she wouldn't be able to play in the finals, she must have been so panicked that she . . .

THAT SHE DID WHAT?

It's the question we've been trying to answer. What would she do? She doesn't have a car. Where could she have gone?

We searched all around the school and the school grounds, but the area yielded nothing. The volleyball team is an emotional mess, but they all got sent home at ten because Mr. and Mrs. Evans said Bridget would want them to rest up and be able to play in the tournament, regardless of whether or not she was there. They protested, but they all knew it's what she would want. The finals are against the school that defeated ours last year, and we all are hoping that Bridget might magically show up at the game.

But to show up and not play? It would kill her.

"Where *is* she?" Mrs. Evans breaks down crying again. There are already Kleenexes littering the floor, and she's sitting on the drool-splotched couch. Two of her closest friends have stayed. Norman is sitting on the couch, quiet. His boisterous personality is gone, and his body seems empty without it. He's petting Chewy on the head and staring at the carpet in front of him, like if he thinks hard enough, the answer will materialize in his brain. Every once in a while, he rubs his wife's back. She seems to barely notice. His neon has gone out. Like a neon sign that has been turned off, he looks like a darkened shell.

"I'm sure she'll be back soon," one of Mrs. Evans's friends says. She tries to smile but also gives a furtive look to the friend sitting on the other side of her. None of us are sure of anything.

Mrs. Evans takes out her phone and dials three digits. It's like we all tense up and sigh, defeated, at the same time.

"Honey," her friend says. "You've already called." The friend tries to take the phone away, but Mrs. Evans stands up and slaps her friend's hand.

"If I bother them enough, maybe they'll care about her!" Mrs. Evans is borderline hyperventilating. Her voice is loud but breaking, and her hair flips wildly as she shakes it out of her eyes. She starts yelling at the 911 operator, and this isn't the first time tonight she's done that.

I'm not sure what's scarier—Cooper's mom's hysteria or his dad's complete shutdown. Both are so out of character for how I've seen them before. I've been thrust back into Cooper's world, but it's all twisted now. It's like the same song but in a minor key. Do I even belong in this world at all? Is there room in this version (or any version) for me?

Cooper grabs the phone from his mom's hand. Her eyes narrow like this is the worst betrayal, and she clambers to get it back.

"Mom," he says. "They said they'll charge you with a misdemeanor if you keep calling. You have to stop calling." He takes her phone with him to the kitchen.

I should go. This isn't any of my business. I tried to leave at ten, eleven, and one, but each time, Cooper asked me to stay. At this point I'm not sure if I'm there for Cooper, for Bridget, or for no reason at all. A quick glance to my watch tells me it's 2:07 a.m.

I'm supposed to be taking the SAT in less than six hours.

My dad went to bed at ten and told me to come home whenever I can. He offered to help, but there's nothing he can do.

That's the hardest part—there's not anything any of us can do. We can try to keep Mrs. Evans rational, but that's about it. And it's not even working. I get up to follow Cooper.

"I want my phone back!" his mom yells from the living room. "She could call any second!"

Cooper puts the phone on the kitchen counter, his eyes wet as he looks at it and then looks at me. "Do I get rid of it?" he whispers.

I take the phone as if I have an idea what to do with it, but I just stuff it in my pocket and give Cooper a hug. "It's going to be fine," I say, though that feels like a lie.

Can I take the SAT on five hours of sleep? Four? None? It's like I'm watching my score drop in front of my eyes, but it seems selfish to care about a test at a time like this. I'm a terrible person. I hug Cooper tighter, as if I can squeeze these awful thoughts out of me. The SAT doesn't matter.

That's not true. It matters to me.

Perhaps my situation right now would have been different if I'd told Cooper sooner. He doesn't know I have the test scheduled for tomorrow, and if I told him now, I would add guilt to the top of everything else he's going through. I might be selfish in my head, but at least I'm caring enough to keep it there. That should be worth something, right?

Can I let it go? Can I let go of something that means so much me in order to help someone who might not even care about me once we find her? After all, I only agreed to help find

Bridget. Neither Cooper nor I have been brave enough to bring up anything past that. Can I stay here in this moment, focusing on Cooper and what he needs, no matter what it costs me? What would my mom do in a situation like this?

For the first time, I realize that what my mom would do and what I should do might not be the same thing.

It is 3:14 a.m. when I decide to leave Cooper's house. His mom and dad have fallen asleep, and Cooper is trying to stay awake, but his eyelids keep closing and then fluttering back open. Finally, he admits that he is tired, and he says he'll take me home. He asks if I'll come over again once I've gotten some sleep.

I pause before nodding. Bridget will be home soon, right? I'll go over as soon as I finish with the SAT. Surely by then all of this will be over.

And then what? Does he actually want me, or does he want what I can offer in a crisis? I don't dare to get my hopes up.

It was 3:50 when I set my alarm for 6:30. I fell asleep without changing my clothes, justifying the poor hygiene by telling myself I'd be saving valuable minutes when it was time to wake up.

Now I'm standing in front of my mirror, clothes rumpled and hair crazy, and I'm wondering if I can get away with ten more minutes of sleep. No one cares about what I look like at this test, right?

As I crawl back into bed, my door opens.

"Happy test day, SkyBear!" my dad says. I groan and roll over, as sleepy as if he just woke me up. "I made your favorite breakfast!"

"You cooked?" I'm in that groggy place between awake and asleep. "Our oven is burned out."

"Perhaps *made* is a loose term. Come on, get up! It's your big day!" His cheery face clouds over a bit. "You didn't stay out too late, did you? You said you were heading home soon when I texted you at ten."

"Right." I rub my eyes. "It wasn't too much later than that."

Which, if you look at the scope of the eternity of time, it really wasn't. It's not a lie if you look at the bigger picture.

"I'll be downstairs," he says. "You don't want to be late." He whistles as he leaves. I groan again.

I heave myself out of bed and throw another glance in the mirror. Yep, my MIT T-shirt is still wrinkled. My jeans have probably left red crease lines on my legs, but I'm not changing.

A quick check to my phone yields no news, and my heart sinks. Cooper will be expecting me at his house this morning.

After about sixty seconds of brushing my teeth and half-heartedly running a brush through my hair, I figure that's about as good as it's going to get.

You know, a shower would probably help me wake up.

Nope, forget it. Let's get the massacre over with.

When I get downstairs, my dad has our best china laid out. A McDonald's bacon-egg-and-cheese bagel sits in the middle of my plate with a hash brown next to it.

"You got McDonald's?" I ask.

"Yep!" he says, his chipper attitude back. "These plates and glasses were in a box in the basement. We never used fancy plates because they're not machine washable, but ha! We don't have a usable dishwasher." He looks proud of this argument, even though there's a pile of paper plates on the counter that we've been using all week.

It's sweet that he cares so much about me. A pang of regret tugs at my stomach—I should have come home sooner. Who goes through this much for an ex-friend? Cooper wasn't even technically my boyfriend, though we definitely seemed more than friends to me. What did he think? What does he think now?

"Shall I pour the orange juice?" My dad holds a McDonald's cup over a crystal glass.

I throw my hands up. "Sure."

The china plates on the dining room table are white with a thin gold ring around the sides. The gold part is starting to tarnish.

"Cheers to you," my dad says, holding up his McDonald's orange juice in its crystal glass. "Today is one step closer to the stars. One day, we'll drink champagne from these glasses. As for today"—he puts on a terrible French accent that sounds like he has a cold—"*Mac-Dohnald's*!" He takes a sip and laughs, his bony shoulders shaking his plaid shirt. His hair is sticking out all crazy like mine, and it's easy to tell we're related.

"Today's a step to somewhere," I say with a shrug, clinking my glass to his. Who knows? Maybe there will be an SAT-day miracle and I'll do well. There could be a fluke in their grading system that gives me a perfect score.

Or I could score less than I did last time. It's hard to swallow my orange juice.

"Dad, if I don't do well . . . I mean, if this goes like last time, or worse . . ." It's hard to look at him, so I study my orange juice. There are little bits of pulp in it.

"You won't. You're the smartest person I've known since . . . uh, the smartest person I know." He takes a bigger swig of orange juice.

"Since Mom. I get it." My ribs pull tighter. "I'm not her. Look at my hair. I'm half your dorky genes." I point to my head, trying to stave off tension.

He puts his glass down, and his mouth is smiling even though his eyes look sad. "I know, SkyBear. Don't worry about the SAT. MIT and eventually NASA would be great. You've always shot for the stars, but it's a big world down on this planet, too. Sometimes I worry you're missing this world because you're so focused on that one. Like how I was so focused on microscopic organisms that I missed the big picture. But, in honor of turning over my new, super-supportive leaf"—he gestures to the table—"test-day breakfast. Because what matters to you matters to me."

After breakfast, my dad gives me a kiss on my messy hair before heading off to work—he's needed at the hospital even on weekends. A glance at our wall clock says I might have time to run a brush through my hair, but I decide not to. Maybe my dad's mad-scientist look will be lucky.

My backpack has my calculator, five sharpened number-two pencils, and a protein bar for sustenance. I'm as ready as I'll ever be.

My eyes are heavy as I drive out of the driveway, but I blink fast to make sure I can stay awake. The test is only a few hours, and then I can crash back into bed.

No, wait—I have to go over to Cooper's again afterward.

This might be a long day.

I look into my rearview mirror, resolute, and say, "You've got this."

I daydream as I drive to the testing site—the students on the MIT website always look so happy. They hold textbooks and laugh as they stroll past the majestic, columned buildings and the sleek, modern ones. It's the mix of old and new that has always appealed to me, even though I've never been there. Dad never had time to take me.

Now things are different. I'll take this test, but before I get my scores back and the dream really dies, maybe I should go. I could fly out there, bring one of my textbooks, and walk around like those laughing students. It would be fun to live the dream, even if it was only for a day. I could find their weird beaver mascot and take a selfie. He's on the MIT website, and a random person in a beaver costume wouldn't care about my admissions status. The idea starts to solidify in my mind: one day of the vision, even a bitter day, is better than none. I've stayed awake on countless nights, dreaming of that campus.

OH MY GOSH.

I think I know where Bridget is. I pull out my phone and try to call Cooper, but then I slam on my brakes to stop for a red light. Oops. The person behind me honks.

No, calling Cooper isn't a great idea. For one thing, I'll get in a crash. For another, I don't know if I'm right. No reason to get his and his parents' hopes up for nothing. Mrs. Evans would immediately go search, and if I'm wrong, she might kill me.

I bite my lip while I wait for the red light to turn green. If she's where I think she is, she'll stay there until after the test, right? I can go after the test.

But what if she leaves? What if I'm two minutes too late, and she does something desperate or runs away forever? What if I miss her by seconds? All because I wanted to chase a long shot?

My car feels very claustrophobic. When did the air get so thick? I'm not mature enough to make these decisions. Missing the SAT means throwing away my last opportunity to shine up my admissions profile, but taking the test could mean missing Bridget.

When I put it that way, the answer seems clear.

I throw on my blinker and turn into the nearest parking lot. The car behind me honks again, and the guy gives me the finger as he passes me.

After a perfect three-point turn, I'm back on the road and zooming toward my destination.

25

"Excuse me? Hi." I say to a random student. This person doesn't look anything like the smiling, intelligent students on every college's website. She looks kind of hungover and stressed.

Come to think of it, so do I.

"Yeah?" she asks. She's wearing a UNIVERSITY OF NEVADA, LAS VEGAS T-shirt and carrying a low-hanging black backpack. Her jeans have holes in them, but they look like the expensive type of jeans that came that way. She has the big, buggy sunglasses that Charli might say are "so this season." I would have asked someone else, but the campus is deserted on a Saturday morning.

"Yes, um, hello. Have you seen my friend?" I hold up a picture of Bridget on my phone.

She takes off her sunglasses to get a closer look. Good—maybe this is sparking a memory. Hopefully she'll say, "Oh yes, she's right over there," and this whole thing will be over.

"Nope, haven't seen her." She puts her sunglasses back on. "Is she a Gamma?"

Gamma rays are strong electromagnetic radiation. They have high photon energy, and they can be harmful to humans in high doses. They can even mutate DNA. Is this some college slang, like "Is she a harmful type of human?"

I shake my head so hard that my hair falls in my face. "No, definitely not a gamma. She's the opposite of a gamma."

The girl with the buggy sunglasses raises her eyebrows and shrugs. "Okay. Yeah, no idea then. Sorry." She heads on, leaving me to look for more advice.

Three people later, no one has seen Bridget. This was a dumb idea, and I want to kick myself. Even if she did come here, how did I think I would be able to find her on this huge campus?

I pass the Robert L. Bigelow Physics Building, and I want to go in. Maybe some scientist could help me organize my search into a more logical pattern. Physicists have always been my people.

Another student passes by, and I stop him. He's a large guy with glasses, and he's wearing a tight, light green shirt. Maybe it's a muscle tee? I don't know. Note to self: ask Charli what a muscle tee is later.

"Excuse me, have you seen my friend?" I ask.

He squints at the phone and says no, as usual.

Then I get an idea. "Where do sports people go around here?"

"Sports people?"

"If I were on the volleyball team, where would I go?"

He folds his arms. "You're on the volleyball team?"

He doesn't have to look so skeptical. Sheesh. So what if I'm five foot two and haven't changed my clothes in twenty-four hours? I clean up pretty nice, and I'm limber.

"I have amazing ups," I offer, emphasizing *ups* so he'll think I'm a savvy volleyball player.

"Okay," he says slowly, unconvinced.

"It means 'to jump high,'" I explain.

"I know." He rolls his eyes. "But if you play volleyball, why don't you know where Cox Pavilion is?"

Oh my gosh. "JUST TELL ME WHERE IT IS," I almost yell.

My crazy eyes probably match my hair, because Muscle Tee holds up his hands and takes a step back.

"Fine. Chill. Sorry," he says. "It's by the library, okay? A two- or three-minute walk from there."

He walks on before I can tell him how unhelpful that is to someone who doesn't know the campus.

Soon, however, I'm standing in front of the building where the volleyball team practices. Part of me wants to rush inside, but part of me is scared. If Bridget's not here, I threw away the SAT for nothing.

I dig around in my brain to come up with another idea of where she might be. If I have a backup idea, then this one failing won't hurt so bad.

Nothing.

My phone tells me that the SAT has already started. No way they'd let me in at this point. This building in front of me is my last hope.

I fill my lungs to capacity and exhale slowly before opening the front door.

It's locked.

"Arrrrgh!" I pound my fist on the door in frustration. What time do they open? I look around until I see the small white lettering on the glass beside the door. Nine o'clock on Saturdays.

Why couldn't today be Thursday? They open at six on Thursdays! And Tuesday! And Wednesday! All the weekdays! WHY ARE COLLEGE STUDENTS SO LAZY ON WEEKENDS?

When I'm in college, I'm going to work out on Saturday mornings. Early. Because all campus buildings need to be open early on Saturdays, and I'll start the revolution. There will be a petition, and my whole exercise club will sign it, and we'll make sure that people getting locked out of the exercise buildings never happens again.

That means I might need to start exercising before college, but I have a semester of high school left. I'll find a fabulous, fit hobby.

I look around to see if perhaps there's a stray open window or other obvious place to break into this building. Unsurprisingly, there is not.

A janitor comes to the door and opens it a crack. "We're not open until nine."

"Oh!" I rush over to him. "Hi. Have you seen my friend?"

He says no before he even looks at my phone.

"Please," I say. "She might have been here. Can I look for her? It will only take a minute."

"No one's allowed in the complex overnight," he replies.

"That's exactly the kind of thing that wouldn't matter to her," I say. "Come on, please? What if she's hiding?"

"This isn't a place for sleepover parties," he says. "She's not here." He tries to shut the door, but I pull it back open.

"Listen. I've been looking for her all night. I'm not leaving here until I look for her in that building, so either I'm going to go literally pound on every door in this building until nine o'clock on the dot, or you can let me in now. I'll be out of your way, and you won't have a headache. It's a win-win."

He looks me up and down, and my desperate appearance works in my favor. "Fine," he says. "I'm giving you ten minutes, and then you leave me alone and scram. Capeesh?"

"Absolutely. Thank you so much." I yank the door fully open and rush past him before he has a chance to change his mind.

My footsteps echo as I run down the long hallway. My first stop is the gym, but it's empty. Then I try the bathrooms, flashing back to when Bridget hid in the bathroom at school during the Andrew fiasco. Nothing—all stall doors open. Maybe there are other bathrooms? I keep running, frantic. She has to be here.

Many office doors are locked, and I don't dare track down the janitor and ask for keys. It's been more than ten minutes before I get back to the front doors, and he'll be looking to throw me out.

Finally, I go back to the darkened gym and sit on the bottom red bleacher. The only light streams in from a few small windows near the ceiling, and it casts long rectangles on the gym floor. I put my elbows on my knees and my head in my hands, like how someone seeking religion might sit in a church. I don't know where else to go to find her.

After a few minutes of silence, the door opens. I jump to my feet.

"Bridget?" I call.

Hope surges through me. Light spills from the doorway into the gym, and whoever's there reaches out and flips the light switches. The faint buzz of fluorescents fills the room as the lights start to wake up for the day.

"You'd best be going," a gruff voice says. "I told ya she ain't here."

Oh. The janitor.

There has to be some reason for me to stay. Maybe I haven't looked in the right places. "There are some offices," I offer. "Maybe we could try there?"

"No." His voice is hard without any room for negotiation. "You said ten minutes. It's been way more."

"Sky?" a voice whispers from behind me. "Is that you?"

I spin around so fast that I feel lightheaded. Only an empty set of bleachers is behind me. Am I having auditory hallucinations? After all, that occurs in almost 8 percent of adults, so it could be that.

"Sky," the voice says again. "Down here."

What the . . . ? Someone is waving, and then I see Bridget's shadowed face under the bleachers.

"Bridget!" I yell. I clamber to hug her but can't get through the bleachers. Dang it. I crawl back out and run around to the side.

She tries to say "Shhh," but I'm not shhhh-ed.

"Where have you been? I can't believe you're here." I'm hugging her so tightly that I might break her ribs. "Are you okay?

What happened? What is *wrong* with you? Why didn't you call your mom?"

My feelings are vacillating between wanting to keep hugging her and to punch her, but I stick with hugging her because that is more socially acceptable. Also, she looks a little pathetic. Her gym clothes are wrinkled, and her hair looks worse than mine. The side she slept on sticks to her head like she sprayed it there.

"Hey!" the janitor calls. "Get out! Who's there?"

"I'm really sorry!" Bridget walks toward the janitor with her hands up like a criminal proving she's unarmed. "I didn't mean to. I fell asleep under there. When I woke up it was dark, and I didn't want to trip the alarms. I was gonna leave as soon as you opened up for the morning—promise. Please don't arrest me."

The janitor throws his head back and sighs, like he can't believe all the stupidity he's had to handle even before the complex opened today. "Get out," he says again. "Both of you. Right now."

"Got it," Bridget says as she sprints for the door. I run, too, but she's a lot faster than I am. By the time we're back outside in the sun, I'm winded and she's fine.

"Where . . . is . . . your . . . phone?" I ask between breaths. "We've all called you a hundred million times."

Bridget gives me a hug. "I thought the night security guard was going to shoot me."

"What the heck? Does he even have a gun?"

Bridget rolls her eyes. "Have you never seen a movie?"

"What kind of movies are there about college-gym night security guards?"

"You know, the security movies." She waves her hand like my question is a pesky fly. "*Oceans 11*, *Heist* . . . *Mall Cop*. Those ones."

The bright sunshine is giving me a headache, and I put my fingers to my temples. There's a red bench outside the rec center, and I sit. "Call your mom."

"I left my phone at school yesterday."

I fish my phone out of my pocket and hand it to her.

Bridget, still standing, looks at it as if it's a grenade. Her voices gets at least three pitches higher. "Um, I don't think so." She attempts to smooth her crazy hair. "The thing is, she might be a little mad at me for staying out past curfew. Will you call?"

Last night's hysterical Mrs. Evans flashes through my mind. "Absolutely not. Your mess, your call."

She sits next to me and puts her arm on mine like we're best friends. "But you're so good with words, Skyler! And people are drawn to you, you know? You always know what to say."

I raise my eyebrows. That's not even a good lie.

Bridget nods and takes her arm off mine. "Right." She puts her hand in her chin and taps her nose while she tries to think of another solution. "Oh! How about I give you ten bucks?"

"No."

"Twenty?"

"No."

"How about—"

I grab her shoulders to cut her off. "Listen, Bridget. I'm not calling your mom. Call Cooper or somebody, but I'm not doing this for you."

Her face falls in defeat. "They're not going to understand."

"Then you might as well get it over with." I pick up her hand and put my phone in it.

"How about I call the Uber driver instead? The one who brought me here? Turns out I totally pass for eighteen. I can start a new life somewhere and pretend this never happened."

"That seems like an ill-formed plan." I'm tempted to point out that getting locked in the gym overnight was also an ill-formed plan, but I resist.

Two girls wearing high ponytails and tight shorts walk past us toward the doors of the gym. One of them is carrying a volleyball.

Bridget looks at them, and a flash of pain crosses her face. She turns to me. "Also, I'm mad at you!"

Her emotional switch from jubilation to sadness to anger is giving me whiplash. "What?"

"Yeah—this is all your fault!" She stands up like she just remembered I have an infectious disease. "How could you do this to me?"

Wait, I'm the one who found her hiding under the gym bleachers. I'm the one who gave up my SAT retake to look for her, and now *she's* mad at *me*? How is anything in this situation my fault? If life had a rewind button, I'd go back to that part where I decided to skip the test. Then I'd keep driving instead. I could be could be answering math questions right now instead of watching Bridget have a meltdown. Someone somewhere in the country is—at this very moment—getting a score that will get them into MIT. That someone could have been me, and I gave it up for this. The thought makes my stomach tighten. The headache comes back.

"How is this my fault?"

"Because . . ." She falters, clearly not wanting to explain why this is my fault. After a deep breath, her words come out in a rush. "You might as well know. I'm not eligible for volleyball anymore, okay? I can't play in the state finals. College scouts will be there, and where will I be? Not there! If I went to the game, I'd look like I was doing the freaking walk of shame, and it's all because you stopped tutoring me in chemistry. If you and Coop had been able to work out your fight about your stupid video, this wouldn't have happened." She folds her arms like this is an airtight accusation.

"I didn't choose to stop tutoring you. You said you didn't want me to do it anymore."

"Argh!" She throws up her hands and starts pacing. "It would have been weird for Cooper, and I am a *good sister*. He got all sad whenever I mentioned you. He was all, 'I love her and can't hold her back,' which is so bogus and never works, and you were all, 'I'm science-y and don't do feelings,' which never works, either, and you're idiots who cost me a scholarship, and that makes me *very mad at you*." She pauses. "I mean you and Cooper. I'm mad at both of you."

"He said *what*?"

Cooper told Bridget he loves me? How long ago? Does he still? My tight stomach now feels a little fluttery. I push some hair behind my ear.

"You are both so *stuuuupid*," she whines. She goes behind the bench and flops down in the soft, green grass, lying on her back and stretching out as much as possible. "You are the one who's bad at chemistry, I swear. And I'm the one getting punished. What's more important in life—knowing when a guy loves you or knowing that there are five carbons in a benzene ring? Huh? Because one of those pieces of information is pointless."

"There are six carbons in a benzene ring."

Bridget holds up my phone and turns her head toward me. "I will throw this. Hard."

"Give me that." I jump up and swipe the phone from her. She could have fought back, but she seems out of energy.

Bridget sighs again and rolls onto her stomach. "Forget it. This is my fault." She buries her face in the grass and says something that is probably "I'm a moron" but ends up sounding like "Ibamohon."

My phone shows a text from Charli. Hi, girlie. Did you see you're a little bit trending? Hope that's okay. I told my manager to hold off posting until I chatted with you, but looks like it went live yesterday. I'll pull it if you give the word!

I'm trending? I'm about to text Charli back when Bridget pulls her face out of the grass and rests her chin on her hands.

"How am I supposed to tell my team?"

"They already know."

"They do?" She props up to her elbows, looking hopeful and scared at the same time. "Are they mad?"

"No. They're freaking out about finding you."

"What?" She looks confused. "I'm not even missing. Everyone knows that you can't file a missing person report until someone has been gone for twenty-four hours."

"Actually, you don't have to wait to file a report about a missing person in Las Vegas," I tell her. I know this only because of all the messages I saw on Instagram in the middle of the night.

"Give me your phone." She holds out her hand. Now she's interested in telling people she's fine? "I don't want stress to affect their game today. They're my team, after all."

The sleeplessness will probably affect their game anyway, but I keep my mouth shut and hand her the phone. At least she's going to tell someone.

"Do you have Bailey's number in here?"

"Who?"

"Bailey DiMarco."

"No."

"Kailey Streetfield?"

"I don't know who that is."

"Ugh. Can I get on my Insta from here?" She starts fiddling with my phone.

"Your family's going to kill you if you don't call them first."

She stares me down. Neither of us speaks for about fifteen seconds. Another person walks toward the gym, but we don't turn.

Bridget blinks first. "Fine. But I'm calling Cooper, not my mom."

"Fine with me."

She dials and holds my phone up to her ear. After about five seconds, she says, "Hi, uh Coop? It's Bridget."

Even though the phone's not on speaker, I hear him yell, "Mom! It's Bridge!" Then he says something indistinguishable.

"Yeah, I'm fine," she responds. "I'm with Skyler."

Bridget listens and looks confused. "No, I'm not taking the SAT. Are you high?" A moment later, she turns to me. "Hey,

Cooper talked to Charli. Did you know you're supposed to be taking the SAT right now?"

I purse my lips. "It has occurred to me."

She turns back to the phone. "I guess she just remembered."

26

Luckily, no one is home when I get home. My dad left a note saying he went in to work, and I'm not sure how to tell him I skipped the SAT. On the bright side, I did find Bridget. That has to make the loss worth something. Noble, in a way.

As I stare at our burned-out kitchen, it's like I'm watching ghosts of my mom and me making our Saturday cookies. The kitchen was brighter then, in so many ways. What would she say if she could see me now? Would her eyes be disappointed? Would she understand?

This fearful uncertainty reminds me of the first time I brought home a test I failed.

Well, I didn't fail it. I got an 87. But still.

I was in second grade, and it felt like a failure. My mom picked up the paper with the giant pink B on it, a history test on the American Revolution, and said, "Honey, it's a silly test. It's okay."

I burst into tears. She knelt down and hugged me, and I cried into her hair. It smelled like her mango shampoo. I told her I was sorry and that I had done my best. It felt like I sobbed for hours. Then she pulled me from her shoulder, looked me right in the eyes and said, "Never be sorry for doing your best." At the time, I didn't believe her—it seemed like a very mom thing to say. I'd never be sorry for doing my best, so as long as my best was better than everyone else.

The thing is, sometimes *my* best isn't *the* best.

"I did my best," I whisper to the burned-out kitchen. Not sure if I'm talking about the NASA internship or making the decision about the test today. I could be talking about getting to the NICER before it comes down or even knowing how to be a friend. But I've done my best, and here I am—no internship, no MIT admission, and a question mark as a future.

Three hours later, something wakes me up from an epic nap. What was that noise? I roll over and grab my phone, which I'd put on silent, and it's blown up with notifications. Texts, calls, Instagram notifications.

There's an insistent knock on my front door. That must have been what woke me up. I groan and roll out of bed. A quick check in the mirror tells me that I look worse than I did yesterday, which is impressive.

I sneak down the stairs so that the person on the other side of the door won't know I'm here if I decide not to answer. I could probably go back to sleep for another three hours.

Cooper is on the other side of the peephole, and he's just started to walk back to his car when I see him. I open the door, only moderately mortified at my appearance. Can I tell him to wait a second while I change into new clothes? Or maybe a few minutes while I shower?

Turns out I have time to do neither. He has heard the door. He turns, and his face breaks into a wide smile when he sees me. "There you are!"

He rushes through the door and gathers me into an awkward hug. "Thank you so much. *Thank you thank you thank you.*"

He pulls back enough to look at me. He looks cautiously optimistic, like he was expecting me to be mad.

"Did I wake you up?"

I could lie, but all the visual evidence points to his conclusion. Plus, I yawn. "Um, a little."

"I'm sorry. Go back to sleep. But thank you." He gives me another hug.

"Did they win the game?" I ask. When I dropped off Bridget, there was a disconcerting number of hugs and cheers and then people yelling at Bridget. They whisked her off to the game so she could support her team (after which she will be grounded for life), and I slipped out at the first available chance.

"Yes," Cooper says, but his smile falters. "They won. Tough for Bridge to watch them do it without her."

"Sorry." I'm not sure what else to say. "Do you want to come in and sit down?"

"Sure."

We sit at the kitchen table. The awkwardness feels thick. Now that I've helped find Bridget, what's left for us to say? Cooper says, "Sorry about—" right as I say, "What was the score of—"

"You go," I say.

"No, what were you saying?" Cooper asks.

"Nothing," I say. "Go ahead."

It's quiet for another second.

"Sorry about the NASA internship. I saw that you didn't get it, and I should have mentioned it sooner, but we were so focused on Bridget that I didn't think to say anything."

My back stiffens. "It's fine."

"It's not. The guy who got it looks like a jerk."

"Thanks."

"I didn't even understand his stupid research topic."

I smile. "You didn't understand mine, either."

He smiles back. The warmth melts the tension that existed a moment earlier. Cooper shrugs. "At least yours sounded cool. And I understood it a little."

"Oh really?" I raise my eyebrows. "What's a neutron star?"

He considers for a moment. "Your life."

I sigh and try not to cry again. "Not anymore."

"No. You don't get it." He puts his hand on my arm. "I know how a neutron star works. There's this star, right?" He holds his hands in front of him like he's holding an invisible star. "And it's huge—so bright that you can't even imagine it. Ten to twenty-nine solar masses." He holds the invisible star in front of his face while looking at me, like I need to see it to understand his oh-so-scientific model. "It's a star, doing star things, shining brighter than everything around it. Then something terrible happens. *Poof-shaww!*" He makes his hands do an exploding motion while he makes this bizarre sound effect.

An exploding star makes no sound because space is a vacuum, but I'll excuse it.

Cooper brushes his hand through his hair before continuing. "The star explodes, okay? And all this matter the star used to have blows off in layers, and the rest of it crumples in on itself, tighter and tighter, until all of the protons and electrons come together to form neutrons. You know what's at the center of the neutron star?"

"No."

"No one does. Yet." He puts his hand on mine. "You're a neutron star. You're going to pieces right now, but I'm going to pieces, too. Can we go to pieces together? One day maybe we'll find the core of this mess, and maybe it's the same type of core and maybe it's not, but I don't think either of us knows right now. We're too busy losing ourselves all over space."

His eyes leave mine only long enough to flicker to my lips before keeping my gaze again.

I should say no—he said no to me. It's close to the same situation really: showing up unannounced and putting ourselves out there. This would be a great time to show him how it felt for me that morning. The way that rejection cuts most when it comes from someone that you . . . love?

"I'm sorry," he says like he's reading my thoughts. "I know it might be too late. If that's the case, I deserve it. But when I saw that NASA announcement and it wasn't you, I was so mad, and

I couldn't imagine how you were feeling, and then it was even harder to imagine you feeling it alone. I already had a countdown to when you were leaving for the ISS so I would be able to watch news coverage and see your face every day and know what was happening in your life. Because I was missing you, okay? *So bad.* The only constant in life is chaos, and we have that in common. I'm sick of trying to pretend I'm over you. I want you to be my girlfriend. Let's give ourselves a chance."

For one second, the white-hot joy of hearing Cooper say those words makes everything else fade. The sting of failure doesn't go away, but it doesn't hurt as much in that moment. In what was possibly the worst scientific demonstration I have ever seen, he made more sense than a degree's worth of lectures.

What *is* at the core of a neutron star? What is at the core of me? Him? Any of us?

Like a scientist certain of a specific theory, I knew my core: it was to follow my mom. No, it was to *be* my mom. Like a copy/ paste function to finish the road she couldn't travel. Now that my theory hasn't turned out the way it was supposed to, I find myself in the footsteps of so many scientists before me and so many still to come: with a broken theory and no fresh one to replace it yet.

"Sky? Hello?" Cooper waves his hand in front of my face. "I'm all in over here, and you're giving me nothing." He tries to laugh, but it's halting and nervous.

"Right." My reverie is broken. "Yes."

"Yes?" His eyes are questioning.

Perhaps he's wondering if I agreed with his theory or if I meant, "Yes, let's give ourselves a chance."

"All the yes."

Before I think it through, my lips are on his. It's a soft kiss, not hungry, even though my nerves are all on fire. He puts his hand up to my face and kisses me back.

"Phew," Cooper says when he pulls away. "I'm so glad we're good. Especially considering Charli's video, I was so worried you'd be mad at me."

"What video?"

He tilts his head and starts to speak but then closes it again. After studying my face, something seems to click. "Oh no. You haven't seen it, have you?"

"Seen what?"

He runs both hands through his hair and rests them on the back of his neck, his head down. When he looks up, he forces a small laugh. "It's funny, if you think about it. And not a big deal at all. It was a misunderstanding, which wasn't my fault. I could have been clearer, I guess, but you couldn't have expected me to know—"

I wave my hand in front of his face. "Know what?"

Cooper looks past me into the kitchen, as if he's looking for someone to back him up while telling me this news.

"You're freaking me out, Coop," I say.

"No—it's seriously no big deal." He puts his hands on both of my shoulders.

His grip is strong and reassuring.

"Didn't mean to make you nervous. It's super great, okay? Remember that. Super great."

His eyes fix on mine as if he can sear the reminder into my brain. Then he sighs and pulls out his phone. He starts fiddling around, talking to me but looking at his screen. "I finished the original video. We weren't talking, but Charli asked to see a copy. So yesterday, I guess she decided to post it, and . . . Here." He hands me his iPhone and taps his foot on the ground.

The video was posted by *Kisses From Charli* twenty hours ago. It's titled "The Gorgeous Story of the Girl Not Going to Space." The corner of the screen has a picture of me. The video has just over four million views.

There are four million people on this planet who have looked at my face?

No, wait—four million views. That's not necessarily four million people. If Cooper was nervous about it, he's probably watched it twenty times. Charli must have watched it a few times, too. Then there's her team who watches to make sure it's not glitchy, and that only leaves . . .

A lot of people.

My hands shake as I push play. Not sure if I want to maximize the screen, so for now I don't. It's as if keeping the screen small will keep the situation small, too.

Charli is wearing a white tank top in front of a purple background. As far as I can tell, she's not wearing makeup. Her hair is in a plain ponytail that drapes over her right shoulder.

"Hi, girlies!" she starts. "Charli here, bringing you a new kind of gorgeous. This is my friend Skyler."

She points to the picture of me in the corner. It's a still from Cooper's video where I'm in the library sitting next to a pile of books.

"Skyler was going to go to space." Charli points to her other side, where a picture of a nebula shows up.

What the heck? I wasn't going to visit a nebula. This is scientifically ridiculous.

Apparently, four million people don't care about that.

"She applied for an internship and got into the top ten candidates, but, unfortunately, she missed out on the final choice." A frowny face pops up at the bottom of the screen when Charli frowns.

For the love of . . .

"I don't know who deserved this chance more than Sky," Charli continues, "but I want y'all to hear her story. It's gorgeous, and not the kind that comes from a perfect contour. This girl"—she points to my picture again—"is more comfortable with herself than anyone I've ever known. She's smart, she's funny, and she's fabulous. Let's check it out."

The picture in the corner zooms in to take up the full screen, and Cooper's video begins.

"She's the Goose to my Maverick." I smile at the screen, pointing to Five while standing next to a telescope. When I peek through the telescope again, my own voice does the voiceover: "I want to finish my mom's research. Deep space travel could be at stake."

The scene cuts to me in the chemistry lab. While I'm messing around with a microscope, Cooper's voice cuts in. "Sky's mom died when she was in third grade, leaving Sky and her dad to bond over the thing they know best: science." A picture pops up of my dad and me after the seventh-grade science fair. We're wearing matching lab coats, which seemed cool when I was ten. We're looking at each other and smiling, and my project in the background is only sort of still smoking.

Where did Cooper get that picture? That wasn't in the first video I saw.

The narration continues. "Skyler's love of astrophysics grew as she used it to feel close to her mom. Renae Davidson was a pioneer in the astrophysics field before her untimely passing." A montage of pictures of my mom floods the screen: her standing next to grad school projects, her giving lectures, the TED talk she gave when I was in kindergarten. "Now, almost as if her mom's spirit has passed into Skyler, Sky can discuss astrophysics at a level that few of the rest of us understand."

Now the footage cuts to me sitting in my chair and lecturing the camera. "When the iron cores of aged massive stars, also supported by this electron pressure, exceed a critical mass and therefore a critical density, some of the electrons will have sufficient momentum to allow their capture onto protons within the nuclei, removing electrons, which softens the pressure exerted, which results in denser conditions, which hastens further electron capture—leading to the gravitational collapse of that iron core."

What's so complicated about that?

The next scene cuts to Vlogalicious, where my dad and I are taking notes. We're an island in a sea of neon colors. Cooper's voice cuts in. "Sky will go anywhere and do anything to support the people she loves, even if it's outside her comfort zone."

The vlog Charli pokes her head in from the side of the screen. "That's Vlogalicious, y'all!" Then she pops out, and it's only the video again.

"She names her lab rats by number, and she treats them as friends. She mourns them when they're gone." The video shows the small mound with Five's candle on top of it.

The video continues, mixing science with personal anecdotes. It's a strange experience to watch my life laid out in a three-minute video. And I have to admit, Cooper does a good job of getting the science right.

"In order to complete the research, Sky needs access to NICER, the Neutron Star Interior Composition Explorer. Tragically, this camera is coming down from the International Space Station next year. This may be Sky's only chance to complete the research and fulfill her lifelong dream."

A shot of the NICER fades from color to black-and-white, as if it has become a thing of the past.

"The mixture of prodigy, loyalty, and personality displayed by Skyler Davidson is unmatched by any other researcher her age. Given the opportunity, she won't just change the world. She'll change the universe."

The video ends, and Cooper is silent. He might be holding his breath. I wait for anger to flood me, or shame, or something. After all, four million people have peered into my three-minute life.

But I'm okay. I might even be good. All of those people heard my mom's story—our story. That may not get me any closer to the International Space Station, but my mom is one step closer to being remembered for the amazing woman she was. It feels like a little pressure has been taken off. If I couldn't put the story out there, at least someone did.

In the interest of keeping Cooper from passing out, I have to say something. "It's a good video," I offer.

"So it's okay?" His green eyes brighten but only slightly, like he's still unsure. "I know it's not the video you wanted."

The phone screen still hasn't darkened in my hand. "I'm sorry I didn't watch the whole thing before."

"Would it have made a difference?"

I think about this. "No, I don't think it would have."

Cooper massages his palms with his thumbs. "Then I'm confused."

"I was different before."

Cooper nods. "That makes sense to me."

"Does it? That makes one of us."

He smiles.

I want to watch the video again, but I bet Cooper has seen it a bunch of times.

My phone rings. It's Charli. I have no idea what to say to her. The last time I talked to her, I was yelling at her outside my bedroom. I'm ashamed at the memory, and *sorry* seems too small. But she's probably calling about the video, not my yelling, and I'm not sure what to say about that, either. She shouldn't have posted it without talking to me, but I also don't hate it. Am I mad? Grateful?

I ignore the call. "I'm so tired."

Cooper kisses my cheek. "Go back to sleep."

"Did you tell Bridget that you love me?"

Cooper's eyes widen. "That was abrupt."

"I told you, I'm tired." Also, I've been dying to know. But I don't mention that part.

Cooper shifts in his chair. "I don't remember everything I've ever said to my sister."

"That seems like the kind of thing you'd remember."

"Bridget can be dramatic."

"Is that what it was, then—just drama? You didn't say it?"

After an eternity, he says, "I don't know." I'm not sure if that means that he doesn't know if he said it or if he doesn't know whether or not he loves me, but either way, I have my answer.

I meet his eyes. He looks worried.

"That's okay," I say. "I'm not sure what I wanted your answer to be."

Which is true. Mostly.

My phone pings. It's a text from Charli. Please call me when you get this? If I don't hear from you soon, I'm going to pull the video.

Cooper sees the text. "You should call her."

"Probably."

We're quiet for a moment before Cooper says, "I'll catch up with you later, okay? I have to meet up with my mom for a stroller thing. Also, as we've established, you're tired." His mouth curls up on one side. "Can I see you later?"

"Definitely."

There's a pang of nervousness about meeting up with him—I don't want things to be awkward again—but something tells me it will be different now.

I should call Charli, but there's so much to say that I don't know where to start. Perhaps we should talk in person. I'm not hungry enough for burritos. I'm not transformed enough to go shopping.

I need an olive branch. Charli's always been kind to me, and she's been met with indifference at best. Now she's trying to support me in my space goals, and I haven't responded to her texts or to her calls. How can I show her that I want things to change? I text her the only peace offering that comes to mind:

Want to go stargazing with me?

After a pause, I add, The video is cool. Thanks.

She responds immediately: Love to, girlie. Followed by a heart emoji.

A week later, Charli is in my living room consulting with me about her new constellation nail designs. "Does this look like Scorpius to you?" she asks. She holds out her left index finger, where she has just finished putting on a clear polish topcoat. The nail color is a deep metallic blue. Tiny rhinestones form constellations. Her right fingers are decked out in Orion, Capricorn, Cassiopeia, Aquarius, and the Big Dipper.

"That is *awesome*," I say. And sure, the angle of Orion's belt is off by a few degrees, but I don't correct her.

"Good," she says. She blows on it. "One of the stones came off, and I'm filming in an hour. I'm going to include some of the information you taught me the other night about how ancient people used constellations for agriculture predictions and navigation. Turns out there's a hot market for science right now." She admires her nails. "Especially cute science."

"People will love them. I love them."

"I could do this on yours!" She offers. "Or you could pick from any of these sketches I'm trying."

She hands me a tiny sketchbook filled with colored designs, each more beautiful than the next. All space-themed. I especially love the one with a planet on each nail, and the thumbs say "RIP" and "Pluto."

"Yeah." I nod. "I'd like that."

"What did your dad say when he found out you didn't take the SAT?"

"Honestly, he didn't freak out nearly as much as I thought he would."

I'd explained about Bridget being missing and how I found her. While my dad didn't go so far as to say "I think you did the right thing," he didn't kill me either. So that's a plus.

"I don't think you give your dad enough credit. He really does care about you as a person, not just your accomplishments."

I shrug and say, "Yeah, maybe you're right."

And really, maybe she *is* right. Maybe I've been the one putting all this pressure on myself, and my dad only cheers me on because he know that following in my mom's footsteps is what I really want.

There's a scratching noise behind the couch. "What's that?" I ask.

"Oh, um, I got you something," Charli says. She looks a little nervous, which is rare for Charli. She hops off the couch and reaches behind it, pulling out a small travel cage. "I hope you like her." She puts the cage on the couch between us.

A small butterscotch-colored rat is sitting in the corner of the cage. She looks up at me with round eyes and wiggles her nose.

"She's so cute!" I exclaim. I open the cage and scoop the rat out. She gives my thumb a tentative lick.

"I thought you could use another rat."

"Thanks, Charli," I say. "I love her."

"I got her from your dad," Charli says, "So it's kind of from him, too. What will you call her? Six?"

Her name should be Six since she's my sixth rat, but naming rats after numbers never kept me unattached to them. Five's funeral proved it beyond the shadow of a doubt. It's science.

Maybe it's not science, actually. It's where science and humanity meet. Like the middle of a Venn diagram titled "My Existence."

The butterscotch color of her fur gives me an idea. "I think I'll call her Chip. Like a lucky butterscotch chip. I could use some luck."

"Butterscotch chips are lucky?" Charli looks a little confused.

"Yes. The thing is, when I was little, my mom and I used to bake cookies—"

My phone pings. I have a new email from a name I don't recognize. The subject line is Research Opportunity in Houston.

Other than the fact that Houston is in Texas, there is only one thing I know about it. But the thing I know is enough to make my hand start shaking before I can even open the email.

NASA has a space center in Houston.

27

Ms. Davidson:

My name is Caroline Burns. I worked with your mother for a year while I was completing my undergraduate studies at the Massachusetts Institute of Technology. She was doing her doctoral research at the time, and I was a lab assistant. Largely because of my work with Renae, I chose to shift my major from physics to astronomy and add a minor in aerospace.

While I am not familiar with your mother's postdoctoral research, I am interested in hearing more about your ideas on how to use the NICER to further our knowledge of deep space. A colleague sent me a link to a fashion video blog in which you discuss your thoughts on neutron star research, specifically in relation to Renae's work. Are you by chance the same Skyler Davidson who emailed me half a dozen times last year? Asking about access to ISS research? If so, my apologies for taking this long to get back to you.

I am now the physics department chair at the University of Texas at Austin. As you may know, we have produced more astronauts than almost any other university in the nation. Because of our proximity to NASA's Space Center in Houston, I work with many of the NASA researchers and have many students interning at NASA. I am sure my fellow researchers in Houston would love to hear more about your ideas. We may have the opportunity to pitch your plan for use by the current team at the ISS.

Would you be interested in coming to Texas for a visit? I would welcome the opportunity to meet you, talk about your research, and show you around campus. Although I assume you will have many college admissions offers, UT Austin offers physics department scholarships that could be of particular interest to you.

I would love to assist in any way, as I owe your mother a great debt of gratitude. While I was saddened to hear of her untimely passing, she is lucky to have you to carry her torch forward.

Sincerely,
Caroline Burns
Department Chair—Physics
University of Texas at Austin

"Is everything okay?" Charli asks. My eyes must be huge.

"Hold on," I say, scrolling to the top and reading again. Is this for real?

She knew my mom. There are never-before-heard memories about my mom, and I'll be able to hear them. And NICER? NICER! I reread that line twice: "We may have the opportunity to pitch your plan for use by the current team at the ISS."

My breathing feels shallow, and my limbs feel shaky. The chance that was so far gone suddenly . . . isn't? Could I finish the research?

I keep reading, though it's difficult to focus. Physics scholarships? I imagine myself going to school in Texas. The picture in my mind looks like my dreams of walking the campus at MIT, but now I'm wearing a cowboy hat. The cowboy hat looks good on me.

The words swim in front of me, and my free hand covers my mouth. So many scenarios are flying around that it's tough to keep them straight. Keep it together, Sky. It's just an opportunity, not a guarantee. I pet Chip and wonder if she's already bringing me good luck.

"Sky?" Charli tries again. "What's going on?"

I hand her my phone.

She's only about a paragraph in when her mouth drops. She reads a few more sentences and then screams. Then she starts jumping, and I don't know how she reads and jumps at the same time.

"Scholarship opportunities!" She shrieks. "And NASA? *Girlfriend!*" She starts to hug me but then stops herself and throws her hands up instead. "This is huge! How are you not freaking out?"

"I am freaking out," I say. "I freak out differently than you." I shake my limbs because adrenaline has made it all but impossible to stand still.

"Ahhhhhhh!" She rummages through her purse. "Here it is. Perfect!" She holds something up that I don't recognize. There's a loud pop, and then confetti rains down on me.

We're both laughing. She's kind of scream-laughing.

"You keep a confetti popper in your purse?" I say.

"For unexpected celebratory moments!" she says, like this is the most obvious thing in the world. "You never know when you might need a confetti popper!"

"My dad's going to kill you," I say, surveying the glitter and bits of paper on our floor. Chip brushes glitter from behind her ears and picks up a piece of confetti with her paw. Then she starts chewing on it.

"Ack! Not food!" I say, picking Chip up and brushing my shoulder off before setting her on it. "Here. Sit up here."

"The man burned down his kitchen and hasn't asked me one question about the remodel I designed. He won't mind." She tosses the popper on the couch. "Does he even know where the vacuum is?"

Good point.

Charli is smiling so wide that I can see every one of her perfect teeth. "The second you know anything for certain, you have to let me tell your fans. They'll be so happy for you."

"I don't have fans."

She crosses her arms. "You didn't read the comments on my last video, did you? I assure you; you have fans."

Of course I read every single comment on the video. She's right—I do have fans. My mom has fans. Even Cooper has fans. *We have fans.*

"Thanks," I say. I'm still trying to keep my hopes low—maybe this whole thing won't work out. But my hopes are not low.

Cooper is going to be so excited. Look what his video did.

Almost as if Charli can read my mind, she says, "You should call Cooper."

"Maybe I'll head over there in a minute." After all, I'd like to see Cooper anyway. If the email happens to come up, we'll talk about it (immediately when I get there). We've been hanging out almost every day. No project, no awkwardness. My stomach flutters as I think of the way his eyes sparkle when he looks at me. Not because we're business partners, but because he simply wants to be with me.

"Head over now," Charli says. "I have to do the measurements for the kitchen before I leave anyway." Charli studies her nails for a moment and then looks at me. "I'm proud to know you, girlie."

I give her a quick hug before I put Chip back in the travel cage and head out the door.

When I arrive at Cooper and Bridget's, they're in the backyard. She's standing near a tall pile of shoes, an impressive number of which are athletic shoes. He's behind a camera taking pictures of it.

"Should I do a hand on my hip?" she asks, trying it. "Does it look better if I cross my arms? No, that makes me look mad."

She's trying arm positions so quickly that I don't know how Cooper's shutter keeps up.

"What are you doing?" I ask.

"Shoe challenge," Bridget says through a glued-on smile. "To raise awareness."

Cooper pops up from his camera and starts scrolling through the pictures he's taken.

I look over his shoulder. There are a lot of pictures of Bridget and shoes. "Raising awareness for what?"

Bridget looks perplexed. "A disease, I think? Or maybe poverty?" She shrugs. "You make a shoe pile as tall as possible and post a pic to your socials. It's been trending all week."

I've never really understood people who do social media challenges just for the trend and not because they care about the cause, but there's a lot about Bridget I don't understand. It's not like she could balance a chemistry equation if I gave her a million dollars to do it. Still, I can be her friend; we don't have to have everything in common.

"What's up?" Cooper says. He snakes one hand behind my back while still clicking through pictures with the other. My body feels like one of those plasma globes where the electric current focuses wherever the hand touches it.

"Nothing much." I try to sound nonchalant.

Now I've waited a full ten seconds. Good. That's long enough, right?

"I got this email." It's already pulled up on my phone.

Cooper looks from his camera over to my phone. He gets through the first few lines and then looks away so that he can post his camera back on his tripod. He grabs my phone so he can hold it closer.

"Are you kidding me?" His eyes are huge, and his mouth is open. "Houston? *NASA?*"

"Because of your video, Coop."

If possible, his eyes get bigger. "Sky," he grabs my shoulders, "We did it." He starts laughing, and there are tears in his eyes. "We seriously did it." He pulls me into a crushing hug.

Bridget runs over to see what's going on. Just then, the back door opens. Chewy bumbles out, and Snickers streaks right for the shoes. He's gleeful as he slams into them.

"Noooo!" Bridget yells. "Snickers! You're wrecking the awareness!"

Snickers picks a dirty Nike and chews it experimentally. Then he moves on to a shinier Reebok.

"Stop it!"

Bridget tries to pull the Reebok out of Snickers's mouth as Chewy finally makes it to the pile. He picks up the shoe closest to him, a brand I don't recognize, and saunters off to the side of the yard.

"Arrrgh!" Bridget scoops Snickers up, shoe still in his mouth, and heads for Chewy. "A little assistance?"

Cooper picks the camera up again. "Don't worry—I'll get it." He starts clicking.

For the next two minutes, Bridget and I chase dogs while Cooper carries in shoes. Every time he comes out to get more shoes, he kisses me as he runs by. I finally catch Snickers, who wiggles around in my arms. Cooper catches me for yet another kiss.

"Get a room," Bridget calls from across the yard.

"Come on, Sky," Cooper says. "You heard her." He picks up two more shoes and heads for the door. I let Snickers loose, and he beelines for one of the leftover shoes.

Cooper and I run to the living room, and he gives me a deep kiss. He holds me so tightly that I might melt into him, and I don't mind at all.

"Houston," he says, still holding me. "I've never been. Might have to visit."

"It's only a three-hour flight."

"You can see yourself there for college?" His eyes show a hint of concern. "It's not MIT."

I picture my cowboy hat again. "Yes. This opportunity would be . . ." I nod. "Definitely yes."

He rubs my back, setting my nerves on fire. "Long distance for us, then. You up for it?" He smiles, which makes me think he already knows the answer.

"Of course. Are you?"

He pulls my waist tighter to his. "I couldn't stop loving you even when I thought you were going to be in space. Houston's right next door." He kisses me again.

He loves me?

I would have thought my body was out of adrenaline at this point, but it's not. It's like that word left his lips and sent a shock to my heart. I think it stops. When we part, I try to read his beautiful green-gold eyes. "I thought you didn't remember saying that to Bridget?"

His face flushes. "I don't."

"But you do mean it?" It feels like my whole body holds its breath at once—like all systems shut down to wait on this answer.

He bites his lip before nodding. "I don't want to make things weird if you're not there yet, but yeah. You're all I think about. You're so driven, you're a frickin' genius, and one day you'll be the first person in history to look sexy in a spacesuit. You make me smile and laugh, and frankly, I'm the luckiest guy in the world to be the one holding you right now. I love you, Sky."

A million words catch in my throat. The skin on the back of his neck is soft and warm beneath my fingers. I think back to the first time we met in the band room, how that first handshake was so electric. If only that Sky could have known what it felt like to be pressed up against him like this. She might have fainted. I feel a little lightheaded myself, but in the best possible way. It's not only the feel of him, either. His words have set off a confetti popper in my stomach. And in my brain. So although there are so many things I want to say, only one line comes out.

"I love you, too."

His dimples run deep.

Then he kisses me. Or maybe I kiss him. By the time we finish kissing, neither of us remembers who started it.

28

NINE MONTHS LATER

My dad's the one who drops me off at the airport. Charli, Cooper, and Bridget all offer, but I decide to go with just him. There was a going-away party last night, and Cooper is flying down next weekend to visit. This feels right for today.

I'm wearing the UNIVERSITY OF TEXAS shirt that Charli bought me when I signed for my full-ride scholarship. It's orange with the longhorn logo on the front.

My mom's dissertation sits at home on the bookshelf, waiting for me to come back someday. In Houston, there will be my own papers to write. One day, I'll put my dissertation next to hers. Who knows what it will be about?

"Here we are," my dad says. "Looks like your flight is on time."

There's a hint of disappointment in his voice, like he's wishing for a delay. He insisted on walking me into the terminal. Now my bags are checked, and we're staring at the bright screen displaying dozens of flights. The airport slot machines clink happily in the background. The Houston airport doesn't have slot machines.

There are people rushing around, talking on phones and looking at watches, and no one notices the lanky man and the girl with the NASA backpack.

"Want a snack?" he says, eyeing a convenience kiosk. "I want candy."

I don't think either of us is hungry, but we're delaying the inevitable. He gets a Butterfinger. I get a Crunch bar.

We sit on a bench, and my dad takes a bite of his Butterfinger like we have all the time in the world to sit here and talk. I wish we did.

"What's Cooper up to tonight?" he asks.

"He has orientation at the community college."

A piece of chocolate flakes off, and my dad brushes it onto the floor. "How's the new guy working out at the store?"

"Cooper will still be training him for a while. After all, it's just a kid from the film club. But he's cheap, he's great with technology, and it gives Cooper's dad another semester to figure things out before Cooper heads to Utah."

"And the kid can stay when Cooper leaves?"

"If they need him to, yeah. He's only a sophomore. Hopefully they'll be able to get someone certified, but they've got the help if they need it. And with Coop's scholarship on the deferred admission, it's not like he'll need money from them." I take a bite of my Crunch.

A few minutes later, we're picking bits out of the bottom of the wrappers as if we could make more candy exist. When there isn't any, we admit the inevitable and stand up. It's time to go.

"I remember the day I dropped you off at kindergarten," my dad says. "You had a NASA backpack then, too."

"That one wasn't actually *from* NASA."

He touches mine, tears welling in his eyes. "Still hard to believe this one is."

"I know." My eyes start to water. "My security clearance should come through just in time for me to start with the research team on Thursday."

"You'd better not skip class to hang out with the researchers."

"I won't." I try to smile, but my eyes are still teary.

My dad hugs me tight, and I'm not sure when I'll next see him. I've changed my mind—people don't hug enough.

"Before you go," he says, "I've got something to give you." He pulls a small box out of his pocket.

"What is it?" It looks like jewelry, but my dad has never bought jewelry for me before.

The box contains a silver necklace. Its pendant is a tiny replica of Saturn. A gold star hangs on a charm from one of the rings.

"It was hers," my dad says. "I gave it to her when she finished grad school. She would want you to have it."

I take the necklace out of the box and close my hand around the pendant. "Thank you so much."

"I love you, SkyBear." He hugs me again. "She would be so proud of you."

You know what? I think she would be.

He clasps the necklace around my neck and gives me one more hug. "I'm always here for you, okay? Promise. Always."

"I know," I say. "I love you, too."

A security officer steps inside the door. "Sir, do you have the silver Subaru? You can't leave that parked out here."

"Okay," my dad says. He turns to me. "Do you need anything else? At all? I can go park in short-term parking."

"I'm fine, Dad. Really." I smile, trying to look less nervous than I am.

I walk away, then turn back and watch through the window as his car leaves. I stand there long after he's gone, touching the pendant of my new necklace and ignoring the weight of my full backpack.

"Excuse me?" A young girl taps my arm. She has braided brown hair and a shirt that says QUEST ELEMENTARY ACADEMIC ALL-STARS. She points to my backpack. "Are you a real astronaut? Cuz we learned about those in school."

"Not yet," I say, and smile.

Then it's time to head for my gate.

ACKNOWLEDGMENTS

Thanks first to God, who doesn't give up on me (even when I would probably give up on me). I'm thankful for the skills to write this story and the opportunity to sell it.

This book wouldn't have been possible without the ideas and inspiration from a lot of different people. Thanks to my wonderful editor Jonah Heller. He has a great eye for story, and this book is undoubtedly better because he was a part of it. Also to Emily Keyes, my agent, who believes in my work and chills me out when I have the occasional author meltdown.

As always, thank you to my writing bestie, Kacey Vanderkarr. We never let each other give up on writing, and it's paying off. Thanks also to Katherine Fleet, who believed in me enough to mentor me and introduce me to the aforementioned writing bestie. I'm forever grateful.

Thanks to Janet Renard, my copyeditor, and Emma Swan, my proofreader, for catching the things I missed. You're the polish on the novel—thanks for making it shine.

Maggie Edkins Willis and Lily Steele, thanks for designing another wonderful cover. I'm so grateful for your creativity and skill.

Thank you Kirk T. Korista, who allowed me to interview him about astrophysics for this project. I assure you that any science errors in this novel are not because of him. He's extremely smart. It was a productive interview in which I admit I did not understand all of the words that were said.

Thanks to Danielle Mai for letting me crash on her couch while I took a writing class in Boston and wrote a big chunk of this novel. Thanks also to my best friends from that class—Shayla Durbois and Eliza Fisherman. Remember how we promised each other we'd go back to that weird speakeasy one day and use our published books as coasters? Well, I've got my coaster. See you there.

Thanks to the people who gave me ideas: Sheila King for suggesting the pedicure gone wrong, Chris DiFranco for teaching me about flipping baby strollers, and Rex Webb for teaching me about keeping pigeons.

Thanks to Bri MacLeod for helping me with some of the chemistry in this novel and to her parents for inspiring me to write a story about a science-y family (though hers is much more functional than the one in the story).

Thanks to the National Endowment for the Humanities for the grant to go study space at Cape Canaveral. I spent the week with wonderful space nerds (like Leslie Austin) who showed me how to be enthusiastic about the universe.

Thanks to my husband, Rex, and my son, Ezra. To Rex: you're my best friend and my favorite reader. Thanks for supporting me in this hobby-turned-career and for the many walks discussing plot points and characters. To Ezra: your birth made me miss a deadline for this novel, and I've never been so okay with missing a deadline. You're the best thing that's ever happened in my life, and I hope you grow up to be a reader (but even if you're not one, I'll still love you).

To the fans of *The Art of Insanity*: thanks for coming along with me on another journey. Thanks for your kind comments about my last book that propelled me to keep going forward with my writing.

Thanks to those who offered moral support and friendship throughout this process: Cara Knasel, Dan and Linda Knasel, the Webb family members, the Koopsen aunts, Aunt Chris and Uncle Kevin, Aunt Lisa and Uncle Paul, Aunt Eileen and Uncle Craig, Uncle Jim and Aunt Jackie, Elle Poustforoush, Lynn and Larson Sholander, Janell and Dave Colao, Lauren Westerman, Leandra Quinn, Sarah Potter, Carly Kellerman, Beth Fryling, Julia Terpening, Krista Moored, the KCMS team family, and Nana and the Fab Four.

You might be thinking, "Phew, that's a lot of people," but I really have been blessed by each one of them on my writing journey. Thanks to all of you for believing in me.

Thanks to you, dear reader, for reading this story. I hope you had as much fun reading it as I did writing it, but that would be difficult to do because I had an awful lot of fun.

See you next time.

ABOUT
THE AUTHOR

CHRISTINE WEBB used to breed rats in college and sell them as pets but is now a middle school teacher and the author of the young adult novel *The Art of Insanity*. When she's not teaching or writing, she enjoys hanging out with her zoo (three goofy dogs, an evil cat, and twenty nameless pigeons). She lives with her husband and son in Michigan.